I0831763

The Leviathan Conspiracy

The Leviathan Conspiracy

Benjamin E. Karp

Cover Design: David Ter-Avanesyan/Ter33Design LLC
Cover Image: Diana Krotova/Unsplash
Editing: Katie Connolly
Book Design: Benjamin E. Karp, Katie Connolly
Epee Publications

ISBN: 979-8-9930583-1-3
EBOOK ISBN: 979-8-9930583-0-6
First Edition: November 2025

To Mom, Dad, and Nina. Thank you for all your help, support, and guidance. But most of all, believing in me.

"During the time men live without a common power to keep them all in awe, they are in that condition which is called war; and such a war is a war of every man against every man."

- Thomas Hobbes, *The Leviathan*

"Artificial intelligence is the future, not only for Russia, but for all humankind. It comes with colossal opportunities, but also threats that are difficult to predict. Whoever becomes the leader in this sphere will become the ruler of the world."

- Vladimir Putin

PROLOGUE

Geneva
Late May Evening
UN Director General's Office

François Mirreaux was alone in a new office. Although François Mirreaux, a Belgian, was the United Nations Secretary-General, his official office was in New York, and he sat in the Director General's office while he was in Geneva. François did not come to Geneva often, as his duties with the UN General Assembly and Security Council occurred in New York. Furthermore, when not in New York, he traveled the world to promote UN objectives.

The Director General's office was on the third floor of the main UN building in Geneva. The office's walls were paneled with laminated Scandinavian maple wood. The office had several windows. The windows directly across from the desk overlooked a green hilly park that overlooked Lake Geneva. The windows to the left of the desk overlooked the open area of the main United Nations building, which was U-shaped. The open area was flat and covered with stone and concrete.

Secretary Mirreaux admired the view and the office. He thought to himself that this was quite a beautiful view. While not discounting the view from his office in New York City, he remembered his work early in his career in Geneva, where he could enjoy a calm busyness that other cities like New York did not afford him.

After a few minutes, Mirreaux looked back at the desk at the papers before him, finalizing the arrangements for the upcoming human rights convention. This human rights convention would be his crowning achievement for his UN career and for society. Since he began to work for the United Nations, he had worked tirelessly for women's rights. In the three years that he held the role of Secretary-General, he brought more conservative-leaning countries to the table, like Iran and Saudi Arabia, to accept rights for women, including allowing all women the right to drive, ensuring pregnant girls could not be taken out of school, and granting women greater access to healthcare. Besides his work, he credited the new young leaders of these countries, who were still conservative but far more accepting of liberal ideas.

The upcoming conference would solidify these goals and devise a strategy for achieving them. This ratification would still not be easy. He knew there would be protests, but the world would be better off in the end.

He looked over the paperwork and took a sip of water from the half-empty glass. As he drank, he started to feel achy in his chest, and soon after, he experienced shortness of breath.

Mirreaux backed away from the desk and tried to get up to call for help. But all of a sudden, a man in a completely unmarked grey outfit, including his hat, appeared from behind Mirreaux and forced him to sit down. The grey-hatted man walked around to the front side of the desk to face Mirreaux, who couldn't communicate because the air in his esophagus was being cut off.

Once the man sat, he saw desperation in Mirreaux's eyes. Mirreaux gazed into the man's grey eyes. "It won't be long now," the grey-hatted man said. He then looked at a few things on the desk but kept everything in order.

"Even though I'm just a hired hand, I don't understand how idealists think they can achieve anything in a realist world. But I guess if they did, I would be out of a job," the grey-hatted man remarked to Mirreaux, knowing he would not get any answers.

Mirreaux started to lose consciousness. "Before you go, remember One Step Forward, Two Steps Back," the hatted man stated as he watched the life leave Mirreaux.

Mirreaux finally slumped over in the chair. The Phantom could now get to work. He didn't have much time to get out quietly and cleanly. He had spent the last six hours in a cramped closet waiting for the right moment. Being cramped for that long didn't bother him. He had spent many nights like this waiting for different marks. The hardest part was making sure Mirreaux used the poison ice cubes. The Phantom had to set them in a certain way in the ice container so that when Mirreaux went for the glass, he would choose those specific ice cubes.

Once Mirreaux was dead, the Phantom then went back to the closet and pulled out a bottle of vodka that he had brought with him. He poured some vodka into Mirreaux's glass and put it on the desk. Finally, the Phantom carefully placed the glass on Mirreaux's body so it would look like Mirreaux died from drinking. Mirreaux was a former alcoholic, so staging a scene that suggested he had relapsed and died would seem plausible.

After a few minutes of setting the scene, the Phantom looked around to ensure he didn't leave anything behind. Then he casually climbed out the window, which had been open all day and night.

CHAPTER 1

Monaco
Same Late May Evening
Jimmy'z Monte-Carlo

Steve Aoki rocked his whole body with his hands up in the air, as he played his song *Turbulence*, getting everyone at Jimmy'z excited. All the people jumping up and down to the music were in cocktail attire, and some had drinks. In the two bar areas off the dance floor, women in bikinis walked around with champagne bottles, topping people off.

Jimmy'z was the world-famous club in Monte-Carlo. It had attracted many celebrities throughout its history. Tonight was no exception, as it was the night before the Monaco Grand Prix. Even with the people packed shoulder to shoulder in the club and a three-block line outside the club to get in, people were partying and enjoying each other's company. At times, the celebrities in the club, like Ana de Armas, Austin Butler, Nina Dobrev, Lionel Messi, and Kylan Mbappé, took selfies with others. Besides the Monaco track being one of the most unique tracks on the F1 circuit, Monaco was still a place to be seen.

Ian made his way off the dance floor; Steve Aoki was still getting everyone to jump up and down. Ian's light blue button-down shirt started showing sweat from the dance floor and all the body heat around him. Ian meandered through the sea of people to get to the bar. Once he arrived, he had to wait a few minutes to get the bartender's attention. The male bartender came close and looked at him.

Ian raised his voice so that he could be heard above the music. "Can I get one Negroni?" The bartender nodded and started to make the drink. Ian took time to look around and observe. All the men were dressed similarly to him, and the women were mostly dressed in either cocktail dresses or tank tops. The dresses were suggestive but not salacious.

"One Negroni. Do you have a tab, or do you want to close out?" the bartender said. Almost immediately, a man in a blazer came up and told the bartender, "Anything this man orders is on the house." The bartender nodded and went to serve other customers while the man in the blazer hugged Ian.

"That is not necessary, Hans," Ian said.

"It's the least I can do for my longtime American friend who is finally moving to Europe. Plus, I'm the manager, and no one will confront me about it," Hans said.

"Still not necessary. It's one of your busiest times of the year."

"Very true. But I have a lot of big spenders here tonight who will definitely cover your charges. Also, after you told me you and Kingsley broke up, you deserve a drink and a fun night."

"Thank you. You might be right about that. This is a hell of a place to be," Ian said as he caught sight of the Jimmy'z bikini bottle girls walking by a table with primarily attractive women.

"Enjoy, my friend. If you have any issues, call me immediately," Hans said and walked off to check in on another area of the club.

Ian returned to enjoying his Negroni and looked at the sights while bobbing his head to Steve Aoki's music. The club had a dark blue light, but more strobe lights were in the dance floor area. Ian's eyes had become accustomed to the dark and light, and he could see others around him. While every area was packed because it was the night before the Formula 1 race, Ian found a spot at the side of the bar to observe. Many women wore black, white, and red sequined dresses, and others wore more risqué halter dresses. Some of the women in the halter dresses could almost be naked, with very little left to the imagination. On the other hand, the men wore slacks, be they khakis, nice dark jeans, or more formal pants with button-down shirts. Some of the younger men had their collars popped, and mostly, the Italians had their shirts unbuttoned halfway down with a couple of necklaces dangling.

After a couple more songs, a long-haired brunette woman

wearing a tight black mini spaghetti-strap dress walked up to Ian and started grinding against his thigh. If Ian had to guess, she was probably in her late 20s. "Would you like a drink?" Ian asked.

"A French 75, s'il vous plaît," the woman whispered in Ian's ear.

Ian turned and got the bartender's attention. "One French 75 and one Negroni." The bartender nodded and asked, "For the French 75, gin or cognac?"

Ian turned back to the woman. The woman smirked and responded to the bartender, "Cognac, as the original recipe called for."

"You're American?" the woman asked.

"Yes. Am I that obvious?" Ian looked at her.

"At first, no, but your accent needs some work if you want to blend in here."

"Noted."

The bartender gave Ian the drinks. Ian then handed the woman the French 75, and he took the Negroni. He raised his glass and tweaked his accent: "Santé."

"Santé," the woman said, clinking her glass with his. "Much better accent. I'm impressed. You are a quick learner." She winked.

Ian took a few sips of his drink and looked at the woman, who seemed to have sought him out. Unlike other girls in the club, she didn't seem to have any guys around her.

"Vanessa, come dance!" three women in their mid-20s called as they approached.

"So, your name is Vanessa?" Ian said to the woman.

"Bien sûr," Vanessa said. The three women started tugging Vanessa's arm. Right before Vanessa was pulled away, she turned to Ian and said, "I hope to see you around. But remember, things aren't always as they seem." Moments later, Vanessa and her friends were swallowed up in the crowd.

Ian took another sip of his drink and wondered why Vanessa would comment on that. He then wandered around to the different dance areas to see if he could find her. He found her an hour later on the dance floor with her three friends. They held the looks of both men and women with their dancing.

Ian started to move toward Vanessa as he worked his way

through the crowd. It took him a couple of songs before he began to dance in front of her. She smirked at him as they started to dance together. He put his hands on her waist as they moved back and forth with the rhythm of the music.

He then leaned towards her ear and said, "I was hoping I'd find you again."

"I was hoping you'd come find me. My friends are crazy, and I'm ready to go." She smirked at him.

He moved his hands to her ass and pulled her close into him, and he leaned in again, "Can I be your chaperone to get you out of here?"

She leaned in and pecked his lips. "Yes, I'd like that very much, Mr. Chaperone."

He smiled and said, "Let's go." As he took her hand, she waved goodbye to her three friends and joyfully followed him.

Once outside, she held his hand while waiting for a taxi to be called. They saw the long line of people waiting to get into Jimmy'z.

After about five minutes, the taxi arrived, and they both got in the backseat.

"Where to?" The taxi driver asked.

"Hotel Hermitage," Ian said to the driver as he put his hand on Vanessa's lap.

"Nice hotel. I walked by it the other day," Vanessa said, smiling.

"Where are you staying?" Ian asked as he looked into her eyes.

"I'm staying at the Fairmont."

"That's a great location for the race."

"Yes, that's why my friends and I chose it. We don't have to leave the hotel during the race tomorrow."

She smiled again and squeezed his hand as the taxi drove to the hotel. Ian and Vanessa kept silent for the ride as they looked into each other's eyes.

Once they arrived at the Hotel Hermitage, one of the nicest hotels in Monaco, they were greeted by a doorman who opened the taxi door as Vanessa and Ian exited. They then entered the lobby with high ceilings, grand marble flooring, and lavish floral arrangements.

Ian led Vanessa to the back and left of the lobby, where they took an elevator. While in the elevator, they still looked at each other in silence, while their eyes scanned each other's bodies from head to toe.

When the elevator doors opened, he took her hand and guided her to his room. He opened the door with his key card and let her go in first. Once he closed the door, he turned, and she stood beside him. They stared into each other's eyes.

"I'd offer you a drink, but I think we can drink later," he said as she smiled. At the same time, he grabbed her by the waist and leaned in to kiss her on the lips. As her lips touched and kissed him passionately, she wrapped her arms around his neck.

As their tongues intertwined during their kiss, he picked her up and carried her to the bed. Once she was on the bed, he noticed her dress rose up her thighs to show a black lace thong with floral-like images. She didn't move to cover up; instead, she reached for him and his waistband as she started to unzip his pants, and she reached under his gray boxers to feel his growing member.

"Putain, tu es incroyable," she started to moan.

"You are beautiful," he said in between kisses and moans.

He leaned into her and started to kiss her neck. She moved her hair to the side to give him better access to her soft skin. He noticed she was relaxed and didn't have any tension.

After a few minutes, she pushed him back and started slipping off her dress. She watched him undress as she slipped off her dress and thong, exposing her C-cup breasts with her erect nipples, then leaned back on the bed. Once undressed, he was naturally in shape with toned muscles, but his body was not over the top like a bodybuilder. As he stood, she bit her lip as she scanned his long, erect member that hung between his legs.

She spread her legs and looked at him. "Putain, I'm so wet." She started to touch herself. "Come join me. I'm getting jealous." Again, she bit her lip and looked at him.

He smirked as he said, "I think that will help my throbbing hardness."

Next, he got on the bed, straddled her body in between his, and leaned to kiss her soft lips. Their kisses and moans grew as he slid into her and started to thrust. Each thrust was deeper, and after their kisses broke from their lips, they explored each other's bodies. Their moans filled the room.

The moans dissipated after both of them were satisfied. Their naked bodies were still intertwined, and they fell asleep in each other's arms.

The next morning, as the sun shone into the room, he rolled over in bed and found that she had already left. His clothes were just left on the ground.

CHAPTER 2

Monaco
Sunday Afternoon
Harbour Front: Grandstand K

Ian sat midway up the grandstands. He viewed the Formula 1 cars zoom down the circuit after exiting the tunnel and right after the cars braked for the Nouvelle Chicane, one of the best overtaking opportunities on the track. A Formula 1 car's top speed was around 220 mph. Thus, sitting in a straightaway, one could only see a blur whizz by, while seeing the cars come out of a corner allowed spectators to glimpse more of the cars themselves.

Just beyond the track was the Monaco harbor. Yachts were moored and docked to each other like a crowded parking lot. On each yacht, people were partying and taking in the sun.

In recent years, Monaco has had its critics, who have stated that the race was boring because there were few opportunities for passing. While that may have been the case, Ian was amazed by the beauty of the location and the fact that this circuit used actual city streets, while most circuits were built just for racing. Ian also thought the Monaco Grand Prix was one of the cornerstone races in F1 history, and it should stay on the F1 season schedule.

Red Bull's Max Verstappen held a confident lead from pole position throughout the race. Starting in fifth position was a two-time F1 Champion, Fernando Alonso, who currently drove for Aston Martin. While Alonso was one of the older drivers in F1, he still passed a couple of cars to make it to third position with 15 laps to go behind Mercedes' Lewis Hamilton. Lewis Hamilton had struggled most of the season as the Mercedes car was not as fast as the Red Bull. Hamilton and the Mercedes team hoped to make some adjustments during the summer break to catch the Red Bull cars.

Two laps later, Alonso came out of the tunnel and had his

sights on Lewis Hamilton. Alonso quickly swerved to pass Hamilton near the Nouvelle Chicane but was unsuccessful. After the two cars passed, Ian and everyone around him cheered. With each remaining lap, Alonso inched closer to passing Hamilton. Alonso and Hamilton approached the Nouvelle Chicane in the third-to-last lap. While in the chicane, the brakes in Hamilton's car locked up, and Alonso took advantage of this, quickly passing Hamilton. Ian and the crowd cheered even louder as Alonso completed the pass. That was one of the race's most thrilling battles and passes, and it occurred just in front of where Ian had been sitting.

ONE WEEK LATER

CHAPTER 3

Geneva
Monday morning
Ian's apartment

The Eaux-Vives district was one of eight districts in the city of Geneva. The famous Jet d'Eau—the fountain that shoots 130 gallons of water per second 460 feet in the air—was located in this district. There were many nice restaurants and apartments in the area. Some of the apartments overlooked the lake and the Jet d'Eau.

Ian's apartment was in the Eaux-Vives area of Geneva. Geneva was one of the most expensive cities in the world, and the Eaux-Vives district was one of the most expensive within Geneva. While Ian's apartment did not overlook Lake Geneva, as those apartments were outrageously expensive, he had found a nice apartment on the 6th floor of a building on Av. Pictet-de-Rochemont. The building had an old classical facade. The interior did not have an elevator, but Ian usually took the stairs. The bottom floor housed several different businesses, mostly banking and real estate firms. Floors two to six were apartments, with two apartments per floor. Ian's apartment had several windows but mostly overlooked other buildings in the area. He was about a seven-minute walk from Jardin Anglais, which overlooked Lake Geneva.

As Ian dressed to go to work, he put on the TV to hear the latest news from the BBC.

"Good morning, this is Hanna Johnson reporting from London. We are following several stories at this hour. Our first story is about the late UN Secretary-General François Mirreaux from Belgium. People who were close with Mr. Mirreaux indicated that he was once an alcoholic but had gone to AA meetings for many years, and they thought he had it under control. But an insider said in private that one never really knows about another man's struggles. A state funeral is planned in Brussels this coming Friday.

"The UN has appointed South Korean Seung Kim as the Acting Secretary-General. Mr. Kim is a longtime diplomat who hopes to continue Mr. Mirreaux's human rights agenda. The major human rights summit is still planned for the end of this month in Geneva. The summit will focus on women's rights."

"Speaking of women's rights, major demonstrations have taken place worldwide both for and against the upcoming UN summit. Men and women in Egypt have clashed over the upcoming UN agenda. In the United States, there have been women's marches around the country, praising the UN for finally making more moves to protect women's rights."

Ian finally dressed in a dark suit and tie. He grabbed his messenger bag, his phone, and his AirPods. Then, he turned off the TV before leaving the apartment to go to the U.S. Mission to the United Nations, located on the other side of the lake. He put his AirPods in his ears and started listening to music as he walked about eight minutes to the Rive bus stop. From there, he caught the 8 bus, which stops at several places, including Gare Cornavin, where most people exited to catch other buses. Ian stayed on for another ten minutes until he arrived close to the U.S. Mission. He got off at the OMS stop and had another ten-minute walk to get to the U.S. Mission.

CHAPTER 4

Geneva
Same Day - 10 a.m.
U.S. Mission to the United Nations

After going through added security, Ian was given his visitor badge. He was then walked by an assistant to the Head of Mission's office. The Head of Mission to the United States was a Senate-confirmed position, currently held by Paul Greene. Paul was Stanford-educated and a career diplomat serving in various positions worldwide.

Ian was brought to Greene's office and told to have a seat. Ian noticed several photos of Greene's family and different international dignitaries. In the corner of the desk with all the photos, Ian noticed a picture of Greene and New York Yankees outfielder Aaron Judge.

A few minutes later, Greene came into the office and greeted Ian.

"Ian, my apologies for keeping you waiting. I hope you made it here okay," Greene said as he shook Ian's hand.

"Yes, it was no trouble. I am settled in my apartment and starting to take in the beautiful sights of this city," Ian responded, taking a seat in his chair after Greene sat.

"Good to hear. I appreciate your willingness to help the United States and the UN with the upcoming Human Rights Summit. I hope we can fulfill François Mirreaux's goal. What a horrible time for relapse, especially with so much riding on the line for women around the world."

"Rights for women are something I've always tried to fight for, big and small. This is also one of the major reasons I've gone on sabbatical from my company. This is for the greater good. I think the public-private partnerships will be even more fruitful after the conference."

"Fantastic. The public sector always wants to work with the private sector, but there's just so much red tape. Maybe you can help us find ways to mitigate this transition. At the same time, there will be some challenges ahead, especially to make sure the summit takes place. I'll get my assistant to issue you a badge and one that gives you full diplomatic status. He will also show you to your desk and introduce you to some other people here. There will be some meetings later about what will happen with finding a permanent replacement for the Secretary-General. Besides your economic advising work, I would like you to sit in on those meetings and report back."

"Of course. Happy to do so," Ian said and stood up to shake Greene's hand as Greene's assistant came into the room to indicate to Greene that he needed to be on his way to the next meeting.

Greene started to walk away. "I would love to chat some more, but this is a crazy time we live in. Please keep me personally updated."

"Will do," Ian said, but he wasn't sure if Greene heard him, as Greene had already walked out the door. Greene's assistant was waiting by the doorway to show Ian around the Mission.

CHAPTER 5

Cologny
Monday Evening
Restaurant du Cheval-Blanc

The Cologny was a commune in the Canton of Geneva. It was situated on the shores of Lake Geneva, just east of Geneva. The area was primarily residential and was known to be very affluent and upscale. It was the most expensive area to live in Geneva. Many of the villas and mansions had grand gardens and views of Lake Geneva.

Restaurant du Cheval-Blanc was an Italian restaurant that sat in the Cologny. While it did not have a view of the lake, it was in a quaint area where there was not too much traffic. It was one of the few restaurants in the area. The main restaurant had two floors and was a warm spot to be in the wintertime. However, during the spring and summer, the restaurant had a large outdoor pebble stone floor with trees to provide shade to the area adjacent to the main building. In the spring and summer, the restaurant was usually crowded with locals. There were some tourists, but not many tourists ventured to the Cologny for dinner.

The outside area was primarily crowded with locals. Not all the tables were full, but the ones that were had two or four people sitting, eating, and drinking. Two men wearing suits but no jackets sat on the far end against the stone wall. No one sat next to them. The two men arrived separately.

When Damien arrived, he requested the table at the back and that no one be seated next to them. Damien gave the maître d' a 50 CHF note to make sure his request was granted. Damien was then seated and ordered a Negroni as he waited for his colleague. Malcolm arrived about ten minutes later.

"Good to see you, Damien. Sorry, I'm late," Malcolm said,

standing and waiting for permission to sit. He knew Damien did not like tardiness.

Damien looked stoically at Malcolm for a moment before nodding his head for Malcolm to sit. Upon sitting down, Malcolm ordered a single malt scotch with just one ice cube. The men mainly sat silently observing the area and the other people in the restaurant.

After the drinks arrived, they sipped them in silence and looked at the menu. The waiter then followed up and took their orders. Damien ordered the foie gras and the veal cutlet. Malcolm ordered the Caprese salad and the perch fillets, a popular fish found in Lake Geneva.

The men still sat in silence before the food came. When the food arrived, the waiter took away their empty glasses, and the men ordered a bottle of the 2020 Martha & Daniel Gantenbein Chardonnay.

Midway through their meal and drinking the wine, the two men started talking.

"The food is very good and the location even better," Malcolm said as he ate his perch fillets.

"Yes, this is one of my favorite restaurants in Geneva, Malcolm, and I try to come every time I am in town," Damien replied as he cut into his veal cutlet.

"I do like the quietness."

"Yes, Geneva may be a quiet city. But it's not as quiet as one would think if one knows where to look and listen." Damien took another bite of his veal and sipped his wine before continuing. "From my sources, the top three candidates to become Secretary-General are from Australia, Kazakhstan, and South Africa."

"That might be the case, but the dark horse candidates are from the Netherlands and UAE. It is these candidates that hold the true light to correct the wrongs in the world and make it right."

"You are quite right. Please tell your clients that there is nothing to worry about. Everything will be taken care of, and they will be protected. My associate will be ready to set phase two in motion."

"See that he does."

Both men nodded and finished their meals and the wine in silence.

"Please let me pay since I was late," Malcolm stated as he pulled out his wallet.

Damien nodded. Malcolm paid for the meal in cash so that they could not be traced, and they departed separately.

CHAPTER 6

Geneva
Monday Night
Hotel President Wilson

The Hotel President Wilson was a five-star hotel along Lake Geneva, across from the Cologny. Many heads of state, including Bill Clinton and Mikhail Gorbachev, had stayed in what was believed to be the most expensive hotel suite in the world. It took up the entire 8th floor and had twelve bedrooms.

Damien returned to the Hotel President Wilson after dinner. He went to his one-bedroom room, which overlooked the lake, opened the safe, and pulled out a phone. He dialed a number, and it rang once.

The Phantom on the other end picked up the phone and only breathed into the receiver.

"Phase two is a go," Damien said. After hanging up the phone, he removed the SIM card and destroyed it.

CHAPTER 7

Somewhere in Switzerland
Monday Night
Undisclosed Location

Upon the phone call dropping, the Phantom removed and destroyed his SIM card.

Next, he walked to his computer in his tight room, which had a nice view of the mountains. He quickly went online, booked a train to Florence, and then a rental car to drive to Como.

Once he received confirmation of both bookings, he shut down his computer and put it in his pre-packed bag. He then brought the bag to his car and got in to drive to the train station in Geneva. Even though it was late, he had a few hours' drive to the train station for the 5:39 a.m. train to Milan, where he then would switch trains to Florence.

CHAPTER 8

Geneva
Thursday
U.S. Mission to the United Nations

Ian did his regular routine in the morning and then took the bus to the U.S. Mission while listening to music via his AirPods. Ian noticed that many people, young and old, had some sort of headphones, either earbuds or full over-the-ear headphones, during the commute. Overall, the bus was quiet.

As the bus approached the United Nations, it stopped at a stop called Nations. This stop was near the United Nations and beside the Broken Chair sculpture. This sculpture was 39 feet high and was a four-legged chair. The front right leg of the chair was broken. It was purposely broken to symbolize opposition to landmines and cluster bombs. Furthermore, the sculpture was placed before the United Nations and reminded politicians and diplomats of this opposition.

Due to its prime location, many demonstrators gathered there so diplomats and politicians could see them. Today was different, though. People presented thousands of flowers and notes to mark François Mirreaux's death. The Belgian and UN flags were hung in various places.

The bus then continued to two more stops, where Ian exited and walked to the U.S. Mission. After he passed through security, which was much easier now that his badge hung from his neck on a lanyard, he got a cup of coffee and then made his way to his desk.

His desk consisted of a computer, a TV, and some papers. Ian had everything in a nice order. He had never been one for a mess. On the days that he had many papers on his desk, he tried to stack them in different compartments.

Today, Ian turned on the TV as François Mirreaux's funeral

occurred in Brussels. Every major television network worldwide covered the funeral.

Ian began to look at some economic data from international governments and put them in a spreadsheet, comparing trends to private sector growth during similar periods. After some time on the computer, he picked his head up to give his eyes a break. He looked over to one of the nearby TVs that was on. He noticed on the TV that the funeral was beginning, and he turned his full attention to it.

The funeral had been a touching tribute to Mirreaux. Several of the eulogies reiterated how he was a career diplomat, and he truly cared about the people whom he worked with and worked for. The eulogies alluded to Mirreaux being very similar to the late Sérgio Vieira de Mello, a Brazilian diplomat who worked on several UN humanitarian projects for 34 years and was killed in the Canal Hotel bombing in Iraq with 20 other members of his staff on August 19, 2003.

Ian noticed Mirreaux's widow, Elena. She was wearing all black. Ian observed that she was very stoic and showed no emotion. Ian knew that people grieve in different ways. But he had a feeling something was off. While the TV showed Elena Mirreaux, he noticed an infinity pendant on her left shoulder. But when he looked away, he felt something was off with the infinity pendant. Ian looked back at the TV, but the TV had already gone on to focus on other dignitaries at the funeral.

CHAPTER 9

Geneva
Friday
United Nations

Acting Secretary-General Kim called the meeting to order. "Ladies and gentlemen, please take a seat. Thank you for returning to Geneva so soon." Kim and the other ambassadors in the room had all been in Brussels yesterday for the funeral. Since this meeting was an emergency, it was best to return to Geneva.

Many of the UN ambassadors took their seats. Lower-level diplomats and translators sat in the background. Ian was included in that group. Ian had a pen and notebook to take notes.

"That was a touching funeral," said Spain's ambassador Gabriela Alvarez.

"Quite right, and now we have to fulfill Mirreaux's doctrine," replied Sweden's Ambassador Erik Andersson.

"Yes," Kim said, "the human rights conference scheduled for the end of the month here in Geneva will be Mirreaux's crowning achievement."

"Point of order, since Mirreaux is no longer with us, shouldn't we wait till a new Secretary-General is approved?" asked Egypt's ambassador Karim Al-Katib. "How do we know Mr. Kim is even up to the task of bringing us all together for this momentous occasion?" Al-Katib knew he was insulting Kim.

Kim retorted, aggravated but diplomatic. "I assure you I am up for the task and I know how François would have wanted the conference to convene."

The Yemeni and Malian ambassadors agreed with Al-Katib. Mali's ambassador, Moussa Tangara, said, "It should be the General Assembly meeting in New York to make this official. Secretary Mirreaux, while his work is admirable, we should make sure the institution is stable before we hold a conference with such magnitude."

"But the General Assembly does not meet till the Fall," said Alvarez.

More of the ambassadors started to talk, some of whom spoke over each other. Ian took notes, but the meeting yielded inconclusive results regarding the next steps.

As Ian surveyed the room, he noticed a similar double cross infinity symbol on the Egyptian and Malian ambassadors' tie clips. From a distance, they looked like the normal infinity symbol, but with a double cross. But Ian could not get a close enough view to examine the symbol. Ian suspected that the symbols on their tie clips and the one on Elena Mirreaux's pendant might be somehow connected, though he could not know for sure. Ian would have liked to believe in coincidences, but from past experiences, coincidences are not always a good thing.

CHAPTER 10

Como
Saturday
Hotel Villa Flori

Hotel Villa Flori was located on the east side of Lake Como, just up the road from the city of Como. It was one of the only hotels in the area on the lake, and almost every room had a great view of the lake and the surrounding mountains.

The Phantom was settled in his room and sat on the balcony looking north up the lake toward Bellagio. The blue hue of the lake combined with the mountains was very picturesque and could not be seen anywhere else in the world.

Since arriving in Como, the Phantom had been a quiet guest, so he did not raise suspicion. When he went for breakfast downstairs on the hotel's patio and left the hotel, he brought a notebook and a pen. To anyone watching, this would seem like someone normal who liked to collect his thoughts with pen and paper rather than being glued to his electronics.

Only if people knew what was in his notebook would they think differently. The pages in his notebook that he constantly looked over during his stay pertained to the subsequent assassination. He had planned out exactly where to place the bomb on the boat and the steps he would need to take to make sure he escaped without anyone suspecting him.

One day, he left the hotel with his car and drove up the road to Villa d'Este. Once he arrived, he parked his car and walked to have lunch in their more casual restaurant on the patio. While he ate his lunch, he looked over his notebook. Written in the notebook was where the hotel's dock was located and how to access the boats. Furthermore, it was noted where there was a closet with uniforms. Much of the information that he had written was provided by the cabal. They gave him the schematics, and he transferred them to the notebook. He then wrote his own notes about how he would accomplish his task and where he thought there were weak points.

Following lunch, he casually walked down to the dock and found his way to the storage area. Using the codes provided, he unlocked the door with a keypad and then saw the boat. The boat was a Riva. It was beautiful. The Phantom looked at the Riva and looked to where he would put the bomb on it in a couple of days. Finding the right place, he made another note in his notebook. Next, he went to the secret closet that held extra uniforms for any hotel boat captain who forgot their uniform at home or had it ruined during the work shift. He took one of the uniforms, which he would need shortly.

Subsequently, he walked back to his car and put the uniform in the trunk without anyone noticing. Then he drove out of the hotel parking lot to see the area before returning to Hotel Villa Flori, again not raising any suspicions.

CHAPTER 11

Multiple Undisclosed Locations
Saturday Night
Via videoconference

Six individuals joined the video conference room. It looked like a Zoom meeting; this system was very secretive videoconferencing software that changed the IP address of every individual, and there was no way to penetrate it or track it. Each individual was a high-level person within their respective government. Five individuals were Kabir Varma from India, Ibrahim Kane from Mali, Zaaeem Farouq from Saudi Arabia, Nakia Ahmed from Egypt, and Jack Samuelson from the United States. The sixth individual was not seen. The sixth screen just showed the double cross with the infinity symbol at the bottom. Everyone's voice was heard except for the sixth individual. When that individual spoke, the voice was scrambled. No one complained about this because if any of these individuals were caught, they couldn't give up the name of everyone in the cabal. The cabal could be reformed if anyone was caught.

"What is going on at the UN? Why haven't they called off the conference?" Kabir asked.

"It soon will. The next phase will happen in the next 24 hours, and I am sure the conference will be postponed indefinitely," responded the scrambled voice.

"There is a strong movement in my country that needs to be extinguished. The leaders of my country are caving to intense pressure," Zaaeem said.

"We need an outside incident to occur for all parties to walk away so that there is no public backlash," Nakia added.

"You esteemed gentlemen will be satisfied with our group's services. We will make sure everything is accomplished. Remember, we have a several-phase approach. Phase two should do the trick, but if not, we have a couple of other options," stated the scrambled voice.

"I don't give a shit about your phases—I just want results. I can't stand this woke crap that's flooding the youth of the United States and the world," Jack called out.

"Exactly," Zaaeem said, "the world was a better place before these freaks and their liberal agendas started infiltrating society."

"Yeah, more walls need to be built and no more globalization. I want my people controlled and don't need them fleeing to other countries or having people come into mine. Let alone having women have so much more power," Kabir opined. "That's what we are here for, doing away with women's power, open borders, and making decisions by what the public thinks it wants."

"Let's just nuke the whole United Nations and be done with it," said Ibrahim.

"It will be better to tear the United Nations down bit by bit, and then it can no longer be rebuilt. Afterward, there will be no willpower to build it again. If one were to bomb the whole thing at once, so many around the world would come to its aid and rebuild it, thus defeating the purpose of the bombing. The slow stabbing will lead to the United Nations' internal bleeding that no one can stop and no one will want to rebuild again," said the scrambled voice.

"We just need feudal states again," said Nakia.

"Gentlemen, I promise you and your leaders will be satisfied. And nothing will be traced back to you or them," the scrambled voice reiterated.

"It's better because if this does not work, we are all fucked," Jack said.

"Once our system is put into motion, and given the people of the world no other choice, a feudalist world will arise and Leviathan will be in control," responded Zaaeem.

"How is the system progressing?" asked Kabir.

Jack cleared his throat before he spoke. "It's going well. I have a team in Silicon Valley working on it, and it is being stored on a secure secret server. They have no fucking idea what they are building."

"Good. But I still reiterate that India could have built it for cheaper," Kabir responded.

"Cheap doesn't mean better or even trustworthy," Jack said.

"You Americans are so smug—no room for others in your worldview," Kabir retorted.

"You're a slimy piece of—" Jack started to say.

"ENOUGH!! Gentlemen. We are on the same side," Nakia said, overpowering Kabir and Jack. "Things are now in motion, and there is no turning back on our actions." There was a long pause, and all of the members seemed to stare at each other like at a table on opposite sides, even though this was a videoconference.

"Thank you," Nakia continued. "We will discuss the system's next steps shortly."

"In Hobbes We Trust," all the members of the videoconference called out.

CHAPTER 12

Como
Sunday Morning
Villa d'Este

The Phantom arrived early Sunday morning at Villa d'Este in the boat uniform he had taken the previous day. Sunday mornings in Europe were quiet since everyone used them as a rest day. No stores were open other than those in a train station or airport. It was even quieter early Sunday morning at a hotel in a tourist area.

Some hotel workers were out and about, making sure everything was clean and ready for the guests to wake up and go about their days. The Phantom took a duffel bag out of the trunk of his car and nonchalantly made his way to the boat storage area. He knew that no one would be in the boat area for the next thirty minutes. The actual boat attendant would arrive and prepare the hotel's Riva boat for the day in thirty minutes. The attendant would make sure the boat was clean and ready, as the first charter of the day would be for a hotel VIP. The attendant had not been told the exact name of this VIP, other than that he was a diplomat from South Africa.

The Phantom looked at the beautiful Riva, then set down his duffel bag and unzipped it. He pulled out a bomb he had created with a timer. He then took off his shoes and stepped onto the boat with the bomb. The boat swayed as he stepped on. Once the boat stopped rocking, the Phantom set the timer for 90 minutes and attached it to the bottom passenger-side seat. The Phantom felt confident no one would notice the bomb under the seat.

After securing the bomb, he exited the boat and put on his shoes. He removed the uniform shirt and put on another shirt that he had in the duffel bag. He looked around to make sure everything with the boat looked normal, and then he took the uniform shirt and hung it in the closet from where he had stolen it the other day.

The Phantom took one final look at the boat and remarked to himself what a beautiful boat it was and what a shame it would be to end up at the bottom of the lake shortly. He then exited the storage area and, with his duffel bag, nonchalantly walked to the veranda restaurant to have breakfast.

As he walked to the restaurant and sat down, no one gave him a second look. He looked as if he were a regular hotel guest. He ordered breakfast and coffee. From his table, he could see the boat attendant arrive and walk toward the boat storage area. "Good timing," the Phantom remarked to himself.

Before his food and coffee arrived, he pulled out his notebook and pen and began to write. When the food and coffee arrived, he continued writing. He drank and ate slowly so as not to draw any suspicion.

As he finished eating, he saw the South African diplomat sit at a nearby table with several newspapers. He asked the waitress for more coffee. He then settled his bill and drank his second coffee while waiting for the diplomat to get up from the table.

The diplomat stood up from the table and walked by the Phantom's table to go toward the boat dock. Just as the diplomat passed, the Phantom took a business card from his journal and stood up.

The Phantom approached the diplomat. "Mi scusi, signore," he said with an Italian accent.

The diplomat turned. "Sì."

"I think you dropped this," the Phantom said, giving the diplomat the business card.

"Thank you," said the diplomat as he took the card. The diplomat did not think he had dropped anything but took it so he did not seem rude.

The Phantom then turned, picked up his duffel bag, and walked toward the parking lot. The diplomat continued walking toward the boat and looked at the business card. The card was white with a black logo. The diplomat raised the card more to study the logo. The logo was a double cross with the infinity symbol at the bottom. The diplomat couldn't quite figure out what this meant and looked for the man who gave it to him, but saw that he had exited the restaurant. So, the diplomat put the card in his pants pocket and proceeded to the boat dock.

The Phantom made his way to the car and drove out from Villa d'Este. He drove south a few minutes in the direction of Villa Flori and pulled over to the side of the road, where there was a lookout point for lake views. He got out of the car and looked in the direction from which he came. After a few minutes, he saw the Riva boat leave Villa d'Este and go toward the middle of the lake before turning north. He looked at his watch and then heard an explosion. He saw a black plume from the middle of the lake, where the Riva once was moments prior. The Phantom smiled and then got back into his car. As he started to drive again, he heard several sirens approaching, heading toward Villa d'Este. He nonchalantly made his way back to Villa Flori.

CHAPTER 13

Geneva
Sunday Afternoon

Ian walked past the tourists taking their photo of the famous garden clock in the Jardin Anglais. He admired the people enjoying the area. While the clock was nice, he thought one of the best views of the lake was just behind the clock. Unfortunately, Ian wasn't the only one with this sentiment. The area beyond the clock had many benches with people sitting and walking along the lake. Furthermore, there was a crowded restaurant; it was one of the few restaurants open on a Sunday.

Ian reached the water, and from the Jardin Anglais, one had a great view of the Jet d'Eau. Even more people were taking pictures with the Jet d'Eau in the background. Ian turned right and walked along Quai Gustave-Ador, next to the water. The area where Ian walked had more casual restaurants right along the lake and the boat docks. The official yacht club of Geneva was further up the lake, but this area had some boats and a dry dock area for people to work on their boats. Ian continued walking and saw a large group of people walking out to a jetty to see where the Jet d'Eau shot from. Ian walked past a couple more open-air restaurants, reaching an open space with trees and benches. He walked to one of the farthest benches away from the crowds and sat.

It was one of his favorite areas of Geneva. He had a great view of the Jet d'Eau, could people-watch, and thought in relative silence. It gave him a peaceful feeling.

Ian sat on the bench and took in the view. He then took out a journal and pen from his backpack. He began to think about the recent breaking news. Before he left his apartment, news broke that there was a boat explosion killing two in Lake Como. There were unconfirmed reports that the South African UN Ambassador was on board.

Ian wondered if this could be a random coincidence. How could two high-level people at the UN just happen to pass away and be killed in a relatively short period? Through previous ventures, Ian noticed that random events aren't always random. What happens if the Secretary-General's passing was natural, but the recent boat explosion wasn't? Who benefits?

Ian continued to look out at the various people walking past him. Many different languages were spoken. While Ian understood some of the languages, none of the brief conversations he overheard interested him to continue listening. There were tourists, people with small children, and some running groups passing by.

One running group stopped and finished their run just past where Ian was sitting. The runners, four men and three women, talked to each other and said goodbye, and each person started to go their own way. One woman in black leggings and a black crop top caught Ian's attention. She looked very familiar. This woman didn't leave when the other runners left. She took her phone from her armband and looked at it. After a couple of minutes, she put the phone back in her armband and started to walk in Ian's direction. At this point, Ian fully saw the woman's face. She looked very similar to Vanessa from Jimmy'z in Monaco.

"Excuse me, are you Vanessa?" Ian called out in the lady's direction.

The lady, somewhat startled, turned her head towards Ian as she passed and stopped. "Yes." Ian then stood up. She turned her head and noticed Ian. "Oh wow! Ian, it was so good to run into you." She stepped closer and hugged Ian, and they kissed each other on both cheeks.

"Want to take a seat? What are you doing in Geneva?" Ian motioned to the bench. Vanessa and Ian sat.

"I actually live in Geneva. I'm a journalist."

"Is that what brought you down to Monaco?"

"No, I had the weekend off and decided to go to the F1 race with some girlfriends. I'm a political journalist for the Financial Times and working on a book."

"What's your last name?"

"Vanessa Dupont. I promise you'll see my articles if you Google me." She smiled toward Ian.

Ian pulled out his phone and Googled her name. Her articles from the Financial Times came up in the first few results. He also quickly saw that she participated in several conferences about women in journalism.

"Well, I'm impressed," Ian said, looking at his phone. "You even reported in Syria during some of the bombings?"

"Yes, I did. That reporting scared the shit out of me. I'm never going into a war zone like that again. I think the people who are war journalists either have a screw or two loose, or they have no fear."

"Yeah, I can't see myself ever doing that. I also never thought I'd be working at the United Nations."

"I have to confess something," Vanessa paused. "In Monaco, I knew exactly who you were." Just then, her phone rang. "Sorry, it's my editor. I need to take this." She stood up and walked a few feet away.

Ian watched her as she talked on the phone. *Wow, she is beautiful*, he thought to himself. After learning a little about her work, she seemed even more beautiful than in Monaco. When Vanessa returned, Ian tried not to show that he had been staring.

"Ian, I'm so sorry. That was my editor, he needs me to write something about the effects of the loss of the South African ambassador in Como."

"Yes, I heard the news just before I came out here. Go. But before you go, would you like to have dinner with me?"

Vanessa smiled. "That would be nice. What about tomorrow?"

"Perfect. Brasserie Lipp? Here's my WhatsApp if something changes," Ian gave her his number.

"Thanks, and that sounds perfect. I'll text you. I've got to run," she smiled and hugged Ian, then started to run towards the Jardin Anglais.

Ian sat back down on the bench. As he put his journal and pen in his bag to leave, he thought about what Vanessa would be writing about. If the Secretary-General and the South African Ambassador were no longer around, what would be the effects, and who would benefit?

CHAPTER 14

Multiple Undisclosed Locations
Sunday Night
Via videoconference

"So, will the conference be canceled?" Zaaeem asked.

"It should be. The excuse will be out of an abundance of caution," said the scrambled voice.

"What happens if not? Kim may have been underestimated," Ibrahim said.

"We have a contingency plan to inflict more casualties that will send the message while keeping each of you safe," the scrambled voice said.

"The Crown Prince cannot be seen as against this conference. He is holding Saudi Arabia together by a thread. Thank the woke United States for this crap," Zaaeem said.

"Don't come here blaming me. The fucking liberals are behind this. I promise when the new president is in power, the U.S. will bring a whole new side to the international stage," Jack said. "It will be much more conservative and one that most of the world agrees with."

"The U.S. is not the only one to blame in this mess," Nakia stated. "François Mirreaux is to blame. He made the U.N. relevant. Remember, the citizens of our countries were questioning the U.N. even more than before after the October 7th Hamas attack on Israel and the U.N. employees who helped with that attack. Mirreaux came to power soon after and started to make amends."

"When can Mirreaux be a name of the past?" Ibrahim interjected.

"When Leviathan is launched, we can be sure to erase Mirreaux," Nakia replied.

Jack cleared his throat. "Leviathan will do much more than

erase Mirreaux. It will rewrite history and show what we want."

"Zaaeem, rest assured there are others in Egypt who will rise against the United States if this fails," said Nakia.

"Gentlemen," the scrambled voice spoke up. "My organization will make this happen. Worst case, we will go after Kim."

"We can't have this become too bloody, then people will know something is amiss," Kabir said.

"People of the world have too short attention spans. No one will see the connection," Jack said. "Or we use it to play in our favor. If and once people start asking questions, we can direct them to Leviathan." There were nods of agreement.

"Don't underestimate people," Ibrahim said. "We just need to give them no choice."

"Well, I hope tomorrow the council will realize they have no choice," said Nakia.

"In Hobbes We Trust," all the members of the videoconference called out.

CHAPTER 15

Geneva
Monday
United Nations

Ian sat and listened in on another emergency meeting. This time, the tone was far more somber.

Ambassador Karim Al-Katib said, "What a horrible time for the United Nations. May God bless the South African ambassador now."

Everyone bowed their heads for a moment of silence. Ambassador Moussa Tangara said, "We need to protect our own and not hold any conferences for the time being. The South African ambassador was on a shortlist to become the next secretary-general." Ian noticed some of the ambassadors nod in agreement, and then another group respectfully waited their turn to speak.

"I respectfully disagree," Ambassador Gabriela Alvarez said. "The job of the United Nations is to speak up when times are tough. Unfortunately, two of our colleagues have been lost, but this is not the time to become isolationists. Random acts of violence and death occur every day, and governments do not retract because these things happen."

Al-Katib responded, "Ambassador Tangara is right. Postponing is the correct call. What happens if these, what seem like random killings, turn out to be more and become a full-fledged attack on one of our countries?"

The Malian ambassador, Seydou Malle, said, " Our national security should be our focus now."

"While national security is always a priority, the individuals in this room are here to uphold and make the international community better," said Polish Ambassador Janina Brzezinski. "We are on the cusp of making monumental movements."

Acting Secretary-General Kim said, "I quite agree with Ambassador Alvarez. We have to stay united. But we cannot become isolationists. That would defeat the purpose of this institution. We must ensure all ambassadors and diplomats have extra security for the foreseeable future. We have to make sure the upcoming conference takes place. The world is counting on the decisions that are being made."

As the ambassadors started to get up, they congregated in several groups. Ian gathered his items to leave, and he noticed one group to the far side, including the Egyptian and Malian ambassadors, who were speaking to each other with the double cross infinity tie clips. Ian again thought something was off with that tie clip; he had seen it before. He still couldn't quite place it, and he made a note to himself to try to find a clip of Elena's pendant. He also realized that those ambassadors were promoting the idea of canceling the upcoming conference.

CHAPTER 16

Geneva
Monday Night
Brasserie Lipp

Ian quickly took the bus back to his apartment to change clothes before walking about ten minutes to Brasserie Lipp. He wore a button-down shirt with his sleeves rolled up and suit pants. He arrived a few minutes before the reservation and was guided to the table. The restaurant wasn't too crowded.

As he sipped his water, Vanessa arrived wearing a white top and black skirt. Ian stood up and hugged Vanessa, holding her chair as she sat.

"May I offer you both a drink?" the waiter asked.

"I will have a Negroni," Vanessa said.

"I will have the same," Ian smiled. The waiter nodded and walked away.

"How was your day? Did you get your assignment done from yesterday?" Ian asked.

"Well, there is never a dull moment in normal times. By the way, everything tonight is off the record." Ian nodded, and Vanessa continued, "But these weeks have been very interesting. I guess the U.N. is taking security even more seriously."

"It's interesting you say that. I was in a long meeting today about that very discussion. It was more about the upcoming conference and whether it should still take place," Ian responded.

Vanessa listened intently. "I promise I will wait for the official news release before I report anything. But can you give me any hints of what happened?"

Ian smiled. "You are a good reporter. All I can say is that everything is going on as normal so far, but the discussions have been tense."

As Ian and Vanessa talked and enjoyed their cocktails, they looked at their laminated yellow rectangular menus and placed their orders with the waiter. Ian and Vanessa ordered the oysters to split as an appetizer. For the main course, Ian ordered entrecôte, and Vanessa ordered mussels. When their main courses arrived, Ian ordered a glass of red wine, and Vanessa ordered a white wine.

"Yesterday, you mentioned that you were writing a book. May I ask what is the subject?" Ian asked.

"Excellent memory. I've been working on it here and there, but I will devote more time to it soon. It's about Secretary-General Mirreaux's wife, Elena. Amazingly, she went from being a Syrian refugee to becoming the Secretary-General's wife. And she has helped shape Mirreaux's rise and agenda."

"So true. I don't know much about her. Something tells me I did know she was a refugee. But otherwise, I don't know much about her." Ian took a few bites of his entrecôte. "Speaking of her, I recall she was wearing some sort of infinity symbol as a pendant."

"Wow, you are the observant type. I don't know many men who would notice and remember that."

"I just found it a little odd for some reason. Something seems to be off with it."

"Well, I have seen her wear it on several occasions. I have a few photos that I can show you."

"I would like that. I am suspicious about something but don't want to jump to conclusions yet."

"Wow, you are like a Poirot." Vanessa smiled. "Speaking of which, I'm interested to know why a successful entrepreneur from America leaves his company temporarily to work for the UN?"

"You are an excellent journalist," Ian said. "Well, that's a longer story."

"Well, I guess we have to spend some more time together. Then you can get what you want, and I can get what I want." Vanessa and Ian smiled at each other.

CHAPTER 17

Geneva
Tuesday
U.S. Mission to the United Nations

"So, what have you heard? Is this conference still on? We have just two weeks to go," Greene asked Ian.

"Well, sir, the meetings have been tense, and a certain group wants the conference postponed. There is another group that wants to continue," Ian replied from his chair across from Greene.

"Let me guess—the Western Europeans say to continue, while the Middle and Far Easterners want to postpone?" Greene said as he leaned back in his chair.

"Correct," Ian said, about to continue, but Greene cut him off.

"This is like the bottom of the ninth in game seven of the World Series. All the players are hurting, and the pitcher has to make a few more pitches, and no other pitcher is left in the bullpen. Now everyone in the outfield has to pay strict attention."

"You're right, I think. I'm more of a football fan myself," Ian responded.

"Interesting. I took you as more of a baseball fan myself. You have a mathematical Ph.D. from MIT. I thought you would be a Red Sox fan."

"Well, I don't like to be a typical mathematician. I like to watch football to unwind. When I start seeing numbers like in baseball, my mind goes into overdrive and comes up with different possibilities."

"Well, I think that is one reason that baseball catches on. One can learn some math while watching sports."

"That's very true."

"Sorry for the tangent. It's hard to find people to talk about

American sports while abroad."

Ian nodded his head and looked at Greene's photos around his desk.

Greene then changed his tone: "This conference has to take place. The U.S. and others have worked too hard behind the scenes to see this fail. I think many of the demonstrations around the world will calm down once all the countries agree at the conference."

"While I agree, I still think enforcement will be a challenge," Ian said.

"True. But this needs to pass, and different methods will be taken to ensure everyone lives up to the expectations," Greene paused. "You know, Ian, with the recent events in the last few years, even in the United States, I didn't think the world would be embarking on this shift for women's rights. But this has shown me that charismatic leaders can bring people together and push people away. François Mirreaux was one of those people."

"Speaking of Mirreaux, Acting-Secretary-General Kim is holding all parties together and staying strong toward making the conference possible."

"Good to hear. It would be nice to have Kim become the Secretary-General. He's a good guy. But I don't think he wants the job. He wants to step in occasionally but doesn't want to always be in the spotlight."

"He is probably trying to come after François Mirreaux and the legacy he left behind."

"Exactly. But maybe the president and other allies can convince him to stay on before the vote in New York." Greene moved some papers around his desk to find a photograph to show Ian.

Greene held a photo of François Mirreaux with the Egyptian and Malian presidents during the Aspen Ideas Festival. "This photo was taken about twenty years ago," Greene said. "There was a diplomacy panel during the Aspen Ideas Festival. I happen to be in the audience. There, Mirreaux brought up the idea of truly bringing change to the UN, starting with women's rights. And both the Egyptian and Malian presidents agreed. That made me say I wanted to work for the United Nations."

Ian examined the photo a little further. While all three individuals smiled, the Egyptian and Malian presidents' tie clips featured double cross infinity symbols.

"Paul, do you mind if I take a photo of this?" Ian asked.

"Sure," Paul answered.

Ian again wondered why this symbol seemed to be more significant. He needed to talk with Vanessa to explain his suspicions and look at Elena Mirreaux's pendant.

CHAPTER 18

Geneva
Tuesday Night
Ian's Apartment

Ian sat in his desk chair and pulled up YouTube. He typed into the search, "Mirreaux UN Funeral." Many video clips were generated. He clicked on a couple of different ones. Most of them were clips of various parts of the funeral, including the procession and the eulogies.

Ian tried to find a video showing a good clip of Elena. After a couple of YouTube pages, he found one that had a good focus on her. Unfortunately, the video clarity wasn't the best. He watched the video a couple of times, then took his cursor, dragged the video clip to a close-up of Elena, and paused the video. He saw that she wore a pendant that looked like the infinity symbol. Due to the lack of clarity, he couldn't tell if the symbol was like that of the few ambassadors he encountered.

Since that led him to no conclusions, he went to Google, typed in the infinity symbol, and looked at the image results. Most of the results were of the infinity symbol, and nothing was peculiar about them. After scrolling, he found an image of a double cross with the infinity symbol at the bottom. This, he thought, was probably what he had seen earlier.

He found several articles about the infinity symbol and its relation to mathematics. However, he had a challenging time finding credible sources that explained what the double cross meant.

Ian leaned back in his chair. If that was the symbol he kept seeing, what was the point? Another meaning could be less well known.

Immediately, he clicked on his email and composed a new email to one of his former semiotics professors at Harvard.

Dear Dr. Sheets,

I hope you are doing well. I'm not sure if you are aware, but I have taken a leave of absence from my company and am working for the next month with the U.S. Consulate and the United Nations in Geneva. I'm helping them with the upcoming human rights conference at the end of the month.

That said, I came across a specific symbol in my work. I'm not sure if there is a name for it. It's a double cross with the infinity symbol. If you have a few minutes, I'd like to call you on WhatsApp to discuss.

Fondly,

Ian

After sending that email, he clicked WhatsApp on his phone and looked for Vanessa's number. He then texted her, "*Good evening Vanessa. You mentioned last night about Elena Mirreaux's pendant photos. Is there a way I could see them soon?*"

A few minutes later, the phone vibrated, and he saw that Vanessa had responded. *"Yes, come by my office tomorrow around lunchtime. I'm renting a space in the shared workspace behind Cornavin."* Ian texted back, *"Great. See you then."*

Ian then stood up and went to take a shower. Afterward, he went to get some water before he went to sleep. When he started to turn off his computer, he noticed he had an email from Dr. Sheets. He opened it.

Dear Ian,

So lovely to hear from you. I'm glad you are doing real work for the people versus being a greedy capitalist.

I'm attending a conference in San Francisco right now. I will be back in Boston on Friday. So, maybe the weekend? Please email me on Friday.

That symbol you mentioned is the Leviathan Cross. It has several meanings….on the surface, at the surface, and below the surface.

Anyways, I have to go on stage to present now.

Respectfully,

Harry

Harry Sheets
Semiotics - Chair
Harvard University

As Ian closed his computer, he smirked when he first thought of Dr. Sheet's email. Dr. Sheets was an academic through and through. He didn't understand why anyone would ever want to become a capitalist. Ian's second thought was about that symbol. If these symbols were starting to appear, what did it all mean?

CHAPTER 19

Geneva
Friday
Cornavin

"*Hey, I'm on bus 20 heading to Cornavin. I'm two stops away,*" Ian texted Vanessa. "*Great. I'll meet you in Coranvin,*" Vanessa texted back.

About five minutes later, the bus pulled up to Cornavin, and Vanessa greeted Ian as he stepped off.

"Bonjour, Vanessa!" Ian smiled, hugged Vanessa, and kissed her on both cheeks.

"Let's grab some food in Cornavin, and then we can eat in my office," Vanessa said, and Ian smiled.

Vanessa and Ian walked into Cornavin together, and it was busy with people going in different directions. Some people were changing buses, some were finding their way to catch trains, and others were going into various stores to shop and eat.

"Want just to get something quick at Pret A Manger?" Vanessa asked.

"That's fine with me," Ian replied. They both walked straight from the entrance to Pret A Manger, which could be seen from the entrance straight back. There was a line of people, but it moved quickly. Both Ian and Vanessa picked the smoked salmon sandwich. Ian then grabbed a bottle of Badoit, and Vanessa grabbed a bottle of green tea. Ian paid for all the items.

"We journalists do have incomes to pay for things," Vanessa said in a friendly protest.

"I know, but you are doing me a favor, so it's the least I can do," Ian smiled.

Vanessa then led Ian from the Pret A Manger to the back of the building and across the street to a building that held a shared workspace. Ian followed Vanessa through the building, passing different people in their offices. Ian noticed that many of the people were not journalists.

Vanessa stopped at one office and opened the door. "Bienvenue to my humble office, please take a seat," she said. The office had one window that overlooked the neighborhood behind them, which was nothing special. Several boxes of documents and photos were right next to the door. Then, there was a glass desk with two chairs on either side and one laptop.

"I wasn't sure what to expect," Ian said.

"Well, it's not like your tech company in Boston. Have a little different budget," Vanessa said.

"True. But I thought there would be some sort of bureau office here," Ian said as he started to open his sandwich and eat.

"There is talk in London about creating a more permanent space in Geneva. One of the reasons I'm in this office," Vanessa said as she ate.

"I don't want to take too much of your time," Ian said.

"It's no problem. I'm still intrigued by you," Vanessa said with a smile. She pulled out a folder from her drawer and opened it for Ian to see. Each photo showed Elena in different dresses, but they all showed her wearing the same pendant.

"You wanted to see these, right?" Vanessa asked.

"Yes, indeed. Thank you," Ian said as he looked at the photos. "Do you have a magnifying glass?"

"Yes," she said as she went to find a magnifying glass. "What has intrigued you about those photos?"

Vanessa handed Ian the magnifying glass, and he began to examine the photos. "Have you noticed anything different about the pendant that she wears?"

"You mean that infinity symbol?"

"I can't understand why she is wearing it."

"Maybe she is a math advocate."

"Maybe," Ian said. "However, recently, I have seen a double cross with the infinity symbol at the bottom. I wonder if there is any connection?" Ian looked at Vanessa. "I took a semiotics course in college. I just emailed the professor to see if he has time to discuss this."

"I will ask her about this when I meet with her next week."

"You're meeting with her?" Ian asked, surprised.

"Yes, next week. I've talked with her over the phone about the book. She is on board with the book. So, it could be an official biography, which I'm excited about. But next week will be my first official in-person interview."

"First off, congratulations on getting her to agree to it. Where is the interview?"

"It's in New York on Tuesday. I'm leaving tomorrow morning, and I'll be back next Thursday. Just in time to start preparing for reporting on the Human Rights conference, which I think she will be attending."

"Interesting. I was thinking about returning to the States to check out a few things before the conference."

"Well, if you're interested and available, you could join me for the meeting, and I can hear why you took a hiatus from your company to work for the UN."

Ian smiled. "Why does it sound like you are trying to write a profile piece?"

"It could be intriguing. And if you give good answers, maybe it can be published as a feel-good piece for our readers," Vanessa paused. "Plus, I've never been to the United States, so I might need a tour guide."

"I know Boston more than I do New York. But I can help with both." Ian paused to think, then said, "You know that professor I had said I contacted? He will be back in Boston this weekend. You can come with me to meet him, and then we can return to New York for your interview on Tuesday."

"Sure, but wouldn't that be complicated and expensive?"

"I'll handle it. What flight are you taking?"

"I'm on the United flight to Newark at 9:50 am."

"Perfect. Let me go back to my place and pack some items. Also, give me your confirmation number, and I'll get the change to Boston."

She texted her flight confirmation to Ian on WhatsApp.

She smiled. "Perfect. This is what I love about journalism. You never know where the story is going to take you."

Ian smiled, threw away his trash, and started to leave. "Let's meet at the airport at 7:00 a.m."

"Perfect," she smiled.

As Ian returned to Cornavin to catch the bus back to his office, he opened his email on his phone and composed an email to Harry Sheets.

Dear Dr. Sheets,

Some unexpected travels just came up. I will be in the Boston area tomorrow evening and Sunday. Will you be around for me to stop by?

Fondly,

Ian

As Ian rode the bus back to the office, his phone dinged with an email notification. He checked, and there was an email from Dr. Sheets.

Dear Ian,

Wow! If it's not too much trouble, let's meet on Sunday at 10 a.m. at my office. I think you remember where it is.

Harry

Ian responded, "*Perfect. Yes, I remember as if it were yesterday.*"

CHAPTER 20

Lyon France
Friday Night
Restaurant Paul Bocuse

Damien and his three dinner guests watched in awe as the waiter seared the fish before their table. The fish was unique to the restaurant as it was served as a whole fish in a puff pastry and then seared by the waiter at the table.

The waitstaff at the three Michelin-starred restaurant were of a different breed. They waited on their guests for whatever they desired and kept watchful eyes on the table as the guests ate. Most guests dined on the eight-course dining menu.

Money drove Damien to succeed. He was very Machiavellian. He truly believed that the ends justified the means. His goal was to be wealthy, but he didn't want to become famous. He wanted to enjoy the finer things in life without having people question his work. He held previous positions in the consulting and investment banking worlds. While he found both worlds appealing, he began to see an untapped market of unsavory individuals and countries that didn't want to be found but had money to burn.

He started a firm that mixed consulting and investment banking. He promised his clients anonymity and that any funds would be spread out in a way that would not raise suspicion. He met with clients to learn their objectives and then try to match them with other clients with similar goals. He ensured there would be plausible deniability by any interested parties. In doing so, his fee was higher than most consultants and investment banks, but his previous track record had proven him worthy. He usually asked for a non-refundable deposit of $2 million for his services and a 10% commission once the job was completed. He didn't take on clients he knew couldn't afford his fees.

Damien was unattached, but this evening, he was having dinner with Annika, a Swedish lady he had seen for the last few months, her sister Malin, and her husband, Nils. He enjoyed their company and discussions. When asked about his work, he noticed that when he said he was a consultant, no one followed up with further questions about his work. They would talk about consulting in general.

Damien's phone buzzed. While he usually would not take out his phone to check who was calling, he knew his clients were still unsatisfied, and the deal was not yet completed. He looked at his phone and frowned.

He then looked at everyone at the table. "Would you please excuse me? Work doesn't stop in the middle of a deal."

"Not a problem," Nils said, smiling at Malin and Annika.

Damien stood up and kissed Annika on the cheek, then walked out of the restaurant and toward the river across the street to answer the phone.

"This better be damn important, Malcolm," Damien said sternly.

"We need to up the ante. My clients are threatening me," Malcolm said worriedly.

"I know you haven't taken on as many big projects as I have, but trust the process," Damien said.

"Zaaeem and Nakia called me and told me he's ready to expose us if things go south. They even threatened my family," Malcolm said.

"Okay, keep calm, Malcolm. I will inform our friend that Python is a go," Damien said, immediately hanging up the phone without waiting for Malcolm's response.

Damien then pulled out a burner phone from his other pocket and dialed a number. The Phantom on the other end picked up the phone and only breathed into the phone.

"Python is a go," Damien said. Upon hanging up the phone, he removed the SIM card and threw it into the river. Damien looked at the calm river and knew more rough waters were ahead. He regained his composure and returned to the restaurant to rejoin Annika, Malin, and Nils.

CHAPTER 21

Saturday morning
Vanessa's office

Just before sunrise, Vanessa looked up from her desk and saw her packed suitcase by the door, next to a daybed that she used if she had to sleep at the office. She knew she had to leave for the airport in a couple of hours, but she had a few more hours of work to rush to get done.

Since leaving Ian, she had quickly returned to her apartment to pack and then to her office to work. She was not on any deadline for an article. Since the discussions with Ian about Elena Mirreaux's pendant, she had to revise some of her questions before her interview with Mrs. Mirreaux in a few days. The stress she was putting on herself was not her everyday writer deadline stress. This stress had to do with two factors. The first is that Elena Mirreaux was her hero and the subject of her master's thesis. This interview would be the first time Vanessa met Mrs. Mirreaux in person. Vanessa thought she had obtained this interview mainly because Mrs. Mirreaux read Vanessa's thesis and was hopefully impressed. The second factor that stressed Vanessa was the idea that her questions could lead to something bigger being revealed.

It was widely known that Elena Mirreaux was a Syrian refugee, and her parents were killed in Syria by the Assad regime. She was orphaned at the age of 15 and traveled through Turkey, living in different refugee camps to get to Germany. While in a refugee camp in Germany, she was able to contact some family friends in London who later were able to bring her to London.

In London, Elena was adopted by her family friends, and she was able to continue her education. A few years later, she was admitted to the University of Oxford, where she completed her studies including an MPhil in refugee studies. Since being a refugee herself, she had taken on the plight of refugees personally and looked for ways to better their conditions. In college, she had a friend who needed to go to Alcoholics Anonymous. When she attended these sessions with her friend, she heard an allegory that stuck with her and made her want even more to be an activist. That allegory was:

This guy's walking down a street when he falls in a hole. The walls are so steep, he can't get out. A doctor passes by, and the guy shouts up, "Hey you, can you help me out?" The doctor writes a prescription, throws it down in the hole and moves on. Then a priest comes along, and the guy shouts up, "Father, I'm down in this hole, can you help me out?" The priest writes out a prayer, throws it down in the hole and moves on. Then a friend walks by. "Hey Joe, it's me. Can you help me out?" And the friend jumps in the hole. Our guy says, "Are you stupid? Now we're both down here." The friend says, "Yeah, but I've been down here before, and I know the way out."

During her studies at a lecture where several UN representatives spoke, she met François, an attractive, nerdy Belgian. François was a few years older than her. He was one of the UN representatives. He was very ambitious but an idealist. When Elena and François started to date, she was able to give him more of a realistic complement to his idealism.

After graduating from Oxford, François took Elena to the lavender fields in Gordes, France, where he asked for her hand in marriage. Their wedding in London was small, with Elena's adoptive and François' families in attendance. They had a short honeymoon in the Maldives, and then they had to move to one of François' many assignments for the UN.

Elena and François lived in many parts of the world as François rose through the UN ranks. Elena was more than just a dutiful wife. She was a wife, an advisor, and an activist. In every assignment, she helped refugees and fought for women's rights.

This, all being known after Vanessa's discussion with Ian, made her think about what she could have missed during her studies of Elena. She reread her thesis and other resources she used for her research. She tried to come up with two sets of questions—one set if it was to be a typical interview, and a second set of questions if the interview went differently. As Vanessa came up with the second list of questions, she wrote a question to herself at the top of her page and circled it. *Was Elena hiding something?*

CHAPTER 22

Saturday morning
Geneva Airport

The Phantom entered the airport with a carry-on and found his way to the British Airways check-in without drawing attention to himself. The airport had a calmness, which the Phantom liked. While Geneva was a critical and busy international city, its airport was small and not close to the size of other big European cities like London or Frankfurt. Yet, since Geneva was at the center of Europe, it was very easy to get a direct flight to any major city within Europe. There were also a few daily flights to the Middle East and the United States.

A few minutes later, Ian entered the airport with a carry-on and a small check-in bag. He looked at the main central board, which indicated which check-in counter he needed to go to. Once he found the counter number, he texted Vanessa to find her ETA. Just as he was doing so, Vanessa came up to him.

"Hello stranger," she said somewhat flirtatiously.

"Hey! I was texting you," Ian said as he hugged her. He then noticed that her eyes looked bloodshot, and she only had a small carry-on and purse. "Busy night packing?"

"Packing was simple, but then I stayed up all night looking into Elena Mirreaux. I have been rethinking my whole approach to the interview."

"Sorry if my observations caused you not to sleep," Ian responded.

"Get me a coffee, and then we might even be," she said jokingly.

"Deal. Let's go check in," he said, leading the way to the United Airlines check-in counter.

The check-in line was somewhat crowded, but it moved fast. Once they got to the counter, check-in was pretty simple for Ian and Vanessa. The United representative then pointed them toward security and mentioned there would be another area closer to the gate where they would have to show their passports since they were boarding a U.S.-bound aircraft.

Ian and Vanessa then proceeded to the escalators, which took them upstairs to the security area. There was only one security area for the whole airport. There were many more people in this line, but the line still moved at a reasonably good speed.

The Phantom was about ten people in front of Ian and Vanessa. The security line then split into several lines. After Ian and Vanessa showed the security agent their passports and boarding passes, they went to one of the open security lanes. The Phantom happened to be in the lane just next to them.

As with European airport security, each individual had to take off their belt and anything metal. In most cases, shoes could stay on. The Phantom and Vanessa were side by side in their respective lanes. Each held a plastic basket with their phones and watches as they waited to go through security. Ian was a couple of people behind, and two people cut in front of him.

Vanessa casually glanced over to the person next to her. She didn't want to spy, but her curiosity got the better of her, and she tried to glance to see what other people were carrying. From her career as a journalist, she learned that sometimes the best and most interesting stories were right in front of her and where no one was looking. In some cases, they pertained to the most obvious of things. For example, the number of people worldwide with iPhones and other smartphones is high. The story there was about how one company, Apple, had revolutionized an entire industry and the world.

Vanessa noticed the man next to her had a grey hat with no markings on it. This man's eyes were grey as well. Also, from what she could see, none of his clothes had any visible markings. He held an iPhone and a very nice-looking watch. She took a double-take at the watch, which had some design on its face. When she took a second look, she put her hands over her mouth and yawned. On her second glance at the watch's face, she noticed a symbol that looked like the infinity symbol. She stopped in her tracks and thought to herself.

Did I see what I thought I saw? She asked herself. She had never seen a symbol like that on a watch face. When she looked up, the man's line moved faster than hers, and she watched him go through security, grab his items, and start to walk to the left and down the hall.

Vanessa finally made it through security and grabbed her bag. She anxiously waited for Ian. Once Ian grabbed his bag and put on his belt, he walked toward Vanessa.

"Good, you made it," she said. "Let's go. I have something to show you." She started walking to the left and down the hall. Ian followed.

CHAPTER 23

Saturday morning
Geneva Airport

Duty-free shops and other Swiss souvenir shops lined the hallway as Vanessa led Ian in a fast-paced walk. Ian didn't know what Vanessa was after other than the food court at the end of the hall. He knew Vanessa needed coffee, but he didn't think she needed it this badly.

Vanessa spotted the man with the watch getting a pastry and some coffee. Vanessa then turned to Ian.

"A man is getting a pastry and coffee at the far end. I need to see his watch. I think it has the infinity symbol on the face," Vanessa said.

"A watch?" Ian paused. "Let me buy some coffee, and you can find a table near that guy."

"Perfect. Play along when you get to the table," Vanessa said. Then she grabbed her bags and started to walk to an open table close to the man with the watch.

Ian proceeded to order two cappuccinos and two croissants. He completed his purchase and put the cappuccinos and croissants on a tray. He figured out how to simultaneously hold his bag and the tray without spilling.

He found Vanessa sitting two tables away from the man she had pointed out to Ian a few minutes before. As he walked up to the table, he noticed the man with the watch was casually sipping his coffee and eating an eclair.

"Oh honey, I'm glad you found me, I need my coffee," Vanessa said in a Texas twang accent.

"Of course, sweetie. Anything for you," Ian said as he sat down and placed the cappuccinos and croissants on the table.

Vanessa thought her accent might grab the man's attention

and cause him to turn towards them, allowing her to see his watch. But the man didn't flinch.

Vanessa started to drink some of her cappuccino and noticed the man with the watch was close to finishing. Her mind went into overdrive, trying to think quickly about how she could get his attention.

Vanessa then looked over to the man with the watch and saw the side of the watch, still not the face, and turned back to Ian.

Vanessa continued in her new accent, "Honey, why didn't you get a watch on our trip? That is what Switzerland is known for."

"I didn't see one I liked," Ian said, looking at Vanessa to avoid drawing too much attention.

Vanessa pointed to the man with the watch and said a little louder, "Look, honey. That man has a super nice watch. Do you think it's a Rolex or a Patek?"

The man with the watch turned towards them and looked.

Without waiting for Ian to reply, Vanessa leaned toward the man. "Excuse me. Can I see your watch?"

The man with the watch then replied, "Désclé madame. Je suis très privé."

"I do love how French people call me 'madame.' It makes it so much more formal than 'misses' in the United States," Vanessa said to try to keep him interested and to indicate more strongly that she was a tourist.

"Please, monsieur. I really need to convince my husband. His birthday is coming up," Vanessa said, winking at the man and touching his arm.

"Oh madame. Ce n'est rien de spécial," he said as he motioned his arm towards Vanessa and showed her the watch.

Vanessa looked at the watch face. "Oh wow, honey, look at this. What is that?"

Ian leaned over and looked at the watch with Vanessa. It had a double cross and the infinity symbol on its face.

"May I ask what is that on the face?" Ian asked. Vanessa scanned the watch and then scanned the man. She saw some boarding passes in his jacket.

The man switched to English. "Sorry, my English isn't so

good. That symbol is a family crest." The man returned his arm to his side, grabbed his tray, and stood up.

"I'm sorry, but my flight is soon. Have a good trip," he said as he walked away.

"Thank you. Safe travels," Vanessa roared.

Ian and Vanessa then went back to their coffee and breakfast in silence. When Vanessa noticed the man had left, she switched to her normal accent and said, "See, that can't be a coincidence."

"Very good catch. I wonder what it all means. I've never seen a family crest like that," Ian responded.

"I also saw he had two boarding passes in his jacket. The first one was the British Airways flight to London. I couldn't tell where his second flight was going to."

"Good observations. Unfortunately, from London, he could fly anywhere in the world," Ian paused. "I hope it's just a coincidence. Yet, I rarely believe in coincidences."

CHAPTER 24

Saturday morning
Geneva Airport

The Phantom walked away from the food court, annoyed. He couldn't believe the audacity of that woman sitting next to him. If he had to guess, the woman was in her twenties, and he thought about the decline of humanity. He thought people should have fun, yet at the same time, they should be respectful and considerate of others. Furthermore, he thought it was ironic that he was having these thoughts because he was in the business of taking people's lives.

He found the gate information board in the middle of the duty-free stores and found that his flight to London had been posted. Next, he read the signs for getting to his gate in another part of the airport.

He walked to the nearby escalators and rode the escalator down to a corridor where he then had to walk underneath the tarmac to get to a satellite concourse. Once off the escalator, he could walk the 400 meters or ride the moving walkway. He opted for riding the moving walkway as he didn't want to draw attention to himself. Many signs along the walkway stated one would not be allowed to turn around to return to the main terminal after Passport Control. There were other passengers along the walkway, some with large carry-on bags and others with small personal items.

Once at the end of the moving walkway, he was greeted by passport control. There were two lanes for people to file into. The first lane was for EU Citizens and the other for non-EU Citizens. The Phantom filed into the E.U. line. This line was long. Before 2020, there was no need for these lines when flying to London. But since Brexit in 2020, Europeans like the Phantom had to have more patience in lines.

After showing his passport to the control agent, he took another escalator up to the gate area. This area was a large circular room with large windows all around. There were many options to sit between the four gates. Unfortunately, there were no duty-free shops or restaurants in this small terminal where you could buy food and snacks. However, there were a couple of vending machines—one for food and the other for drinks.

Not long after the Phantom found a seat near his gate, the gate agent stated, "Good morning, ladies and gentlemen, British Airways Flight 4235 to London Heathrow will be boarding in a few minutes."

The Phantom watched his fellow passengers start to stand up and gather their belongings before boarding commenced.

The gate agent announced five minutes later, "Thank you for your patience. At this time, we would like to invite Priority Group 1 to board." The Phantom stood up to ensure he had his items and continued to people-watch.

Another five minutes passed, and the gate agent announced, "Now, we would like to invite Priority Group 4 to board at this time." The Phantom then started to get into line to board. Once the gate agent scanned his ticket, he boarded the A320 aircraft and found his seat next to the window. He always liked areas where he could have nice views. He loved how the mountains surrounded the city of Geneva and the lake. He also loved the A320's climb into the air, as he could see the Alps below him getting farther away. He could also see the Jet d'Eau in the distance for a brief minute before the plane slid above the clouds.

Once the plane reached its cruising altitude, he went to grab his personal item. He then pulled out his journal and pen. He turned to a few pages in the middle of the journal. If anyone happened to look over his shoulder, all they would see were sketches of a large ship. He studied each page intently and then turned to a few subsequent pages that showed sketches of a ship's interior.

When the flight attendant came by offering drinks, he asked for sparkling water. After being handed the sparkling water, he drank it while staring into the white clouds. He had a long day of traveling to go. Once he arrived at Heathrow, he had to spend the night in the airport to await his next flight tomorrow to Gibraltar.

CHAPTER 25

Saturday morning
Geneva Airport

Vanessa looked dazedly out the window of the United 767-200 as it taxied from the gate to the runway. Ian noticed and then tapped her shoulder. "Hey. Are you a nervous flier?"

Vanessa slowly turned away from the window towards Ian. "No. I am thinking about my upcoming interview and that guy's watch we saw in the food court."

"Yes, that was strange. I don't think it was a family heirloom. Just curious, how did you become such a good actress? That American accent earlier was pretty good," Ian said as the plane started to position itself on the runway, ready for takeoff.

"I picked it up while covering the last U.S. political elections. It was my first assignment with the Financial Times. I covered the southern states. I spent a few weeks in several southern states. Most of the time, I was in Florida and Texas."

The plane started gaining altitude. "I always found it interesting that Europeans think all Americans are like Texans. Why is that?" Ian asked as he looked at Vanessa.

"Maybe it's just a stereotype that comes from TV," Vanessa said.

Ian looked at Vanessa like a lightbulb just went off in his head.

"What is it?" Vanessa looked intrigued.

"Do you have your dissertation with you?"

"Yes, it's in my carry-on. I'll get it when we are allowed. Why?"

"I'd like to read it," Ian paused. "I also want to see something. We were talking about stereotypes. Refugees have a certain stereotype." Vanessa nodded. "What happens if Mrs. Mirreaux wasn't a stereotypical refugee?"

"Well, she wasn't a stereotypical refugee. Look at the career she has had. Overcoming all those obstacles and making a difference."

"I do commend her for that. However, if memory serves me correctly, I think in the city where she came from and where her parents were killed, there were supposedly no survivors except her. She's a teenager. The Syrian government at the time did not show any mercy when they attacked their citizens. Yet, she survived."

"So you think someone protected her?"

"Well, I think there could be three theories. One, she was fortunate and used her wits and strength to survive. Two, someone could have protected her. Or three, someone or some group saved her from getting killed and now is using her."

"You can't be serious, Ian. That's very cynical. Don't you believe in good outcomes and heroes?"

"Of course I do. Just from personal experiences, coincidences similar to this aren't usually random. There's more than meets the eye, especially when the next person in line to be Secretary-General is killed in close proximity," Ian said, and then the plane made two dings.

The captain's voice was heard over the intercom before Vanessa could reply. "Good morning ladies and gentlemen. My name is Captain Larry Palmer. I am joined by First Officer Martin Edelson. We want to welcome you aboard United Flight 44 to Newark, New Jersey. We will fly northwest over the Swiss Alps towards Le Mans, then veer toward Brest, where we will start our way across the Atlantic Ocean. We will then turn south around St. John's Newfoundland, proceed toward Nova Scotia, then fly along the coast of Maine, pass Boston, and over the state of Connecticut; we will begin our descent into Newark, New Jersey. Our flight time is nine hours and twenty minutes. We expect a smooth flight but maybe a few bumps along the way. Please keep your seatbelts fastened while seated. If you need anything, any of our flight attendants will be more than happy to assist you. I will speak to you again as we approach our arrival in Newark. Please sit back and enjoy the flight. Thank you for flying United." There was a brief pause. Then Captain Palmer started to speak the same message again but in French.

After the captain finished his announcements, the flight attendants started getting up and preparing for the beverage service. Vanessa looked at Ian to continue their discussion.

"Do you think she's involved? And why now?" Vanessa asked.

"Well, I don't want to go accusing anyone yet. I just want to be cautious. Unfortunately, power and money manipulate people," Ian responded.

"Sex, too, can make people do crazy things," Vanessa added as she started to get up and open the overhead compartment. She pulled out her bag to get her dissertation, which looked more like a textbook with yellow tabs throughout. Vanessa put up the bag, and as she sat back in her seat, she gave Ian the dissertation.

As Ian grabbed the dissertation, he smiled, "This brings me back to my college days. Looks like my textbooks and notes before an exam."

"Weren't you at the top of your class at MIT?"

Ian blushed, "Yes, I was. But many things didn't come easy for me at first. It was in the second half of my sophomore year at MIT that everything started to click."

"I think you humble yourself," she said and winked. "I read an article about the company you started, and a few people are quoted stating that you always had the drive."

"You're a good investigative journalist. Still checking up on me, I see." He paused. "Yes, I was always driven, but the professors made me better. Much to the chagrin of Dr. Sheets, who you'll meet. He thought academia was the only noble profession."

"I just haven't figured out why you would leave your company to help the United Nations. Even if it's temporary, like you said, it may not be a coincidence."

A flight attendant arrived at their row. "May I offer you something to drink?"

"A coffee with cream and sugar, please," Ian responded.

"Gin and tonic, please," Vanessa said, looking at the flight attendant.

The flight attendant gave the drinks to Vanessa and Ian and moved to the next row.

"I've got some reading to do," Ian said as he sipped his coffee.

Vanessa sipped her gin and tonic. "But you didn't answer my question."

"That's a longer story and for another time," Ian started to page through the dissertation, reading each part carefully. Vanessa finished her drink and rolled to the side, closer to the window, to sleep.

CHAPTER 26

Multiple Undisclosed Locations
Saturday
Via videoconference

"Yesterday, the Nasdaq and the S&P 500 closed higher for the seventh straight day," said American Jack Samuelson.

"Isn't that a good thing?" asked India's Kabir Varma.

"Yeah, if you are fucking blinded by false optimism," responded Samuelson.

"The U.N. is finally acting on its missed promises," Saudi Arabia's Zaaeem Farouq said sarcastically.

"It won't be for long if we have anything to do with it," Samuelson said. "Plus, imagine all the returns we will get as we short the stocks and hope for peace."

The scrambled voice from the infinity symbol started speaking: "The next phase will come at a more significant price for each of your countries. My man is getting in place as we speak, and by early next week, the ramifications should be felt."

Mali's Ibrahim Kane said, "I don't know how long we can hold out. Our governments are all prepping to go to Geneva."

"The terrorist groups in Egypt are losing members so fast. This is not normal. International peace is not the answer. Chaos is what is needed, and only the local governments can bring about the correct peace. Plus, we don't need some archaic globalist group to tell everyone else what should and shouldn't be done. The Leviathan must rise," Egypt's Nakia Ahmed opined.

"When will Leviathan be ready?" asked Kane.

"The president will be traveling to California next week, and I will be able to stop by to see Leviathan," Samuelson said. "I will send it to you if it works as intended." There were nods of agreement.

"Leviathan will rise. All Hail Hobbes!" Kane said.

"In Hobbes We Trust," all the members of the videoconference called out.

CHAPTER 27

Newark Airport
Saturday Afternoon

"Good afternoon, ladies and gentlemen," Captain Palmer said via the airplane's PA system. "On behalf of myself, First Officer Edelson, and our Chicago-based flight crew, we want to be the first to welcome you to Newark, New Jersey. Thank you for flying United Airlines, and we look forward to welcoming you on another United flight."

As the 767-200 taxied from the runway to the gate, Ian closed the dissertation and turned to Vanessa. "That was an impressive dissertation. If you weren't a journalist, I would hire you to work for me."

Vanessa smiled. "Thank you, but I'd rather report and dig up something interesting about something or someone versus selling a product."

"Fair point. I can respect that. Journalists have an important role to play keeping people and institutions honest."

The plane made one final turn as it pulled into the gate.

"So, did I write anything revealing that I might have missed about Mrs. Mirreaux?" Vanessa asked.

"It depends. You paint a glowing portrait of Mrs. Mirreaux. She overcame many obstacles and succeeded. But is there more? Could she have been after something else?" Ian asked.

Vanessa stood up to get her carry-on. Ian stood up a few seconds later and grabbed his carry-on. Vanessa looked at Ian as they waited to disembark.

She quietly asked Ian, "What do you mean after something else? Yes, she became the wife of the Secretary-General, but she was not just a wife. She continued to be an activist."

"I am not questioning her activism role. She should be admired for that. But your dissertation focuses on how she and her husband's career goals intertwine and complemented each other. But is there another way of looking at it, as if she had other goals?"

Vanessa looked at Ian, perplexed. "I don't understand what you mean. Maybe my English isn't so good."

"Sorry, my thoughts might not be clear. What I mean is Mrs. Mirreaux has always been a determined person. And she found her husband, who complemented her. But what would have happened if she had never met François Mirreaux? Was there something she wanted to keep going in her old life?"

Ian and Vanessa started to walk off the plane toward customs. "So you're saying to question my idol?" Vanessa asked.

"Yes and no. You need to probe a little more when you see her in person."

"What do you mean 'me'? You are coming. As my research assistant, you need to see this hypothesis through."

"So, I'm your research assistant?" asked Ian.

"Possibly. If your hypothesis turns up with nothing, you'll be my procrastinator," Vanessa smirked.

CHAPTER 28

Washington D.C.
Saturday Afternoon

Jack walked to his study in his home, which he barely frequented as his duties in the White House had him working nonstop in preparation for the Geneva conference. He walked to the back wall, where a Miró print hung. He moved the print to the side, and there was a safe. He entered the combination and opened the safe to retrieve a phone.

He hit the recent calls and clicked on the first number. The phone rang a few times before someone answered.

"Jack, good to hear from you," the man on the other end stated.

Jack wasn't in the mood for any small talk. "I'll be coming to see you on Monday. Will Leviathan be ready?"

The man on the other end always enjoyed small talk before business, but Jack seemed overly agitated. "Yes, it is basically ready," the man responded.

"I don't want fucking basically. I want a definite answer," Jack retorted.

"Yes, it's there unless you have some tweaks, and we will be ready to launch."

"What about the takedown of the other systems?"

"Once you approve Leviathan, I will upload the bugs for the other systems. It will be nearly impossible to repair when implemented."

"Good, good. That's what I like to hear. There can be no glitches."

"There definitely won't be. Once we hit initiate, there will be no turning back. But I can give you a small presentation of it."

"Fuck yes," Jack said with a little more ease. "So, regarding the meeting place, this cannot be associated with the Presidential visit to your company and others in the area."

"Of course. Let's meet at the Rodin Sculpture Garden at Stanford."

"That would work. The President's last stop is Stanford before returning to San Francisco for a donor dinner and then returning to Washington. I can go without anyone noticing."

"Great. There's a bench on the west side of Rodin's 'Gates of Hell'; I'll be there at 4 p.m.," the man said.

"See you then," Jack said and clicked off the phone. He breathed a sigh of relief but knew the most challenging parts were about to start. He put the phone back into the safe and locked it. He made sure the print was back in its normal position. Then he grabbed a few items off his desk and returned to the White House.

CHAPTER 29

New York City
Saturday Night
The Polo Bar

Ian climbed out of the Uber car and opened the door for Vanessa in front of The Polo Bar. Vanessa thanked the driver and then thanked Ian. Ian then held the door for Vanessa as they entered the restaurant. Almost immediately, they were greeted by a man in a black suit holding an iPad and looking sternly at Vanessa and Ian.

"May I help you?" the man said snarkily.

Ian and Vanessa stopped and looked at the man. "Yes, we have a reservation for 9 p.m. for two under the name Ian Steele," replied Ian.

The man took a few moments to find the reservation. Once he saw it, his tone became more welcoming: "Mr. Steele, welcome. Please walk past the bar and check in with my colleague at the desk by the stairs."

"Thank you," Ian said, and he and Vanessa started to walk past the somewhat crowded bar to the desk by the staircase that led downstairs to the main restaurant.

"Good evening, Mr. Steele. So nice to see you again. It's been a few months," the female maître d' said welcomingly.

Ian smiled. "Thank you. Nice to see you again, Scarlett. How many times have I told you to call me Ian? I've been abroad for work. But it's nice to be back." Ian then motioned to Vanessa. "Scarlett, this is Vanessa, a dynamite European journalist."

Scarlett smiled. "I just don't want to show any preferential treatment. Nice to meet you, Vanessa."

"Nice to meet you too, Scarlett," Vanessa smiled.

Scarlett looked at her iPad on her desk. "Mr. Steele, your table is ready. But feel free to grab a drink at the bar if you want first."

Ian looked at Vanessa. Vanessa replied, "It's been a long day of travel. I could use a drink, but maybe at the table."

Ian smiled and nodded. Scarlett replied, "Of course, would you both please follow me?"

As Ian and Vanessa followed Scarlett down the staircase, the dark walls were covered with paintings of horses and people playing polo. But once they arrived downstairs, the lighting was much brighter than by the bar, and while there were more paintings of horses and those playing polo, every inch of the restaurant, from the floor to the ceiling, was varnished in mahogany. Leather seats and couches surrounded the tables. In a way, it looked like an over-the-top country club restaurant.

Scarlett showed Ian and Vanessa to their table near the side of the main dining area. Vanessa sat on the leather couch, and Ian sat in a chair across from her. A giant mirror above Vanessa looked out at the rest of the restaurant. While Vanessa could look out at the other dining guests, Ian could do so through the large mirror.

"I apologize for not seating you in the main area, Mr. Steele. We are busy tonight, and with your last-minute reservation, this was the best I could do," Scarlett said after Vanessa and Ian sat.

"Please, no worries," Ian said. "I'm just happy you could find us some space."

"It's not a problem. It's nice to have you back with us. Please enjoy your meal." Scarlett said as she walked away.

Vanessa and Ian observed the room for a few minutes before the waiter arrived. The restaurant was crowded, but the noise level was manageable.

The waiter arrived a few minutes later with the menus. "Good evening. My name is Daniel. I'll be your waiter. Can I get you both started with something to drink?" Daniel looked at Vanessa first.

"I'll have a Manhattan. When in New York," she said and smiled.

Ian then said, "I'll have a Vesper martini."

"Perfect. I will have those right out to you," Daniel said as he walked away.

Vanessa looked at Ian. "That nap helped. Maybe from not sleeping last night and sleeping some on the plane, combined with my anxiety about the interview, I needed that nap. I feel better now."

Ian smiled, "I'm glad. The food here is worth the visit. And this place has seen some celebrities more than others."

She smiled. "Only some celebrities make my mouth drop open. Otherwise, I want to figure out what the story is."

"I don't know much about journalists besides what they write."

"Well, I'm still trying to crack one celebrity—if you would call him that."

He smiled. "Who's that?"

She smirked. "I think you know him. He's well-known for a company he started but has suddenly stepped away from his normal duties to help the United Nations. And just today, I found out he likes to frequent this restaurant when he visits New York City."

Daniel arrived back with the drinks and said, "Please enjoy. I'll come back in a few minutes to take your food order."

Ian raised his martini. "Cheers to uncovering secrets. Even if they take time to unfold." Vanessa raised her Manhattan and clinked glasses. Vanessa smirked in frustration as she took her sip and opened her menu.

They looked at their menus for a few minutes, picking out what they wanted. Then Daniel returned to the table, asking, "Have you both decided?"

"I will have the Polo Burger," Vanessa said.

"I'll do the same. And can we have a dozen of the raw oysters to start?" Ian piped up.

Daniel jotted it down on his small handheld computer. "Of course. Please let me know if you need anything else." He then walked to check in on a few other tables.

Vanessa sipped her drink and looked around the restaurant. Although it was almost 9:45 p.m., most tables were still pretty crowded. From a distance, Vanessa saw a large group of men and women who looked like they were from one of her last Netflix binge. When Vanessa looked to the other side of the restaurant, she saw a few people she recognized from the U.S. political world.

Ian took some time and looked around in the mirror without it becoming obvious.

"I guess this is where Hollywood and politics come together," Vanessa remarked. "If I was on another assignment, I might be digging for a story. This city has a different vibe than Florida and Texas."

Ian laughed. "Definitely compared to those places."

Ian and Vanessa again looked around the restaurant. They began to overhear a conversation at another table.

"Look at it this way: even if the United Nations is successful in this women's conference, it won't last," said a man in a white button shirt.

The woman at the table responded, "The U.N. has made some incredible strides since Mirreaux took office. It's such a shame he passed."

"Yeah, a damn shame. But again, even if he were around, the U.S. would find some way not to follow the U.N. directives."

The woman became somewhat unnerved by that comment. "So, you think the U.S. is superior to the U.N.?"

"Basically, yes, I think members of the U.N. have to pay their fair share to be part of an organization. Like a membership to a country club. And since the U.N. has its headquarters in the U.S, that membership fee should go to the U.S."

The woman squirmed a little in her chair. "Wow, you are really showing your true colors, I see. I didn't know many MAGA people were in NYC."

"You'd be surprised, sweetie," the man arrogantly retorted.

The woman stood up, picked up her purse, and walked away. The man looked smugly around and got up to pursue the woman.

Vanessa looked at Ian. "Well, if that was a date, I don't think he is getting any dessert."

Ian replied, "Yeah, true. At least they find their true colors now versus later in the relationship." Ian paused. "Or let's hope they were at the start of a relationship versus being a long time together."

"True. In any relationship I've been in, I don't mind differences of opinion, but I didn't like the guy's smugness. I think he does a lot of mansplaining."

"You are right; he probably does."

Daniel arrived and placed the raw oysters in the center of the table, and Vanessa and Ian began to eat. They began to hear another conversation from another table.

"I'm not sure about Artificial Intelligence. There are so many privacy concerns with it. Plus, the biases it has. Shouldn't we get some legislation before putting things out in the public?" an older man stated to others at the table.

"Those are fair concerns. But the government knows shit about AI. The private sector has to lead the way and tell those intellectual midgets in D.C. what to do," said a younger man at the table.

"I've just heard something new on the horizon, and it will launch very soon. Word on the street is that it will put OpenAI and others out of business. It's going to blow them out of the water," another young man said.

Ian and Vanessa observed that this larger table of men seemed to consist of Wall Street traders. As they continued listening, Daniel cleared the oyster platter, with shells remaining, and brought out their burgers. Vanessa took a first bite, and Ian could tell from her face that it was scrumptious.

"What Sam Altman did with ChatGPT was incredible." the older man stated, "but before you young bloods go investing with the firm's money, don't believe all the hype sometimes. That hype can be bullshit. We sometimes trade on speculation, but I have friends who lost millions investing in Theranos."

"Yeah, we know the Elizabeth Holmes stories. But we won't be that stupid," said one of the young men.

"Don't say that. My advice from decades in this business is that all entrepreneurs are crazy about taking risks. But some take the crazy to very different and darker levels," the older man said as he sipped his wine.

Vanessa and Ian turned their attention back to each other and their hamburgers as they finished eating. "I have to say, this restaurant has been quite eye-opening on several fronts," Vanessa said to Ian.

"Very true. Sometimes you learn more by just listening," Ian said.

Daniel then cleared the plates from the table. "Looks like you both enjoyed the hamburgers. They are some of our best sellers.

Would you both care to see the dessert menu?"

Vanessa looked at Ian and then at Daniel. "No, thank you. I'm still tired from the flight, and I've eaten so much already."

Daniel nodded and brought the check to Ian.

Ian and Vanessa returned to the stairs and told Scarlett good night before catching an Uber back to the hotel. Vanessa turned to Ian in the Uber and said, "That was an impressive evening with some amazing company. I can't promise tomorrow's library outing will be as exciting as that."

Ian looked at Vanessa. "You never know. It just depends on what we find."

CHAPTER 30

Amsterdam
Sunday Afternoon

Damien kissed Annika goodbye and shut the door behind her. They had been spending the past several nights together. He enjoyed her company. He told her that she should walk to the Rijksmuseum because it was a beautiful day. He said he had an important work call and would call her to join him. When Annika asked why he had a work call on a Sunday, Damien replied that his recent client was based in the United States, and they didn't understand weekend boundaries like people in Europe.

Damien walked around the apartment nervously, waiting for the phone to ring. He knew who was about to call and what the phone call would be about. He looked out the large windows that overlooked the canal, hoping to find some peace. He saw many people walking around and boats going up and down the canal. All of the boats were leisure boaters since it was a Sunday.

He didn't even look at the unknown number when the phone rang. Before hitting the answer button, he sat in his Eames chair.

"Hello. Good to hear from you," he said.

The voice on the other end was scrambled so that if anyone tapped Damien's phone, it would not be tracked. "Sorry to bother you on a Sunday, but this is urgent."

"I know things haven't gone completely as planned; or should I say, not as fast as you would have liked?"

"I thought my part was the hardest part, and everything else would have fallen much faster."

"It has shaken the tree. There needs to be an extra couple of shakes."

"Yes, have you heard when the system will be ready?"

"I have heard the system is working, but the necessary people will look into it next week. Final payment will not be given until everyone is happy with the product."

"Good. I like your attention to detail and setting limits. That, combined with your impeccable references, is why I hired you."

"I'm grateful for that," he said, hoping it was a genuine compliment, though he couldn't be precisely sure since it was not the actual voice of his superior.

"If everything works correctly, I will send you the next installment to the same account," the scrambled voice said.

"Thank you. Do you have my asset to start the final phase?"

"Yes, but have your asset stand by. I know the phase you have planned will be far more harmful to surrounding economies. But if the phase does occur, I want your asset back in Geneva in case other measures have to be implemented."

"I fully understand, and I will inform the asset," Damien said and paused. "Is there anything else you will need?"

"Yes, how well do you know this developer?" the scrambled voice asked. Damien's business model operated on compartmentalization, which would lead to plausible deniability from his clients. Damien never told his clients who would fulfill their needs but reiterated that they would be the best people for the ventures. Furthermore, if something ever went wrong, Damien could easily cut the bad part out altogether or replace it and continue with the rest of the venture.

"I have used him on other ventures, and he is one of the world's brightest minds. He hasn't been fully recognized as such, but he will once the system is out there. I am one of the angel investors in the company that will be launched."

"You will be well compensated when this works—not just from the company."

"I thank you for the opportunity," Damien said, as if he were responding to a military superior.

"In Hobbes, we trust," the scrambled voice said, and immediately disconnected the phone.

Damien breathed a little relief as he thought the call could have had worse outcomes, but it would seem he was still in good graces.

He then sat up from the Eames chair and walked over to his desk, unlocking one of his drawers and pulling out a burner phone. He dialed a number, and the phone barely rang once when he could hear a couple of breaths from the other end.

"Python, hold fire. I repeat, Python, hold fire," Damien said and paused. "Operation is still workable, but party conditions have to be achieved. Ready Python, but hold fire."

"Roger that," the Phantom said and hung up the phone.

Damien put the phone back into the desk and locked the drawer. He then pulled out his main phone, and with a smile, he texted Annika to find out where he could meet her.

CHAPTER 31

New York City
Sunday Morning
The Morgan Library

Vanessa and Ian walked around the room, looking at the books bathed in the warm red and light-colored hues of the library. There were tons of books in the main room, all enclosed with fencing so that one could see the books but not touch them. There weren't many people around, so it was an even more peaceful place to be, away from the city's main streets.

The library had three levels, but visitors could only visit the first floor. When one looked up, one could see the other two levels. The arched ceiling had an Italian theme. Even though this was a museum, it still felt like a personal library rather than one open to the public.

"This is one of my favorite places in the entire city," Ian stated as he walked closely behind Vanessa. "There's a sense of peace in the middle of the busy city."

"You are right," Vanessa said. "I always equated Boston to being the more literary city, but New York has some good places, I see." Vanessa looked with amazement at the books on the shelves.

Ian nodded. "So true. Both cities are different in their own way and have some similarities. However, you'll see that the architecture here differs from that in Boston."

Vanessa walked to the center of the room, where a glass case held several books open to specific pages. She almost stopped in her tracks when she saw the middle book.

"Ian, come take a look at this," she whispered towards Ian.

He then came over and looked at what Vanessa was pointing at. In the center, a painting showing God pointing down was displayed, and below were two large creatures. The watercolor by the poet William Blake was titled "Behemoth and Leviathan." When Ian read the name of the watercolor, he started to back up.

"What is it with this Leviathan?" he asked Vanessa, but she wasn't around. He looked around to see where she had gone.

A few moments later, Vanessa returned with someone who worked at the library. "Pardon me," she told the lady in a red jacket with the Morgan Library logo. "This watercolor, what's its history?"

The lady looked at the watercolor and then looked at Vanessa and Ian. "This work was purchased by Mr. Morgan in 1903. The artist is William Blake. He was famous for being a poet, but he was also an artist. This watercolor was part of his illustrations for the Book of Job. In this specific watercolor, God shows Job the monsters of earth and sea, the Behemoth and Leviathan."

With a thick French accent, Vanessa said, "Pardon, but my English isn't so good. But this Leviathan is a monster?"

Ian listened intently as the lady responded, "Yes, the Leviathan is the monster of the sea. You can tell from the depiction of the dragon figure at the bottom."

Ian added, "Do you know if British philosopher Thomas Hobbes influenced William Blake?"

The lady looked a little confused. "I'm not entirely sure."

"How long has this watercolor been on display?" Vanessa asked.

"It just recently came on display this month. It was on display several years ago. One of our benefactors wanted it on display."

Ian asked curiously, "May I ask who is the benefactor?"

"This exhibition is made possible through the generosity of Elliot and Stephanie Brooks," the lady said, pointing to the plaque with the benefactors' names.

"Thank you for the information," Vanessa said, and Ian nodded.

"If there is anything else, please let me know. Enjoy the rest of your visit," the lady said, then walked to the front of the museum.

Vanessa turned to Ian. "As you said, you don't believe in coincidences. Can we track down Elliot and Stephanie Brooks?"

Ian pulled out his phone and immediately Googled the benefactors' names. He found something in his search and seemed to have purchased something where a QR code came up, and then Ian locked his phone. He then looked at Vanessa. "Let's go—I think I know where to find them."

CHAPTER 32

New York City
Sunday Afternoon
Madison Avenue

Ian and Vanessa walked out of the Morgan Library, turned right on Madison Avenue, and started going up Madison at a fairly brisk pace. Vanessa kept in stride with Ian, but she had no idea where they were going.

"I meant to ask, do you know Elliot and Stephanie Brooks? Aren't they like mega-donors in U.S. politics?"

"Yeah, well, sort of. Elliot Brooks operates one of the largest hedge funds in the world. His firm is one of the most secret groups, and they avoid the headlines as much as possible. But he does want to be known in the political circles."

"Do you know him personally?"

"I did go to his firm once for an investment opportunity. He turned me down and said he wanted something more leading edge."

"Well, it's his loss. Your firm has done very well since."

"Thanks. I know what I do isn't for every investor. This was before I knew how far right he and his political views were. While an investment is an investment, I've found out he wants his investments to reflect his political views."

As Ian finished his thought, Vanessa's eyes lit up. "Oh, I think I remember reading about him. Stephanie—isn't she like a supermodel who tweeted about pro-gun rights right after a few major shootings?"

"Yes, that is her. However, she isn't a supermodel. She is beautiful, but I don't think she thinks much before speaking. So, in my mind, she isn't that attractive."

Vanessa smiled, giving Ian some credit for his taste in women.

"So, where are we going?"

"Are you interested in listening to some chamber music?"

"I guess. I don't usually listen to classical music. If I do, I prefer to see it live."

"Well, today is your lucky day. We are going to a concert. It's only a few more blocks. I found a private concert starting shortly, and they are the sponsors. From what I could tell, they are going to be there. Might be a good opportunity to talk with them."

"Perfect. Who's performing?"

"David Finckel and Wu Han. From what I quickly read, it's a summer salon series that the Brooks are sponsoring."

"Sounds nice."

Ian and Vanessa stopped in the middle of the next block. A small line was in front of one of the luxury apartment buildings. Typically, there wouldn't be a line as the buildings were not open to the public, and the doormen would have people move along. However, since a concert was being held in one of the apartments, a man in a suit next to the doorman checked everyone's tickets before guiding them to the elevator.

The man in the suit scanned Ian's phone and showed them to the elevator. Ian and Vanessa rode up with one other couple. The other couple nodded to Vanessa and Ian but said nothing else during the elevator ride to the apartment.

The elevator doors opened. The other couple walked out first and went to the right. Ian and Vanessa followed. About fifty feet from the elevator, one of the apartment doors was open, with a sign in front of the door stating "Brooks Concert Series." Ian and Vanessa crossed the doorway into the foyer and were immediately greeted by a server offering champagne. They each took a glass and looked around the foyer. Guests circulated in the foyer and in the adjacent rooms. The marble foyer looked out onto Madison Avenue and was decorated with modern paintings and sculptures. Closest to the window were two couches facing each other, with a coffee table and two chairs on either side creating a closed rectangle.

The room to the left of the foyer was where the concert would occur. Folding chairs were set up with a piano at the far end of the room and a chair to the side for the cellist. While the event had open seating, no one had yet claimed their seats. The room to the right of the foyer led to the rest of the apartment. Only two doors were closed at the far end of the apartment. The guests seemed to mingle and drink champagne like patrons in a museum. Several servers came around with more champagne and some small bites.

Ian and Vanessa looked around the apartment and made some small talk with each other as they tried to see if they could find Elliot and Stephanie Brooks.

After about twenty minutes, there was a clink of a glass from the left side of the foyer. Everyone turned toward the noise of the glass, where they were greeted by Elliot Brooks, who wore a blazer with a white button-down shirt and khaki pants. "Excuse me, if everyone can make their way to their seat, we can start the concert. There will be more champagne and bites later." Elliot then walked toward the piano, where Stephanie was seated in the front row.

About eighty people then made their way to find seats. Ian and Vanessa found some open seats in the middle section. One-page programs were printed on each chair.

Once everyone was seated, Elliot stood up and took Stephanie's hand to stand next to him. Stephanie wore a blue Lilly Pulitzer dress. Her long blonde hair stood out even more as it fell on the blue dress. Elliot grabbed a microphone with his free hand and started to speak. "Stephanie and I want to thank you for coming to the inaugural Brooks Summer Chamber Series. We are so excited that David Finckel and Wu Han are our first performers. We will have these salon concerts throughout the summer in different homes around the city. The proceeds of these concerts will go to children's education in artificial intelligence."

The crowd clapped, and Ian and Vanessa looked at each other. "Isn't that somewhat of an oxymoron?" Vanessa whispered to Ian.

"Yeah, it would seem so."

"Thank you," Elliot continued as the applause quieted. "I know everyone here didn't come here to hear me talk. Without further ado, let's welcome David Finckel and Wu Han."

The crowd started to clap, and Elliot and Stephanie took their seats. Then Wu Han and David Finckel, carrying his cello, walked out to the center and bowed. Wu Han wore a long black and gold dress, and David Finckel wore a dark suit with a bow tie.

Wu Han positioned herself at the piano, and David Finckel positioned himself with his cello in his chair to the side of Wu Han. They then began their performance. The program entranced everyone with the way David Finckel and Wu Han played their instruments. Their movements looked like they were conversing with their instruments rather than just playing them. The program focused on the complete cycle of Beethoven's cello-piano duets.

There was a short intermission. Vanessa looked at Ian. "Wow! That was incredible. I've heard a few of these pieces but always in a much larger concert hall and on Spotify, but never in a home environment."

Ian nodded. "So true. I still couldn't stop thinking about what Elliot said about A.I. I know it has been a hot topic, but I think it is already well-funded. There are many more problems in the world, especially regarding education."

"So true. It seems like a wealthy person's problem," Vanessa replied.

"Yeah. Yet it fits what I know of the Elliots. I want to talk with them before we leave."

"Definitely."

The guests started returning to their seats for the concert's second half.

The concert ended in a standing ovation. Then, the guests mingled with more champagne and bites, joined by David Finckel and Wu Han.

Ian and Vanessa found their way to Elliot and Stephanie. Stephanie hung on Elliot's arm like arm candy.

"Hi Elliot, it's Ian Steele." Ian stuck out his hand, and Elliot shook it. "This is my friend Vanessa Dupont." Vanessa then stuck out her hand and shook Elliot's hand.

"It's very nice to see you again, Ian, and meet you, Vanessa," he paused as he shook their hands. "This is my lovely wife, Stephanie." Stephanie smiled and shook their hands.

"What brings you to the city? I thought I heard you left your company. Still looking for money?" Elliot said.

"My company is doing very well. I am taking some time off to work with the United Nations at the upcoming women's rights conference," Ian replied.

Elliot and Stephanie both laughed. "Who cares about women's rights? Artificial intelligence will replace us all. And no one will have to work," Stephanie said.

Vanessa made a slight scowl before she spoke. "Artificial intelligence may change some things, but it still won't solve women's rights problems around the world."

Elliot held Stephanie tighter. "I think Stephanie means that a bigger revolution is coming, and then we can sit back, have peace, and not worry anymore."

Ian thought he dodged a bullet by not having Elliot invest in his company. While Elliot may have been successful, he and his wife were very aloof. Ian thought on his feet to change the course of the conversation. "So, Elliot, I assume you are investing in A.I. companies?"

Elliot's eyes became wider, and he made a large smile. "Fuck yes! I'm an angel investor in a company that is about to launch. They are finishing the research and development phase and will soon hit the market. It's going to blow all the competition out of the fucking water."

Stephanie smiled. "We will be so rich from this." Vanessa thought about what Ian had said earlier; Stephanie did not think before she spoke. She wondered what Stephanie would do if she were really in some of the undeveloped parts of the world.

"May I ask the name of the company?" Vanessa asked.

"Leviathan. That name is just so powerful," Elliot smugly said. "Stephanie and I donated a Leviathan painting to the Morgan Library. You should check it out."

"We just came from there," Vanessa said.

"Isn't that painting so evocative?" Stephanie said, still holding Elliot's arm.

"If you say so," Ian said. "But I think there could be a warning."

"You don't take risks, Ian. See the bigger fucking picture, and you will see the things on the horizon are closer than you think and will change the world. No one wants the United Nations," Elliot said. He looked at Stephanie, who said she was bored and wanted to move on to the other guests.

Elliot looked at Ian and Vanessa and said, "It was nice seeing you, Ian, and nice meeting you, Vanessa. We need to tell some of our high-level donors hello."

"It's good to see you and Stephanie," Ian said. Elliot and Stephanie walked hand in hand as they schmoozed with other guests, including David Finckel and Wu Han.

Vanessa turned to Ian. "That is an interesting couple. I think they wouldn't survive without money."

Ian laughed. "You are right. And the unfortunate part is, Elliot hasn't changed." He paused, then looked at Vanessa. "I've not heard of Leviathan as a new company. We need to look into that."

"Definitely," Vanessa said. "Let's get out of here. Elliot and Stephanie aren't worthy of presenting music like what we heard."

Ian smiled and nodded his head. They finally made their way out of the apartment and building.

CHAPTER 33

Palo Alto
Monday Morning
Rodin Sculpture Garden

Jack entered the open-air sculpture garden on a beautiful California blue sky morning. He was overdressed, in a suit and sunglasses, and admired Rodin's magnificent works. Many college students were around since the sculpture garden was on Stanford University's campus. Some of them looked at Jack. If anyone asked him why he was dressed in a suit, he would say that he was part of the presidential visit, which would be occurring in the afternoon.

Jack stopped to admire Rodin's *The Three Large Shades*, each one six feet tall. The sculpture depicts three souls of the damned at the entrance of Hell who all point to one inscription that states, "Abandon hope, all ye who enter here." Jack found the inscription ironic as he was about to see a system that would give the world even more hope. He was not an artist, but he was always amazed at how marble and bronze could be molded to seem lifelike and extremely detailed.

He walked about fifty feet to the center of the sculpture garden, which displayed *The Gates of Hell,* towering over twenty feet high. All the sculptures in the garden were in *The Gates of Hell* but on a smaller scale. Jack again admired the gates. Since he was admiring the sculptures, once he sat down for his meeting in the garden, no one would question his intentions.

He continued walking to the left side of the gates, where there was a long bench occupied by a man wearing a black polo shirt, jeans, and a San Francisco Giants hat.

"Nice suit," the man in the hat said.

"Remember, I'm here on official business. I can't just change when the president will be on site soon," Jack said, not looking at the other man. He looked out and said, "So, is Leviathan ready?"

The man in the hat eagerly pulled out an iPhone, opened an app, and gave the phone to Jack.

"Can anyone find this fucking app?" Jack said aggressively.

"No. It's made into an app after you download it from the server. It looks like an app, but it's much more than that," the man calmly replied.

Jack looked at the phone and the app. The screen showed the name Leviathan with a search bar underneath. "This looks like a Google search."

"Well, it is, and it isn't. After you type in a search, the results will show deepfakes, algorithmic biases based on bad data, and other social manipulation tools. It will seem so real and much better than any other search engine to the general public."

"And the plan is in place, too?"

"Yes, after approval, I will bring the companies out here to their knees, and Leviathan will rise."

"Good," Jack said. "Now let me test this." Jack typed in *United Nations Women's Conference* into the search. Within milliseconds, every result showed different anti-women messages. The first few results pertained to how the Middle East was breaking down and war was imminent. There were deepfaked photos of the Middle Eastern army getting ready to launch offensives. There was even data claiming that women staying at home made men more productive and gave them higher incomes.

Jack skimmed a few more pages of results and saw there were hundreds more pages of results. "Wow! This is really impressive. I think the group will be impressed."

The man took Jack's computer and started to type. "Let me show you another cool feature." He pulled up a screen of Arab militants. "This is a live image taken from a drone that the CIA is currently watching." He paused and hit a few more keys on the keyboard. "The CIA has some of these militants' phones tracked. I've been able to upload a ghost version of Leviathan through the CIA's database and got access to these militants' phones. What do you want to happen to their phones?" The man looked at Jack.

"Ideally, what about blowing them up? But if not, maybe

send them a message." Jack said as he looked at the man.

"You are of little faith, my friend." He then hit a few more buttons on the keyboard and looked up at Jack as he hit the enter button. "Watch 'em and weep." As Jack looked at the screen, four of the militant phones started to vibrate and catch fire. The militants began to scream and throw their phones down on the ground. In the middle of the screaming, the man cut off the feed. "Those Arab bastards and the CIA bastards will have no idea what happened; even if they look through all the code, they won't find any traces of my software." He said, and he started to put away the computer. "I think your group will be more than impressed."

Jack smirked, "They are going to be truly impressed."

The man smiled smugly and said, "Not one of these companies out here initially gave me the time of day. But who is going to have the last laugh now?"

"We will make sure you do," Jack said, returning the phone to the man. "How can I get a copy of this?"

"I will send you the link on the server, and then you can share it with the others."

Jack pulled out his phone and typed a few numbers in an app. "The second part of your payment has just been sent. The remaining will be sent after the launch."

"Much obliged. You know where to find me."

Jack stood up and walked out of the sculpture garden without saying goodbye to the man in the hat.

CHAPTER 34

New York City
Tuesday
3 Sutton Place

Ian and Vanessa approached the four-story building, which had traditionally been the residence of the United Nations Secretary-General. It overlooked the East River and Roosevelt Island and was about a mile north of the United Nations Headquarters.

Right before getting to the building, they were met by two policemen who asked them for their identification and what was their purpose.

"We are meeting with Mrs. Mirreaux. My name is Vanessa Dupont, and my colleague is Ian Steele," Vanessa said as she gave her ID, and Ian gave his.

The policeman scanned their IDs and looked through his computer. After a couple of minutes, he raised his head. "Thank you, Ms. Dupont and Mr. Steele. Please walk to the front door, and someone will greet you."

Vanessa and Ian took back their IDs and walked toward the front door. The door opened, and they were greeted by a young lady in a black blouse and a black skirt. "Hi, Mr. Steele and Ms. Dupont. My name is Emily. I'm Mrs. Mirreaux's assistant. Please follow me."

Vanessa and Ian followed Emily into the building and up the stairs. "I hope you didn't have any trouble getting here," Emily said.

"No trouble. But I've been busy working on a project with a deadline and exploring the city," Vanessa said.

"Oh. Is this your first time in the United States?"

"No, I've been to the United States before. But this is my first time in New York."

"I've been to New York often, but I live in Boston and Geneva currently," Ian said, as Emily looked at him.

"That's great," Emily said as they approached the fourth floor and entered the library. The library had many books and a seating area with a coffee table. There were some half-empty moving boxes near the bookcases. "Please excuse the mess," Emily continued. "Mrs. Mirreaux is in the process of moving, as you are aware."

"No problem at all," Ian said, and Vanessa nodded.

"Please feel free to take a seat, and I'll let Mrs. Mirreaux know you both are here. Also, can I offer you both anything to drink?" Emily said.

"If it wouldn't be too much trouble, can I have a coffee?" Vanessa asked.

"Not a problem. Mr. Steele, can I get you a coffee as well?"

Ian looked at the books and then turned toward Vanessa and Emily. "Sure, a coffee would be great."

"Great. Please wait here," Emily said as she exited the room and closed the door.

"A trick I learned in my short career," Vanessa said as she looked at Ian.

"What's that?"

"Sometimes, by asking for a drink before the subject is in the room, you can have a little extra time exploring the room for clues."

Ian smiled. "Good point."

He and Vanessa started to look at the bookshelves casually. Most of the books were in several different languages. Their subjects pertained to global issues of the day and history. One shelf was dedicated to literary fiction. One of the bottom shelves displayed larger coffee table books. Another shelf had books focused on economics, while the other had books on artificial intelligence.

"I'm impressed by the level of detail that went into each shelf. Similar subjects together," Ian said.

"I know," Vanessa said. "My work office can be this way, but my apartment is another story. It takes me forever to find a book I'm looking for."

"Anything seems out of place?" Ian asked as he still looked at the shelves.

"Not that I can see," Vanessa said. "Just seems like a savvy diplomatic residence."

Vanessa and Ian looked for a couple more minutes, and then Vanessa tapped Ian on the shoulder. "Check this out," she said and pointed to a book on a philosophy shelf.

Ian looked at the book she pointed to: Leviathan by Thomas Hobbes. "Interesting. Always keeping the philosophers of the past relevant," he said.

The door began to open, and Mrs. Mirreaux walked in, wearing a black jacket and a black skirt. She also wore the same infinity pendant from the funeral and other photos. Both Ian and Vanessa took notice. "Ms. Dupont and Mr. Steele, sorry to keep you waiting." She walked over to shake Vanessa and Ian's hands.

"Not a problem. I'm so sorry for your loss," Vanessa said as she shook Mrs. Mirreaux's hand.

"My sincere condolences. Your husband was a great man," Ian said as he shook Mrs. Mirreaux's hand.

"Thank you. Please come have a seat, and please excuse the mess," Mrs. Mirreaux said as she sat on the couch. Ian and Vanessa followed behind and sat in two leather chairs across the couch.

"Please don't fret," Ian said.

Mrs. Mirreaux smiled. "Seung Kim has graciously let me stay through the women's conference, given what has happened. Or maybe it is because the conference is in Geneva, and Seung doesn't need a New York residence yet."

"I'm sure Mr. Kim would have let you stay a little longer even if he needed to be more in New York," Vanessa replied.

"I wouldn't be too sure. While the United Nations tries to be high and mighty, there are certain people there who will do anything for their best interest," Mrs. Mirreaux said. There was tension in the room for a few seconds, then Mrs. Mirreaux changed the tone. "Were you both offered something to drink?"

"Yes, Emily did say she was going to get us some coffee," Ian said.

A few moments later, Emily opened the door and carried a large tray with three cups and a pot of coffee. She set the tray on a table near the door and poured the coffee.

"My apologies for the wait," Emily said. "Would any of you like any cream or sugar?"

"Emily knows how I like my coffee," Mrs. Mirreaux said. "Ms. Dupont and Mr. Steele, how do you take your coffee?"

"One sugar and cream, please," Vanessa said.

"Just sugar for me, and black is fine," Ian said.

Emily poured the coffee and added milk and sugar to the three cups. She then gave the first cup to Mrs. Mirreaux, the second cup to Vanessa, and the third cup to Ian.

"Thank you, Emily," Mrs. Mirreaux said as she sipped her coffee. Emily then quietly exited the room and shut the door.

Mrs. Mirreaux shifted her attention to Vanessa and Ian. "Ms. Dupont, I read your dissertation and was very impressed. I hear you want to write a book about me."

Vanessa smiled. "Thank you. You have an important voice that needs to be highlighted—one that your late husband does not overshadow."

Mrs. Mirreaux nodded and turned to Ian. "Mr. Steele, I was surprised when I heard you would join Ms. Dupont. I took you for an entrepreneur."

"Well, I am an entrepreneur and am taking some time to help the U.N. with the upcoming conference," Ian responded.

"That's admirable," Mrs. Mirreaux said. "But I'm sure you will miss the private sector soon enough. How did you and Ms. Dupont connect?"

"Well, I guess I'm her assistant at the moment. I like research adventures," Ian replied.

"He's been invaluable," Vanessa said and tried to change course. "So, Mrs. Mirreaux, you have a beautiful pendant. I've recently seen you wearing it at your husband's funeral and other functions. Does it have any special significance?"

Mrs. Mirreaux picked up her coffee cup, took a sip, and then put it on the table. She let the pause take up the room. "Well, it's a symbol for me to keep pushing on. Everything has a way of working out."

"What does this mean for you? Has this helped you during your time as a refugee?" Vanessa asked.

"Yes and no. I have always had to keep pushing to get to where I am and to escape the bad connotations of being a refugee."

"But how can something change? It would seem that everything stays the same." Ian asked.

"That's a good point," Mrs. Mirreaux replied. "But if you look closely, one must continually adjust to keep going and pushing forward."

Ian sat back and drank some of his coffee. Vanessa then asked, "Besides the information I've written about you in my dissertation, what is something that I didn't write about and/or something that most people don't know about you?"

Mrs. Mirreaux took a few seconds to pause before answering. "There is a Syrian proverb that says 'dwell not upon thy weariness, thy strength shall be according to the measure of thy desire.'" Mrs. Mirreaux paused to let the proverb sink in, then added, "I think I had a drive of not wanting to always be a refugee or always designated as such."

As Vanessa wrote down some notes, Ian replied, "I think many people who become refugees have this same drive. But not nearly as many are as lucky as you."

Mrs. Mirreaux looked at Ian. "I think having family friends that I knew in the United Kingdom helped my mental state. Like that light at the end of the tunnel, as you Americans like to say."

Vanessa began to realize where Ian's line of questioning was headed. Then she asked, "When your family was killed, where were you? How were you able to survive?"

Mrs. Mirreaux wiped a tear from her eye, then replied, "My parents were big proponents of women's rights in Syria. At the time of their assassination, they were creating women's health clinics."

"They must have known the dangers," Vanessa added.

"Of course. But they knew the risks and still believed in the greater good. I think that is why I have tried to press the U.N. to work on this women's conference. It is an homage to the work my parents and many others, especially in war-torn areas, have died trying to do."

"That is very admirable," Vanessa said. "After the conference, what will you do?"

"That's an excellent question; I will start a foundation in my husband's name and continue his work. I have not made that announcement public yet, so please keep that information confidential, but you can add it to your book," Mrs. Mirreaux stated.

Vanessa smiled, "That's great. I will be sure to keep that confidential. Maybe the last part of the book can focus on this new foundation?"

"Yes, that would work. Before you leave, I will give you the contact information of a few people at the foundation who could be helpful in your writing. Before I forget, I will tell Emily to get that information for you." Mrs. Mirreaux then stood up.

"Thank you, that would be very helpful," Vanessa said as Mrs. Mirreaux walked out of the room.

Vanessa looked back at Ian, who had a quizzical look.

"What's wrong?" Vanessa asked.

"Mrs. Mirreaux seems different. I know her husband just passed, and she is probably stressed with the conference coming up, too. But she seems different from what I've seen her before. Granted, I've never actually met her till now. But just something feels off," Ian replied.

"I think you are right. She does seem a little more arrogant. I don't know if that's the right word."

Mrs. Mirreaux walked back into the room. "Emily will bring that information to you shortly."

"Thank you again," Vanessa said.

Mrs. Mirreaux nodded, and Ian asked, "For your foundation, will you still work through the U.N.?"

"No, we will be working through the private sector. I have a group of investors and family who would prefer no governmental oversight." Mrs. Mirreaux paused and looked at her watch. There was a knock on the door, and Emily entered with a piece of paper.

Emily walked over to Vanessa and gave her a folded paper. "Here are the names Mrs. Mirreaux requested that I give you."

Vanessa unfolded the paper, and Ian looked over Vanessa's shoulder and saw the foundation people's names, phone numbers, and emails handwritten. At the top, though, was a Leviathan cross.

Emily then whispered something in Mrs. Mirreaux's ear, and she stood up. "Ms. Dupont and Mr. Steele, thank you both for coming. I've just been informed that my next appointment is on his way here."

Ian and Vanessa stood up. Vanessa said, "Thank you so much for your time. This has been quite helpful."

"Before you go, the symbol at the top of this note is unique," Ian said.

"Oh, that's the logo for the foundation. I think it's unique and strong," Mrs. Mirreaux said. After briefly pausing, she continued, "I will be happy to talk to you more about your book. Please send some questions, or we can talk in Geneva during the conference."

"That would be lovely. I will coordinate with Emily," Vanessa said.

Vanessa and Ian then shook Mrs. Mirreaux's hand as she left the room. Emily then showed Ian and Vanessa out.

They walked for a couple of blocks in silent thought. "We need to see that professor of yours to find out about the cross," Vanessa said.

"Yes, definitely. I don't think that cross is unique, as she told us. Plus, I thought all her family was killed in Syria. We need to investigate more about her time in the U.K. and find out who those family friends were or are."

CHAPTER 35

New York City
Tuesday Afternoon
3 Sutton Place

"What time did he say he would be here?" Mrs. Mirreaux asked Emily.

"He said in about an hour. He just landed in LaGuardia and is coming right over," Emily responded.

Mrs. Mirreaux nodded and said, "When he arrives, show him to my private office. And please, don't disturb me when I meet with him."

Emily looked at Mrs. Mirreaux. "Of course, ma'am."

Mrs. Mirreaux then walked to her private office without saying another word to Emily. While waiting for the next appointment, Emily stayed put and looked through her phone at Mrs. Mirreaux's emails.

Mrs. Mirreaux walked into her office and sat at her computer, reflecting on her conversation with Ian and Vanessa.

About an hour later, Emily was notified that the man Mrs. Mirreaux was going to meet had just arrived and was heading to the front door. She met the man at the door and showed him to Mrs. Mirreaux's private office.

As Emily left, she asked, "Would you care for anything to drink?"

Before the man could respond, Mrs. Mirreaux said, "We are fine. Please no disturbances." Emily then nodded and closed the door.

Mrs. Mirreaux waited a few seconds to make sure Emily did not return. Then she turned to her guest, who was seated across from her. "Jack, were there any complications?"

"No, ma'am," Jack said as he sat up straight.

"Good, can I see it?"

"Of course, may I?" Jack said as he motioned to her laptop.

"Yes, please," she said as she moved her laptop toward Jack. She watched him work on the computer, and a few minutes later, he turned the computer back toward her.

Without saying a word, she started to investigate the program. She spent the next twenty minutes in silence. He did not say a word either. He was hopeful the program would pass her inspection. If not, he tried to think about how he could get back to California without raising suspicions from the president.

She then looked up at him. "This is very good. This will have lethal consequences. It's exactly what the investors want. Please show the investors and tell them it comes with my approval."

"Yes, ma'am."

"Is everything in place when it goes live?"

"The developer said yes and is ready to act when called upon."

"Good," she said and sat back in her chair. "I will call Damien to let him know the next phase should go ahead, and he will also inform the investors."

"Yes, ma'am. Anything else?" he said as he stood up.

She stayed seated and said, "No, that is all." She then turned to her computer as he walked out.

CHAPTER 36

In between New York City and Boston
Wednesday Morning
Acela

The train wasn't too crowded for a weekday morning. Vanessa and Ian sat across each other as they worked on their computers.

"I've been searching for those family friends in the U.K. There isn't much to be found," Vanessa said. "I see that Mrs. Mirreaux mentions them occasionally, but there are barely any photos of them."

"Maybe they just aren't into being photographic," Ian said.

"No, this is different. I have this feeling they are hiding something, or someone is trying to hide them."

"Interesting. Keep digging," he said. He glanced at his computer and then looked up again. "Also, I've been looking into this Leviathan A.I. company that Elliot and Stephanie were enchanted by. It, too, is very secret. However, several Wall Street message boards indicate it will be a game changer when the company goes public. Although the product is said to be unseen by anyone, there are rumors that certain high-level government investors have been given access to it."

"You know Wall Street better than I do. Is that normal?"

"Not exactly. In most cases, it is normal to see what type of products a company works on before it goes public. Even if they want to stay under the radar, they will tease one of their products to the public so that their IPO will stir up some talk. Then, the hope is when it goes public, the IPO prices will open and shoot up, thus making the institutional and initial investors very, very satisfied. On top of that, A.I. is a hot topic."

"Do you think Mrs. Mirreaux's foundation is one of the investors?"

"I'm not sure. If they were, I don't see the connection. Plus, what does this have to do with the Secretary-General's assassination?"

"For one, it could be about money. But who stands to benefit?"

"I'm not exactly sure," Ian said, as they looked quizzically at each other.

After a few minutes of further research, Ian told Vanessa, "I'm going to email my professor to see if he can meet with us earlier than the weekend." Vanessa nodded.

Ian opened his Gmail account on his laptop and composed an email.

Dear Dr. Sheets,

I hope you are well. I'm reaching out to let you know that a colleague and I are arriving in Boston earlier than expected. We are actually on the train from New York right now to Boston.

By chance, are you in town so we can meet a little earlier than originally planned?

Fondly,

Ian

A few minutes later, Ian received an email notification. It was from Harry Sheets.

Dear Ian,

I'm glad to receive your message.

I'm on my way back from San Francisco right now. As we speak, I am in the airport, waiting for my JetBlue flight.....a long cross-country flight.....but I'm happy it's nonstop. I have had to leave the conference earlier than expected.

That said, I will be in my office tomorrow from 11 a.m. to 1 p.m. and again from 3 p.m. to 5 p.m. I'm juggling my teaching commitments and deadlines for my new book....which is past due!!

Respectfully,

Harry

Harry Sheets
Semiotics - Chair
Harvard University

Ian quickly wrote back again.

Dear Dr. Sheets,
We will be at your office at 11 a.m. tomorrow.
Best,
Ian

After sending the last message, Ian looked at Vanessa. "11 a.m. tomorrow with the professor."

Vanessa smiled in relief but wondered if they were racing against the clock about a conspiracy or overthinking this whole scenario.

CHAPTER 37

Cambridge
Thursday Morning

Ian and Vanessa hopped out of their Uber in Harvard Square as a bustling group exited the Harvard T stop. Some people turned behind them toward the Starbucks, while others kept walking towards the Harvard campus.

Ian and Vanessa walked across the street from the T stop through the opening in the stone wall, which officially led them to Harvard's campus. Many students exited their dorms with backpacks and headed to class. Some students walked with breakfast and coffee in their hands. As they passed the sculpture of John Harvard, a group of tourists admired it and rubbed the foot of John Harvard, which is believed to give people good luck.

Vanessa watched the people take turns rubbing the sculpture's foot. "Shouldn't we go rub the foot for good luck? At least that is what I've read about Harvard."

Ian smiled at Vanessa as he continued leading the way. "The students know that sculpture as the statue of three lies."

Vanessa looked puzzled. "I don't understand."

He continued, "The first lie is that the person in that sculpture is not John Harvard. In 1884, the French sculptor used another model since John Harvard had no living representation. The second lie is that John Harvard was not the founder of Harvard. He was the first major benefactor of the university. And the third lie is that Harvard was founded in 1636, not 1638."

"Interesting. Why not correct these things?"

"Maybe it just adds to the Harvard mystique."

She admired the red brick buildings with white trim on the Harvard campus as they continued to walk. "Isn't the architectural style of these buildings Georgian Revival?"

He looked at her. "Impressive. You are right. How did you know that?"

"Something I recall from one or two architectural history classes I took for fun at university."

He smiled. "I'm impressed. A few other parts of campus have other architectural styles." He paused as they crossed the street. "We have just about a block left till the archeology department. After we meet with Dr. Sheets, we will have to go down by the river; it's an amazing view."

She smiled as she followed him into one of the red stone academic buildings and proceeded up the stairs. There were a few students, but not too many, as it was summer. Once they reached the third floor, they walked down the hall past different professors' offices.

He stopped in front of the office, which said, "Dr. Harry Sheets Semiotics—Chair." He collected himself and knocked on the door.

A man with a commanding voice called out from behind the door, "Come in."

As Ian opened the door, he said, "Good morning, Dr. Sheets." Vanessa followed.

Dr. Sheets smiled, stood up from his chair at his desk, and stuck out his hand. "Ian Steele, it's so good to see you. Thank you for taking the time." Dr. Sheets had broad shoulders and wore a button-down shirt with rolled sleeves. He wore black pants and had a goatee. As they shook hands, Dr. Sheets turned his attention to Vanessa. "Hi, I'm Harry Sheets," he said.

Vanessa smiled and shook Dr. Sheets' hand. "I'm Vanessa Dupont. Ian and I are helping each other on a special research project."

Dr. Sheets looked at them and motioned toward the open chairs across from his desk. "Please have a seat," he paused. "Vanessa Dupont, are you a journalist?" The desk was covered with stacks of books and research papers. There was a small desk behind him where a MacBook sat open. The rest of the office had two significant bookcases filled with books from the floor to the ceiling.

She smiled as she sat down. "Yes. Ian must have told you."

Sitting in the chair, Ian said, "Dr. Sheets has a photographic memory."

Dr. Sheets smiled. "Yes, I do have a photographic memory. I recently read a few of your articles. I was impressed by your style and conclusions."

"Thank you. I'm not really at the level yet of writing opinions; I'm just reporting the news."

"You'll get there soon enough. You have talent," Dr. Sheets said and then shifted the topic. "So, you came here to talk about the Leviathan Cross."

Ian and Vanessa nodded. "We have been seeing versions of it come up in places that we've been traveling, from Geneva to New York," Ian said.

"Well, as I said in my brief email, there's an interesting and long history with that symbol."

"Dr. Sheets, just remember this isn't one of your classes where you can space out the lecture," Ian said, and Vanessa smirked.

"Yes, I know some of my students, like you, grasp the topics discussed more quickly than others." Dr. Sheets paused, stood up, picked out a book, opened it to the middle where it showed the Leviathan Cross, and put it on his desk for Ian and Vanessa to see.

"I'll try to be brief," Dr. Sheets said as he sat back in his chair. "The cross has a complex history, drawing on alchemic, mythological, and religious influences. It does have an association with Satanism, which has given it somewhat of a controversial reputation in today's culture. Some people call it the Cross of Satan."

Dr. Sheets took a sip of water as Ian and Vanessa listened intently as if they were in a college lecture. He continued, "It is believed to have originated in alchemical texts. Alchemy was an ancient practice of seeking spiritual transformation through natural substances. 'Leviathan' in alchemy refers to the primal state of nature before transformation. 'Leviathan' is also mentioned in the Bible, referring to a sea monster that only God could tame in the Book of Job. There is also a Leviathan mentioned in the Book of Isaiah.

"This Leviathan Cross," he said as he pointed to the cross in the book, " see, combines the Christian Cross and the infinity symbol. The cross can also signify the balance between good and evil or other opposing forces.

"In today's culture, besides being associated with Satan, it is also used as a symbol of defiance, independence, or rebellion against traditional religious beliefs."

Vanessa interrupted Dr. Sheets. "Pardon me. But does this Leviathan have anything to do with Thomas Hobbes?"

"You have a very perceptive colleague, Mr. Steele. You might want to keep her around," Dr. Sheets said towards Ian, then turned to both of them. Ian and Vanessa smiled.

Dr. Sheets continued, "First, the actual name of Thomas Hobbes' book is *Leviathan: Or The Matter, Form and Power of a Commonwealth Ecclesiastical and Civil.* It has been commonly referred to as *Leviathan.* It is believed that Hobbes chose Leviathan because he wanted an image of strength and power to uphold its sovereign. I think it is also believed that Hobbes wanted something memorable.

"It was not lost on Hobbes that Leviathan came from the Bible. Yet, in the scenes where the Leviathan is mentioned in the Bible, the Leviathan tries to bring chaos to the world while God can bring peace and order. In Hobbes' work, he established his Leviathan as a 'mortal god' who can bring peace by overruling rebellions."

"So, does the Leviathan cross symbol have anything to do with Thomas Hobbes?" asked Vanessa.

"Insofar as the Leviathan is a powerful figure, they can be considered connected. But under the surface, I don't see how they can be connected."

"Have you heard of a new company named Leviathan?" Ian asked.

"Oh, now Mister capitalism comes into view," Dr. Sheets said with a smirk, then changed his tune. "Sorry, I am more of an academic, and I don't care for money and greed. Though if it brings peace, I'm for it." He paused again and was in thought. "Now that you mentioned it, I did hear some grumblings somewhere about a potential Artificial Intelligence project called Leviathan. I don't know whatever happened to it, and it very well could have been a working preliminary title."

"Do you recall where you heard about this project?" Ian asked.

Dr. Sheets thought for a moment more, "I think it was in passing from a few other professors. I think someone from the U.S. government was seeking A.I. experts to help with a national security project. I believe no Harvard professor joined, at least not to my knowledge."

Vanessa took out her phone, opened her Notes app, and wrote,

Leviathan = Government + Mirreaux (others killed) + wife + finance (meaning ?????)

CHAPTER 38

Cambridge

Ian and Vanessa walked out of the building without a word. Ian turned away from the direction they had originally come, and Vanessa followed. They walked toward the Harvard Museum of Natural History in the same general quad. As there weren't too many people around, Ian and Vanessa turned to each other.

"Something is amiss," Ian said.

Vanessa nodded in agreement. "Vraiment. Where can we go where we can think and not draw any attention?"

Ian thought momentarily, "How do you feel about rowing?"

"Well, I did row stroke in a double in university but haven't practiced much since."

"Let's go. I have a friend who works at the Cambridge Boat Club. He can help us get a shell, and then we can row that part of the Charles River where there isn't too much traffic."

She smirked. "Well, since we aren't doing any racing, why not?"

He pulled out his phone, texted, and requested an Uber. Within a few moments, the Uber pulled up to the street corner nearby, and Ian and Vanessa hopped in. Shortly into the ride, Ian's phone dinged. He checked it, replied, and then looked at Vanessa.

"We are all set. My friend said there will be a double waiting for us."

She smiled and looked out the car window at the Charles River. Although she usually enjoyed the sights, her mind went blank as she wondered how these puzzle pieces fit together.

The Uber ride took about ten minutes and had little traffic. Then, a car pulled into the U-drive parking lot, where Ian and Vanessa exited to see a two-story boathouse. They walked to the entrance, where a lanky white-haired man greeted them.

"Thanks for your help, Fred. And this is my colleague, Vanessa," Ian said, shaking the lanky white-haired man's hand and motioning to Vanessa.

Vanessa smiled and shook Fred's hand. "I know it might be a lot to ask, but do you have any workout clothes I could buy?"

Fred smiled. "Yes, we have a small shop this way." He showed Vanessa and Ian the options.

Ian and Vanessa picked out some clothes and went to their locker rooms to change. A few minutes later, Ian changed into a white T-shirt and black spandex, and Vanessa changed into a red shirt and black spandex.

Fred then guided them down to the dock, where a yellow double Empacher shell with four oars was already set in the water. "I don't usually set this out for people before their row, as I think the setup is part of the rowing experience. But for you, Ian, I'll do it." he said, as Vanessa got in the stroke seat and Ian in the second seat.

As Fred pushed the oars away, he said, "If you want less traffic, I would go through the Eliot Bridge." The Eliot Bridge was just to the right of the boathouse.

Vanessa and Ian nodded, and once all four oars touched the water, Vanessa looked back at Ian to see if he was ready.

"Ready," he said, ensuring the shell was pointed in the correct position through the bridge.

"Ready at the catch," she said as they rolled up the slide to the catch position. They squared their blades and let them rest in the water for a few seconds. Then she said, "Ready row." Immediately, they both gripped their oars; their feet pushed off their foot stretchers so that their legs strengthened as they pushed their oars into the water, immediately followed by their body rocking backward by hinging at their hips and bringing the oar out of the water and the handle into their chests. Once the oars were out of the water, they did the exact opposite motion with the oars out of the water to get back to the catch position. Then, they did the exact same movements. Contrary to what some may think, a rowing shell is only moving when the oars are out of the water. The oars create some momentum, and then the shell takes it the rest of the distance.

They rowed continuously for about ten minutes, and then

she called out, "Weigh enough in two." They took two more strokes and then feathered their blades on top of the water as the boat came to a stop.

"You're a very good stroke," Ian said.

"Thanks," Vanessa said as she turned slightly to look at Ian while balancing the boat with her oars. "So, do you think there's some conspiracy, or all these Leviathan signs just happen to be one super coincidence?"

"As I've said, I don't necessarily believe in coincidences. At least at this level, something else must be going on."

"I still don't see how and why Mrs. Mirreaux would be involved. She has influence."

Ian took a couple of light strokes to move the shell slightly. "Well, most conspiracies I've found boil down to money and power. Mrs. Mirreaux had much power with her husband. Public service isn't where one goes to make an exorbitant amount of money. So, it must be about the money."

Vanessa then took a couple more strokes. "Or maybe she was coerced?"

"Well, that is plausible, too." Ian looked out onto the embankment and saw some cars whizzing by and a few cars stopped near some parks.

"My journalistic gut tells me we must look at her adoptive family and her time before university." She slowly took a couple more strokes. "I think that will answer if she is involved in any way."

He nodded. "Do you have information about that family from your dissertation?"

"Not really. I have a few things, but they are back in Geneva in a box in my office. However, I think I have a phone number of a contact who can help in my phone. I'll look it up when we get back to the boathouse."

Whizz! Whizz! Pop! Pop! Whizz! Whizz! Pop! Pop!

"What was that?" Ian said as he looked around towards the embankment.

"IAN!!! Merde!!! Look!" Vanessa started to squirm in her seat as she saw the stern of the shell breaks. She looked toward Ian and saw the bow breaks in two, and then water quickly engulfed them.

Ian took a quick look towards the left embankment and saw someone lying on the top of a car with what looked to be a gun. "Fuck! Vanessa, take my hand and take a deep breath."

She let go of her oars, and he grabbed her hand. They both then took a deep breath and submerged underwater. They both quickly got their feet out of the foot stretchers. While holding her hand, he guided her to the opposite embankment.

Whizz! Whizz! Pop! Pop! Whizz! Whizz! Pop! Pop!

They could hear and see the bullets go by them as they started to swim away. The adrenaline in both of their bodies kept them going to the other embankment without coming up for a breath.

Whizz! Whizz! Pop! Pop! Whizz! Whizz! Pop! Pop!

Vanessa looked at Ian and motioned for him to come to the surface but in a floating position. Taking her lead, they started to float and came up with their backs to the water's surface. Both of them were able to cock their heads slightly to get fresh air into their lungs. They floated for about five minutes before she grabbed his hand, and they started to swim to the embankment.

CHAPTER 39

Cambridge

Vanessa and Ian lay still on the embankment for a few more minutes in the hope that whoever was shooting at them had left.

Ian then looked at Vanessa. "I think it's safe."

"What the hell was that?" Vanessa said as she and Ian stood up.

"I have no idea. But we need to get to England," he said as he looked around. "We need to get back to the boathouse to grab our phones and such."

"Yeah, but how will we get back? Is it safe to walk? We have no idea who shot at us."

"Let's walk back casually on this side and then we can cross over at the bridge near the boathouse." He reached out his hand toward her.

She took his hand, and they started to walk back toward the boathouse. They walked in silence as they observed their surroundings.

As they reached the boathouse, Fred pulled up in his truck. Ian and Vanessa walked to Fred.

Fred looked at Ian as he stepped out of his truck and started laughing. "It must have been a while since you've been rowing. You do know you are supposed to stay in the shell."

Ian made a small smile. "That's the thing. I owe you a new shell. It's in the middle of the Charles upriver. It's in pieces. You're going to need someone to retrieve it."

"What the hell happened?"

"Well, it would seem like someone tried shooting at us," Ian responded calmly.

"I don't understand."

"It would seem that we ticked someone off," Vanessa said.

"Are you both in some sort of trouble?" Fred asked, looking at both Ian and Vanessa.

"Well, not sure. I think this has something to do with what we are investigating," Ian said.

"I see. Why don't you both shower, and I'll take you back to your hotel."

"Are you sure? We don't want you involved," Vanessa said.

"I think you'll be much safer with me versus someone else. Go change, and I'll take you all back."

Ian and Vanessa nodded and went into the boathouse to change. Fred waited for both of them in the boathouse lobby.

Once Ian and Vanessa stepped into the lobby, Fred said, "Let's go. I'll survey the damage later."

Fred drove them back to the hotel, mainly in silence. Before getting out of the truck, Fred said, "Stay alive. I need to make sure you pay for that shell."

Vanessa and Ian smiled and responded, "Yeah, I'm looking forward to the day I pay for that new shell. Maybe I can get the naming right, too."

"Stay alive, and then we can talk about it." Ian and Vanessa smiled as they closed the door, and Fred drove off.

Ian and Vanessa walked to the elevator. "Let's grab our things and find a flight to London," Vanessa said.

Ian and Vanessa headed to Boston Logan in an Uber twenty minutes later. Ian directed the Uber to Terminal E, the international terminal. Afterward, they calmly walked and stood in line for British Airways, which had a main hub in Boston.

Fortunately, the British Airways agent found two seats in business class on the final flight out of Boston. As they waited for the flight, they booked a car at Heathrow for when they arrived and planned to drive to Oxford.

CHAPTER 40

Multiple Undisclosed Locations
Friday morning
Via videoconference

Everyone listened eagerly as Jack presented his findings: "I have tested Leviathan, and it is better than we could have imagined. I will upload Leviathan to the secure VPN for everyone to access. It will be similar to the VPN used for these meetings."

The scrambled voice then spoke up: "I will make sure Swan tests the program as well."

"Has Swan been notified about what is happening?" Ibrahim Kane asked.

"Yes, I assure you Swan knows all of your concerns," the scrambled voice said.

"Mr. Kane does bring up a good point. We are supposed to be similar to a board of directors for Leviathan, and Swan is the CEO," Zaaeem Farouq said.

"Swan will have this under control. Remember, this is their idea," Nakia Ahmed said.

"It is their idea, but we are the stakeholders," Farouq said.

Kabir Varma said, "If Leviathan works, we must tell Swan that this must be rolled out to the masses. We cannot wait too much longer. The conference starts late next week."

The scrambled voice said, "I have my contact setting things up for the next phase. Shall I go ahead and tell the contact to continue?"

All the members discussed this further as the scrambled voice listened. Everyone knew the next phase would have enormous economic implications for their countries.

Kane had the last word in the discussion, "I think everyone here is concerned that the last few attempts to stop the conference haven't worked. We need to try something more drastic." Everyone nodded. "And if Leviathan works how you say it works, we want Leviathan rolled out to the masses at the same time as the next phase."

The scrambled voice took notice and responded, "I will express to Swan that this is your wish."

"They are more than wishes; they are orders," Kabir said.

CHAPTER 41

Oxford
Saturday Afternoon
The Randolph Hotel

Ian and Vanessa took turns freshening up in the bathroom. They were fortunate to find a room in Oxford on such short notice. They could only get one bedroom with two twin beds because of the short notice.

Vanessa walked out of the bathroom, looking freshened up from the flight. "The bathroom is all yours."

Ian smiled as he walked to the bathroom. "I'm sorry the hotel didn't have two rooms or bigger beds."

"It's not a problem. I haven't slept in a twin bed since I went to summer camp as a teenager." She sat on the bed, pulled out her laptop, and connected to the Wi-Fi as he freshened up in the bathroom.

About five minutes later, he walked out of the bathroom and asked, "So, do you think we can find anything about Mrs. Mirreaux's time in England here?"

She looked up from her computer and smiled at him. "I believe her adoptive parents passed away a couple of years ago, but I believe some of her papers have been collected and given to the University of Oxford. On top of that, I believe an Oxford classmate of hers, Dr. Viyan Hadid, will be speaking here tomorrow."

"Isn't Dr. Hadid speaking at the conference in Geneva?"

"Yes, she is one of the leading cardiac surgeons in Germany, and she will be leading a presentation at the conference called *Empowering Women and Refugees: Building Resilience and Opportunities*."

He laughed. "Wow, do you have a photographic memory? That's pretty specific."

She turned her computer screen to face him. "Here is the

announcement that she will present that topic at the Geneva conference. Tomorrow, she will present a similar topic at the Refugee Studies Centre called *Building Bridges: Empowering Women and Refugees for Change.*"

"We should definitely go to that. What time tomorrow?"

"It's at 2 p.m. The announcement does indicate that the talk is open to the public, so we shouldn't have any issues getting in. Then, after we talk to Dr. Hadid, we head to the library."

"Sounds like a great plan. But the university has about 30 libraries. How will we know where to look?"

"When I wrote my dissertation, a librarian at the Bodleian Library was a major help. I wrote her just before we got on the plane to see if she could help us. Hopefully, by the time we finish with Dr. Hadid, we will have an answer about which library to investigate."

"Perfect. There's still some light out; let's go walk around a bit before dinner," he said as he grabbed a few items from the desk.

She smiled, put her computer on the chair beside the bed, and stood up. "Sounds great."

A few minutes later, they walked out of the Victorian-style hotel. The entrance from where they exited had a sizeable ornate doorway framed by stone carvings and decorative moldings. The lampposts in front of the hotel had flowers growing on them.

Once they reached the main street, they turned right, which took them toward the central part of the city.

Vanessa had spent some time in Cambridge, and as they walked, she thought about how the University of Oxford was in the city of Oxford. On the other hand, the is in the city of Cambridge.

As they walked, they passed Balliol College and Trinity College. They saw many students in white shirts and black robes, their outfits indicating they were in the middle of the examinations. Others carried open champagne bottles, and they were more lively. Both Ian and Vanessa assumed that those students had just completed their exams.

They made their way to the eye-catching Radcliffe Camera. It was one of the University of Oxford's most iconic buildings. The neoclassical circular building with a dome at the top was 135 feet tall.

After Ian and Vanessa admired the building in their own

thoughts, Ian turned to Vanessa. "I know the Radcliffe Camera is a library. But is that the Bodleian Library?"

Vanessa looked at Ian and said, "The Bodleian Library is across the street. The Radcliffe Camera is mostly a reading room just for the students. I have never been there during my research, but I am sure it is impressive."

Walking back to the hotel, they stopped to look at the Bridge of Sighs, part of Hertford College. Vanessa turned to Ian and said, "Did you know that this Bridge of Sighs is named after the one in Venice?"

Ian turned toward Vanessa, "Yes, I did know that due to the similar neoclassical architecture style, but I am unsure if there is any other connection."

She smiled and responded, "The bridge connects the old side of the college to the new side, though not like the prisoner element, which was the purpose of Venice."

There was a sign on the door near the entrance to Hertford College. Ian and Vanessa were both drawn to it. *Thomas Hobbes: The Oxford Years - Hertford College, Thursday 20:00.* There was an image of Thomas Hobbes and the Leviathan.

"Merde, we just missed it," Vanessa said.

Ian looked at the flyer and then at Vanessa. "I know we missed it, but maybe there is a recording of what was said, or your library contact can help us."

"Good thinking. I know tomorrow is Sunday, but maybe we can get lucky with a response."

CHAPTER 42

Oxford
Sunday Morning
The Randolph Hotel

"Agh!!!!!" Ian groaned as he woke up and tried to turn in the twin bed. When he saw that Vanessa was still sleeping in the other twin bed, he quietly grabbed some clothes and went to the bathroom to shower and change.

When he finished showering, he dressed in the small bathroom so as not to disturb Vanessa. He then quietly opened the bathroom door and noticed Vanessa slowly getting out of bed.

"Good morning, Vanessa," Ian said with a smile. "How did you sleep?"

Vanessa looked at Ian as she stood up and shrugged. "It wasn't the best sleep, but it wasn't the worst."

"Yeah, these beds don't do this hotel justice. But that happens when we book a room with a day's notice."

"Let's hope that this trip is worth it," she said as she grabbed some clothes and went to the shower.

"So true. I have a good feeling," he said, then turned on the TV to BBC News, and sat on his bed.

"Good morning, this is Hanna Johnson reporting from London. This morning, we are following several stories. The top story is far-right protests clash with women's rights groups in Hong Kong, Istanbul, and Washington D.C. These protests come just before the major international women's rights conference that will be taking place in Geneva next week. Many reasons for the clashes stem from whether domestic policies must adhere to international U.N. resolutions.

"The next story we are following is San Francisco-based tech company OpenAI, which is being summoned to Brussels next week to go in front of the European Commission to answer questions regarding how OpenAI gathers their information. The European Commission has been seeking fines against OpenAI if their sources are not revealed. One member of the Commission is even threatening expulsion."

Ian then turned off the TV as Vanessa returned to the room. Her hair was still wet but pulled back into a ponytail. "Anything we missed on the news?" she asked, putting away her clothes and grabbing her phone.

"Nothing out of the ordinary, fortunately, I guess."

"Good. Let's get something to eat before we go to the lecture. There's a place that I've heard is good called The Ivy," she said.

"That sounds great. I'm all ready," he said as he grabbed his wallet and phone.

They then left the hotel, and Vanessa guided him to the Ivy Brasserie, about a ten-minute walk away. It was on High Street, one of the busier streets in Oxford.

They were able to get a table almost immediately. The dining area had a bar to the left and many tables and booths. The chairs were decorated with green flowers, and the walls had painted trees. There were a couple of areas with real green plants. Ian thought the ivy name was consistent with his impression of the restaurant's interior. Furthermore, he felt the restaurant's interior could fit perfectly in Miami or Palm Beach.

The waitress handed them the menus and asked what they would like to drink.

"Double espresso, please," Vanessa said, picking up the menu.

"I'll take a cappuccino, please," Ian said. The waitress nodded and walked away to take their order. Ian then looked at the menu.

A few minutes later, the waitress came back with the coffee. "Now, do you have any questions, or would you like to order?" she said, looking at Vanessa and Ian.

"I'll have the Avocado Benedict," Vanessa said, handing the waitress the menu.

"And I'll have the Eggs Royale with cured smoked salmon," Ian said, handing the waitress the menu.

Before walking away, the waitress wrote both orders down and asked, "Would you like anything else to drink?"

"Not today, we're working," Vanessa said. The waitress then walked away. Vanessa then turned to Ian. "We'll have to find another time together for a more peaceful and relaxing brunch." She smiled at him.

"Of course," he smiled, and her phone rang.

She smiled as she answered the phone. "Yes, this is Vanessa." As she listened to the caller on the other line, her smile turned into a frown. "But just listen. You can't be serious. You don't understand...I'm onto something."

A few seconds later, she put her phone on the table and mumbled, "Putain!"

Ian looked at Vanessa. "What's going on?"

Vanessa regained her composure and said, "I've been fired, and my book deal is no longer valid."

CHAPTER 43

Oxford
Sunday Afternoon
The Ivy and Refugees Studies Centre

Ian and Vanessa ate their meals silently, and then Ian said, "Were you given any explanation?"

Vanessa, still upset, said, "They just said that effective immediately, my services are no longer needed, and someone will pick up any stories I've been assigned. On top of that, the book deal is terminated since the *FT* was paying for the book."

He sat back, eating his food. "This doesn't make sense."

"This was supposed to be my big break. When else can I write a book and get paid before it gets published?"

"Well, if it's money you're worried about, I'd be happy to be your investor. I think there's something deeper going on."

"It's not that. Thank you. It's not the money necessarily. It's the access. Being with the *Financial Times* gave me access I wouldn't normally get if I worked independently."

"An old American writer, Elbert Hubbard, once said, 'The man who has no problem is out of the game.' I think we're in the midst of a game, but I can't figure out the end of the game."

"Yeah, I think you are right. Let's see what Dr. Viyan Hadid has to say. Maybe she can provide some insight into what is going on."

Ian nodded as they finished their brunch and then started to walk to the Refugee Studies Center, which was about a 10-minute walk north. They walked mostly in silence, passing the Radcliffe Camera. Again, they saw another flier for the recent Thomas Hobbes lecture.

The Refugee Studies Centre was located on Mansfield Road near Balliol College and was part of the University of Oxford's Department of International Development.

As they approached the tan stone building that housed the Centre, they noticed a line of about 40 people. Vanessa approached the man at the end of the line and asked, "Excuse me, are you waiting to see Dr. Viyan Hadid?"

"Righto," said the man, looking toward the front of the line. "I hope there are enough seats."

"Just curious," said Ian, "is it usual to have speakers on Sunday?"

The man turned more toward Ian and Vanessa. "It is rather unusual. This talk was supposed to be during the week, but it had been rescheduled to today."

"Do you think there will be enough seats?" Vanessa asked.

"Hope so. There are a couple of large rooms in the Centre. I don't think they have started to let anyone in yet."

"Thank you. I hope so, too," Ian said. A few minutes later, the line started to move. They finally made their way into the Centre. They walked past a large foyer with couches, chairs, books, and magazines. Ian thought this area must be where students come between classes. As it was a Sunday, no students were around except those in line headed to the guest lecture.

Once Ian and Vanessa entered the auditorium, they found a seat near the back of the room. Most of the seats were already filled with students, but there were also a few older people. After a couple more minutes, a man stood up, approached the lectern, and spoke into the microphone.

"Good afternoon. My name is Dr. Lewis Goodenough. I'm the head of the Refugee Studies Centre. Welcome to today's guest lecture with Dr. Viyan Hadid. To briefly introduce Dr. Hadid, she is a refugee from Syria. She grew up in Germany and attended the University of Oxford for her studies focused on cardiac surgery. She has a medical practice in Munich and has worked with the United Nations on several refugee medical missions. Furthermore, she is a major proponent of women's rights. She will speak about women's rights at next week's major U.N. conference in Geneva. And there has been talk in U.N. circles that she is being considered as the next head of the UNHCR. Let us welcome Dr. Hadid."

The crowd started to applaud as Dr. Goodenough stepped aside. Dr. Hadid approached the lectern and shook his hand before turning to the audience. She was about 5'10" with long black hair and olive-complected skin.

"Thank you, Dr. Goodenough," Dr. Hadid said as she spoke into the microphone. "That was an excellent introduction, but I am unsure about those UNHCR rumors. While it is probably my dream job, I don't want to cause any ill will towards Francesco Tarantino. He is doing a great job leading the organization."

Dr. Hadid took a breath and continued, "Ladies and gentlemen, we live in a time where health is not just an individual concern but a societal one. Today, I want to discuss a topic that affects us all: health. In a world marked by constant change and challenges, we must build bridges and provide women and refugees with the tools to effect change.

"Women play a crucial role in ensuring the health of their families and communities. Empowering them is, therefore, vital.

"At the same time, refugees face unique health challenges. They often have limited access to medical care and suffer from traumatic experiences. Their integration into the healthcare system is crucial to ensure they receive the support they need.

"Therefore, working together to empower women and refugees is imperative. Please provide them with the resources and necessary support to improve their health and well-being. Building bridges and fostering collaboration can create positive change and create a healthier, more inclusive society for all."

At the end of the speech, there was another round of applause. As people started to stand up to leave, Ian followed Vanessa, who quickly meandered her way to the stage where Dr. Hadid and Dr. Goodenough spoke. A few students also came up to the stage and thanked Dr. Hadid. After the students walked away, Vanessa caught Dr. Hadid's attention.

"Dr. Hadid, my name is Vanessa Dupont. I work for the Financial Times. Do you have time for a few questions?"

Dr. Hadid smiled. "Sure. I have a few minutes. Let's go to the classroom next door."

Vanessa let Dr. Hadid lead the way. Ian followed. "I hope you don't mind," Vanessa said to Dr. Hadid, "my colleague Ian Steele will join us."

Dr. Hadid turned and shook Ian's hand. "Of course. Nice to meet you, Mr. Steele."

CHAPTER 44

Oxford
Sunday Afternoon
Refugees Studies Centre

Dr. Hadid guided Ian and Vanessa to an empty classroom. The classroom had two long tables in front of a white dry-erase board. Dr. Hadid motioned for Ian and Vanessa to sit across from her.

"Please call me Vivi," Dr. Hadid said. "So, what would you like to know? I'm not big on press interviews because I want my work to speak for itself. Yet, since I can't find an excuse to escape, we can talk for a few minutes."

Vanessa straightened in her chair and said, "Well, Vivi, this isn't for an article per se. I'm working on a book about Mrs. Mirreaux. I understand you were close to her when you were both students here."

Vivi looked at Vanessa and Ian and said, "I feel so sad for Elena with her husband's passing. His legacy will be cemented in history when the conference occurs next week. We haven't spoken in years, even though we both work similarly."

"How did you and Mrs. Mirreaux become acquainted?" Vanessa asked.

"We are refugees from Syria, and we met on one of the first days upon arriving at Oxford. She had migrated to the United Kingdom, and I had migrated to Germany. We didn't know each other before Oxford. I believe she is from Damascus, and I am from Aleppo. I came from a wealthy family, and Elena's family did not come from wealth. Most of my family was slaughtered by the Syrian government. They thought the people of old wealth were the cause of many of the problems in the country. My mother, brother, sister, and I escaped."

Ian then spoke, "But you didn't grow up wealthy in Germany?"

Vivi responded, "Correct. My dad gave my mom some money and items to sell when we got somewhere safe. But when you become a refugee, there's an element that you lose some of your humanity. Some people we met along the way treated us nicely, but others treated us like dirt." Dr. Hadid paused. "In a way, I'm glad I didn't have that wealth. When we settled safely in Germany, I told myself that I wanted to find ways to help fellow refugees. I didn't care about wealth since that point."

"If I may ask, you mentioned that Mrs. Mirreaux didn't come from a wealthy family. So, why was her family killed?" Ian asked.

"Yes, she didn't come from wealth, and I think that bothered her, especially at Oxford. Her family supported another candidate for president. So, when the government in power came to be, they executed anyone against them, even if they didn't come from wealth."

"Did you ever visit her adoptive family in the U.K.?" Vanessa asked.

"No. She was secretive about her family. We were close the first two years, but in the latter years, we grew apart. When I accepted a speaking role at the upcoming conference, I sent Elena a message saying it would be great to catch up in person. She responded curtly, saying 'definitely,' but she had to check her schedule. And then when François passed, I sent her a condolence message, and she responded by saying thank you and nothing else."

Vanessa said, "What happened when you and her grew apart?"

"We were part of different colleges. But Elena would always try to go to parties at other colleges. She never seemed happy where she was. I think Americans say something like the grass is greener on the other side. She was astute, but she wanted to climb that social ladder. Right before we grew apart, she joined a Leviathan rowing club. She asked me to join."

"There's a Leviathan rowing club?" Ian asked.

"Well, it wasn't an official university rowing club. There was a boat called the Leviathan that was used for training. I went to the first couple of practices or gatherings. The boat was from 1951 and did look like a monster. Meaning there were sixteen people in the boat. Eight people on each side, and the coach could walk up and down the middle of the boat, coaching everyone. So, it looked like a leviathan in the water."

"So, this was a learn-to-row type club?" Vanessa asked.

"That's what I thought at first and why I decided to join Elena. I thought rowing would be fun, even though I didn't have the body to row competitively. The first couple of practices were learning to row. Then it became more political. They would row in the middle of the river and stop and have these political discussions. Many of them concerned Thomas Hobbes, wealth and technology, and the world's problems. It became a bit too radical for me, and when I decided not to return to the club, Elena became very upset with me and didn't talk to me again till years after our graduation."

"Who were the other members of this rowing club?" Ian asked.

"I don't recall exactly. Most of the people seemed to have something against the wealthy and/or wanted to join them at the parties and secret societies."

"Do you think this boat is still around?" Vanessa asked.

"I have no idea. Probably not. I think the university was getting rid of it since it had been around from 1951, and the rowing clubs have more up-to-date equipment." Vivi looked at her watch. "I have another commitment I have to go to, but here is my contact." She handed Ian and Vanessa her card.

"Thanks," Vanessa said. "Your insights have been extremely helpful as I write my book."

"Well, happy to help even though I don't know much about her life more recently than what I read in the news." Vivi stood up, followed by Ian and Vanessa. She shook each of their hands, and before she turned to leave the room, she said, "I recall a couple of times I was in her room, and she had stacks of mail, and it was addressed to someone named Hanna Assad. I asked Elena a couple of times about that name, and she would brush me off and say I didn't need to know. I'm not sure if that can be of help either."

"Thank you. Your help has been very invaluable," Vanessa said.

"If you are in Geneva for the conference, please let me know." Ian and Vanessa nodded and Vivi walked out.

Ian and Vanessa looked at each other. "Let's search for this Hanna Assad," Vanessa said.

Ian nodded and said, "Mrs. Mirreaux seems more complex than we originally thought."

CHAPTER 45

Multiple Undisclosed Locations
Sunday Evening
Via videoconference

"Swan was very impressed with Leviathan," said the scrambled voice.

"I'm thrilled that Swan is pleased. I hope everyone else on the call is pleased with Leviathan," Jack said.

Kane was the first to speak up. "Yes, Leviathan shows some great promise, especially in the tests I ran. It does have amazing capabilities for producing deepfakes, algorithmic biases, and other societal manipulative tools. If this can be rolled out correctly, the public will have no idea what has hit them, and Leviathan can control the narrative." Everyone made sounds in agreement.

Zaaeem Farouq then spoke up after everyone quieted. "Leviathan is why we are here, but I'm sure I'm not the only one still worried. How will we make sure the implementation will work?"

Jack cleared his throat. "The developer in Silicon Valley is ready to make the necessary moves to ensure Leviathan rises above the rest."

Zaaeem tried to cut Jack off. "I understand that. But what is going to happen and when?"

Jack cleared his throat again. "If you let me finish," he said curtly, "I'll explain." He used a few seconds of silence to collect himself. "The developer will set his moves in motion and install his bugs, which will activate on Tuesday. There will be a massive market upheaval."

The scrambled voice added, "Furthermore, before the developer sets his motions into action, my contact will have instigated the upheaval on this side of the pond. Thus, we will all be in disarray by Tuesday night and the early trading sessions on Wednesday."

"Leviathan then will roll out through carefully placed ads and social media influencers. So, Leviathan will look like a phoenix and savior by Wednesday night. Furthermore, by Thursday, our shares will be worth billions."

The scrambled voice added, "The turmoil that will ensue and the messages that Leviathan will address by Thursday will cause the conference's demise before it even begins."

"In Hobbes We Trust," all the members of the videoconference called out.

CHAPTER 46

Oxford
Sunday Afternoon and Evening
Bodleian Library

Ian and Vanessa walked back to the Bodleian Library. They thought it could be a good place to start their research into Hanna Assad. When they arrived, they requested to see yearbooks and university enrollment lists from the years Elena Mirreaux attended the University of Oxford. The librarians were very helpful and brought them a couple of boxes of documents from those years. While Ian was very good at speed-reading, Vanessa wasn't as quick.

"Nothing here mentions Hanna Assad," Ian said as Vanessa finished reading a few documents.

"Could this Hanna Assad have been part of that Leviathan rowing club?" Vanessa asked as she put down the documents.

"For a university club, I don't see anything about it in any of these documents," Ian said as he looked through another yearbook. A few minutes later, Ian opened the new yearbook and leaned toward Vanessa.

"Look at this. Here, a mention of the Leviathan Club and some photos is included." Vanessa looked over at the yearbook that Ian left open. "This was the same yearbook as the others we've been looking at, but this one had an insert for the spring activities."

She looked at the photos. "Look at this," she said, pointing to a small emblem on the rowing shell. "I think that's the Leviathan Cross."

He squinted at the photo.

"I think you are right. It is rather distinctive."

She looked over and saw there was one group photo. She recognized Elena Mirreaux in the photo from her research. When she looked at the names of the individuals underneath the pictures, she noticed an error.

"Ian, look here," she said, pointing to Elena's photo. "That is Elena, but when you see the names printed below, it states Elena is Hanna Assad. And Elena is three women away."

As they both leaned back in their chairs, lost in thought, an older librarian came by and asked, "Do you all need anything?"

Vanessa grabbed the open yearbook and pointed to the photo. "Actually, yes. The person in this photo—why is this the only photo of her? I don't see any information that she was a student."

The librarian looked at the photo briefly and then looked up at Vanessa and Ian. "I'm not sure. I have seen many students come through these halls." She paused to look at the photo again. "That name does sound familiar. There was a murder later that year on campus. The deceased person, I believe, was a student. I remember the student was in her freshman or sophomore year, and the university didn't think she had completed enough credits to qualify for being recognized as part of the class. There was an uproar within the student body, but the university wouldn't be swayed."

Ian replied, "Is there any information about that murder?"

The librarian thought momentarily, then said, "I don't think so. But from what I recall, there were rumors that the deceased might have been a spy from the Middle East."

"Oxford is certainly not unknown to the spy world," Ian replied.

"Exactly. If this is true, the university didn't want to be caught in another Cambridge Five situation," the librarian replied.

"Is that why this student disappeared from any school records?" Vanessa asked.

"Could be. The university tried to act swiftly to sweep it under the rug. I think the upset students didn't know the full story," the librarian responded. "Is there anything else I can help you with?"

"No, I think we are good. We will be leaving soon," Vanessa said.

"No worries," responded the librarian, and she walked off.

When the librarian disappeared, Ian looked at Vanessa. "Wow! Talk about keeping calm and carrying on. That must have been tough for the community."

Vanessa looked at the photo. "Very sad. But why are the names mixed up?"

"Probably a typo," he said as he looked through several other documents.

The librarian walked by with a library cart and grabbed some books to put away.

"Excuse me, ma'am," Vanessa said to the librarian.

The librarian walked over. "Yes, you have another question?"

"Yes, just one more quick question," Vanessa said, opening the yearbook to the Leviathan team photo. "Do you know why these two names are mixed up?"

The librarian looked quizzically at Vanessa and Ian. "I'm not sure. Are you sure the names are mixed up?"

Vanessa pointed to the photo. "I am researching Elena Mirreaux, who, as a student at Oxford, used her maiden name of Aziz. I have seen some photos from when she was here and know this person is her. But the name under the photo says she is Hanna Assad. And the girl a few places from her says she is Elena Aziz."

"Let me look at another yearbook and see if that shows the same thing; I'll be back momentarily." The librarian said and walked away.

Just as Ian and Vanessa started to look at the other items on the desk, Vanessa's phone vibrated. She looked at the phone and then up at Ian.

"I just got a Google Alert notification about Elena," she said as she opened the notification on her phone.

She spent the next couple of moments reading the message. Ian waited patiently to hear what Vanessa was reading. "So, anything of interest?"

She looked up and said, "Well, I think we need to get to Gibraltar."

"Gibraltar? What's there?"

"Look at this," she said as she handed him her phone.

He took a moment to start reading the article that initiated the Google Alert.

Page Six: Elena Mirreaux Spotted on Gibraltar Yacht with Mystery Man: New Romance for U.N. SG's Widow?

This morning, Elena Mirreaux, widow of the recently deceased United Nations Secretary-General François Mirreaux, was seen boarding the new 170-meter yacht Leviathan. Heesen, one of the world's premier yacht manufacturers, recently built this new yacht. It is one of Heesen's largest yachts ever produced. The owner is unknown, but sources say the owner is single and interested in Elena Mirreaux. Could this be a budding romance?

He looked up from the phone and handed it back to her. "Wow! That can't be just a random coincidence."

She nodded. "Definitely. Let's get to Gibraltar to find out."

He nodded as the librarian returned with two yearbooks. "As you can see from these other yearbooks, the photo shows the names in the same places as your copy."

Vanessa and Ian looked at the other yearbooks. "I guess we are mistaken," Vanessa said as she looked up at the librarian. "Thank you for all your help. You have been extremely helpful."

"Happy to help. Is there anything else I can help you find?"

"No, you have been a great resource. We unfortunately have to go," Ian said as he and Vanessa stood up.

"But of course. If you need anything again, please let me or any of the library staff know," the librarian said as she started to pick up more books and put them on the cart.

Once Ian and Vanessa exited the library, they walked faster to the hotel. At the hotel, they quickly packed and found a last-minute morning flight on British Airways from London Heathrow to Gibraltar. They then checked out of the hotel and drove to Heathrow.

CHAPTER 47

Gibraltar
Monday Morning
Leviathan Yacht

The bright white 170-meter new Heesen yacht was docked in the Mid Harbour Marina outer wharf. It was one of the few areas in the harbor that could accommodate super yachts. While the outer wharf had 500 meters of dock space, the Leviathan yacht was the only one docked. The inner harbor had around 200 smaller motor-boats and sailboats docked in various slips.

Elena was mesmerized by the view as she walked out on the balcony of the main bedroom. She overlooked the Rock of Gibraltar, predominantly limestone, gray, and white, which rose about 1,398 feet above sea level. The Rock had a steep, elongated ridge in which the highest point was on the north end and gradually sloped downward to the south. The Rock's southern end had more greenery and vegetation patches than the northern end.

After a few minutes of looking at the rock and thinking, she returned to the main bedroom. The bedroom featured an unmade king-sized bed on one side of the room with identical mahogany end tables, each with iPads on either side. Behind the bed, there was a large walk-in closet. The other side of the room had a long rectangular mahogany dresser with a large flat-screen TV that hung above. The large windows gave the room much natural light, and the ocean breeze could be enjoyed when the windows were open.

On the opposite side of the bed from the balcony was a table with two chairs facing each other. One of the chairs had a man's blazer with a briefcase on the table. She walked past the TV and pressed the wall that opened into a door that led to the hallway, which she walked down. The hallway went the length of the yacht. She walked by several bedrooms and a gym, all with great views. She stopped three-quarters of the way down, where there was an office. She opened the door, and a man sat in the chair behind the desk. His back was to the door, and he was on the phone, looking at the view.

"I promise I will be in Geneva in a couple of days. I have some business that I need to attend to." He paused as the person on the other line spoke. "Yes, Mr. President. I will be sure to have that ready for you when you arrive at the hotel." He spent a few more minutes on the phone, and as he put down the phone, Elena came up to him, put her arms around his neck, and kissed his cheek.

"So, does the President have any idea where you are?" she said, smiling, as she wrapped her arms around his neck.

"He has no idea. Policy wise, he is top-notch, but socially wise, he has shit for brains. He really has no idea of this plot." He said and smiled at her.

"Where does he think you are?"

"I have no idea. It's great being at my level, and I can pay the Secret Service off, and Paul takes care of the rest. Who would have thought public service had these benefits? Power is some thrilling shit," he said with a smirk.

"Kissinger was right. 'Power is the great aphrodisiac,'" she said with a smirk.

The man reached his hands to her waist to pull her into him, and he gave her a peck on the lips. She smiled as he pulled away. "You're going to make me late. I do have a schedule to adhere to. Not like your people telling the President some lie for you," she said as she started walking to the other side of the room.

He watched her. "You have nothing to worry about. The longer you stay, and if the operation goes into the next phase while you are here, you most certainly will have plausible deniability."

She smiled at him, "You really are the perfect political strategist."

"It's more than being a political strategist. It's about being a politician and putting yourself in the right place at the right time."

She looked at him. "So, do you think the next phase should take place?"

"I think it's definitely necessary."

"It will definitely cause a big stir even from our investors."

"Don't worry. Everyone knows the risks. Furthermore, remember Thomas Hobbes. If these individuals acted separately on their self-interests, there would be all-out wars with each other."

"If this doesn't work, there will be a big mess to untangle."

He looked at her more sternly. "It will work. There will be a mess, but that is the point. And we can lead in the shadows. Something that Locke probably never envisioned."

She looked at him and smiled. "You're right. Hobbes really couldn't foresee the 21st-century Leviathan. One Leviathan controlled by another in secret."

She felt invigorated. She picked up her phone and dialed a number. After one ring, she said, "The next phase is a go. The sooner, the better." She then hung up the phone and looked at him smugly.

A few minutes later, her phone started to ring. When she looked at the caller ID, she immediately picked it up. As she talked on the phone, he noticed her smug smile had turned to a frown, and her forehead had wrinkled.

"Fuck!" she said as she threw her phone on the sofa and looked out at the Rock.

"What's wrong?" He asked from the other side of the room as he started to pick up his briefcase.

"It concerns a problem I've been having since I was in New York recently. It seems to have followed me here."

"Do you want me to take care of it? I could easily order the CIA or NSA to take care of this problem."

Her frown faded into a faint smile. "That won't be necessary. I have a better idea, one that won't alert anyone."

He smiled. "Even better. Now, who's the political strategist?"

CHAPTER 48

Gibraltar
Monday

Once the Phantom hung up the phone, he started to get to work. He knew the call was coming, but he didn't know when. Yet, he knew he would have some space, especially when instructed to hold fire. This made him thankful, as he could fly into Malaga and rent a moving truck. This latest task would be different than previous jobs. This task would be multilayered and take some precision. He painted a construction logo on the truck so as not to raise any suspicion. Over a few days, he visited various stores in Malaga and the surrounding area to obtain materials to build several naval mines. He did not start building the mines until he crossed the Gibraltar border. He was able to hide some of the materials for the mines from the authorities.

Once he obtained the materials, he spent a little time acting as a tourist in Malaga, then drove to Marbella and Puerto Banús for a few days. He enjoyed the tranquil mindset. It gave him time to think and write about the upcoming task in his journal. He then carefully drove to Gibraltar so as not to raise any suspicions. He passed through the border without any problems. The border patrol inspected what he had in the truck, but no suspicions arose.

After receiving the call, he picked up another burner phone and called a boat rental company he had identified a few days prior. When he called the rental group, he told them he had orders to deliver items to the *Emma Maersk* that would be passing and mooring in Gibraltar later in the day. He needed a relatively large boat with big engines to carry the heavy weight that would later act as a mine planter.

The boat rental company told him that there would be a forty-foot boat next to the cruise terminal with four engines. He then looked on Google Maps to see the route he would take with the truck to get to the boat. Before going to the truck, he opened the MarineTraffic app to find the *Emma Maersk*. It was just entering the waters of Gibraltar. He couldn't have asked for better timing.

Upon getting to the dock, he saw the *Emma Maersk* moored in the distance. The *Emma Maersk* could not be missed. It was one of the largest ships in the world. It was the first E-class series for Maersk. Its length was 1,302 feet, carrying nearly 15,500 twenty-foot containers. He looked at the ship in amazement that it could even float.

He then turned his attention to finding the rental boat. He quickly found it. The boat had "Rent Me" on its hull and four large white Yamaha engines.

Next, he went back to the truck and drove it next to the boat, and carefully started to transfer the completed mines, still in crates, from the truck to the boat.

CHAPTER 49

Gibraltar
Monday

Ian and Vanessa arrived in Gibraltar around 11 a.m. after taking a 6:55 a.m. British Airways flight from London. This was both of their first visits to Gibraltar. The plane made a short taxi to the terminal. When they walked off the plane, the Spanish border greeted them on one side and the Rock of Gibraltar on the other. They also saw tourists walking across the active runway from the Spanish border to the city, which was about 500 meters.

They retrieved their bags quickly, as their flight was the only one at the terminal. Gibraltar Airport was one of the smallest international airports in the world. In addition to civilian aircraft, the Royal Air Force used the airport for military operations.

They then quickly found a taxi that took them to their hotel. They reserved a room for two nights at the Bristol Hotel. The hotel was in the more populated part of Gibraltar, next to one of the main harbors. They didn't know how many days they would spend in Gibraltar, but they thought two days would be a good estimate.

After checking into the hotel, they put their bags in the small room with two twin beds, which looked more like a ship's cabin than a hotel room. They then walked a short distance to the harbor.

Looking around the harbor, Vanessa pointed across the harbor to the white yacht. "There is *The Leviathan*."

Ian looked to where she was pointing. "Good, it's still here. I'm no James Bond, but how do you think we could figure out if Elena is still on board?"

Before she could answer, her phone rang. She turned to pick it up. "Hello, this is Vanessa."

"Hi Vanessa, this is Elena Mirreaux." Vanessa's face turned white. Ian wondered who had called. "I hear you and Ian are in Gibraltar. I happen to be in Gibraltar. But you already knew that. Why don't you come aboard *The Leviathan*."

Vanessa's face remained white as she spoke into the phone. "Sure. We are following up on a lead, but would be happy to come aboard."

"Good, I was hoping you'd say that. Come in an hour." The phone then clicked off.

Vanessa then turned to Ian as the color came back to her face. "Well fuck, no need for spy theatrics. That was Elena. She wants us on the yacht in an hour." She paused, then asked, "How the hell did she know we were in Gibraltar?"

Ian looked at her. "Sounds like we are being watched."

CHAPTER 50

Gibraltar
Monday
The Leviathan Yacht

Ian and Vanessa walked up the yacht's gangway to be greeted by Mrs. Mirreaux.

"If you don't mind, would you both remove your shoes and put on these boat shoes?" Mrs. Mirreaux said as she pointed to the blue shoes on the side. "Also, please leave your phones on the table," she said with a polite yet firm tone. "For security reasons. We wouldn't want any interruptions now."

Ian and Vanessa said, "Of course." After they changed their shoes and put the phones on the table, Mrs. Mirreaux said, "Let's go to the living room, and we can discuss this lead that brought you both to this small peninsula."

They walked by several large sculptures and paintings as they followed Mrs. Mirreaux to the living room. The living room had three couches in a U-shape that overlooked the large windows overlooking the water. In the middle of the couches was a coffee table with a small maquette portraying the Leviathan Cross.

"Please have a seat. May I offer you both something to drink?" Mrs. Mirreaux said as she watched Ian and Vanessa take a seat on the couch.

"No, we're okay," Ian and Vanessa said.

Mrs. Mirreaux looked at both of them. She displayed a calmness as her fingers lightly tapped the armrest. Despite the tension in the air, she seemed unperturbed, almost as if she enjoyed the suspense. "So, how can I help you both? I know you have been checking up on me since the book deal was canceled, Ms. Dupont."

"Well, I still think I have a story that will be worth telling," Vanessa said firmly.

Mrs. Mirreaux turned her gaze to Vanessa and smiled, "You must be careful who you trust. Not everyone has your best interests at heart." She paused and then looked at Ian. "It's interesting," she mused, "how we all have our vulnerabilities. Some are more personal than others. Isn't that right, Mr. Steele?"

"I'm just trying to help bring more justice to the world," he said.

"Why would you care? That is what I haven't been able to figure out. Why would someone who runs a successful company leave for the sake of the upcoming conference?"

Vanessa looked at Ian, and they both wondered how the conversation had become more of an interrogation of them rather than of Mrs. Mirreaux. Ian cleared his throat and then replied, "Well, there are some things I think should be left in private I'm not a governmental official but still a private citizen."

"Touché, Mr. Steele. But I think I'm entitled to some answers since you and Ms. Dupont have stalked your way onto this yacht," she said firmly as she looked at Ian and Vanessa.

"We didn't exactly stalk our way onto the yacht. I believe we were invited," Ian said, looking at Vanessa, who nodded.

Vanessa tried to think on her feet quickly and change the direction of the conversation, which almost led to an interrogation. "Mrs. Mirreaux, who is Hanna Assad?"

She smirked and looked calmly at Vanessa. "So that's what this little rendezvous is about?"

Vanessa and Ian stayed silent and didn't say anything right away.

Mrs. Mirreaux looked out the window briefly, then looked back at Vanessa and Ian. "If you must know, she was a good friend who didn't deserve what happened to her."

"I don't quite understand," Vanessa said.

Mrs. Mirreaux looked at Vanessa and said, "She was a roommate of mine while at Oxford, and we rowed together, but then she met her demise by being at the wrong place at the wrong time."

Vanessa continued, "Do you mean the murder during your time at Oxford?"

Mrs. Mirreaux looked out the window again and then back

to Vanessa. "Yes, she was a sweet girl who was murdered, and the authorities never caught the people who did that unthinkable act."

There were a few moments of silence, and then Ian spoke. "I'm sorry to hear about your friend. But speaking of the rowing club, we discovered that the boat you all used was called *The Leviathan*. Is that why this yacht has the same name?"

The whole conversation felt like a game of chess. Whenever there seemed to be an opportunity to pin Mrs. Mirreaux, she returned with some defense, which made Ian and Vanessa go back on the defensive.

Mrs. Mirreaux smiled and calmly looked at Vanessa and then at Ian. "This is just a big coincidence. You might have heard there is a new company about to launch called Leviathan. They own this yacht, and they had some business they wanted to talk to me about as I was in the area. I would have introduced you, but they left before you arrived."

"We have heard about the company, but we don't know much about it," Vanessa composedly said. After a brief pause, Vanessa tried to shift the conversation to see if Mrs. Mirreaux would offer any other information. "While in Oxford, we met your classmate, Dr. Viyan Hadid. She mentioned she was part of the rowing club but left because of their views," Vanessa said.

"I hope Vivi is doing well. I miss her. I think she will be attending the conference in Geneva." Mrs. Mirreaux paused and then looked at Vanessa as she answered more directly. "During the practices, there were discussions about reshaping the world order, often through dramatic measures. Almost everyone steered clear of those methods as most conversations were purely philosophical. I don't think Vivi understood that the conversations were just that and nothing more."

Mrs. Mirreaux pointed to the Leviathan Cross on the table. "The symbols like the rowing club and the pin I wear represent a school of thought that has existed for centuries. Yes, it began with noble intentions, focusing on unity and progress. However, over time, some factions within this school of thought have taken a more radical approach away from just the philosophical."

Ian asked, "What do you mean by radical?"

"They believed in reshaping the world order, often through drastic measures. François and I tried to steer the society as a whole towards more peaceful methods. Yet still, some disagreed with us." She paused. "But this new Leviathan company will help bring more peace and try to settle some of the more radical factions."

Ian and Vanessa looked at each other, and then Vanessa turned towards Mrs. Mirreaux and asked in a journalistic tone. "Do you believe that the ends justify the means?"

Mrs. Mirreaux calmly looked at each of them. "I admire your dedication to uncovering the truth, but sometimes the truth can be dangerous." She paused and kept her composure. "I'm suggesting you be cautious with your next steps. Some truths are buried for a reason, and digging them up has unintended consequences."

Vanessa looked at her. "I think we understand now."

There were a few moments of silence as Vanessa and Ian looked at Mrs. Mirreaux, and then she broke the silence, "Is there anything else I can do for both of you?"

"No, I think we have what we need," Ian said as he cleared his throat. He tapped Vanessa's shoulder, saying, "I think it's time we headed out."

Vanessa nodded and stood up to join Ian as they left. Mrs. Mirreaux watched them as they walked back the way they came in. As they put on their shoes and grabbed their phones from the table, Mrs. Mirreaux said, "Good to see you both again. Remember, once you unpack what's hidden, there is no going back."

CHAPTER 51

Gibraltar
Monday

Ian and Vanessa walked in silence after exiting the yacht's gangway all the way back to the hotel. Once they got back in the room, Vanessa looked at Ian. "Mon Dieu. Mrs. Mirreaux is really involved in some conspiracy."

Vanessa sat on the bed, and Ian grabbed two water bottles on top of the boudoir cabinet, which was located between the entrance to the bathroom and the closet. He handed her one of the bottles. As he sipped water, he said, "Something is going on. But I can't quite figure it out. What's the connection?"

She grabbed a pen and notebook from her bag and started writing quickly. After a few moments, she gave the notebook to him.

Leviathan = Government?? + Elena + People Killed + late-Hanna
Mirreaux Assad

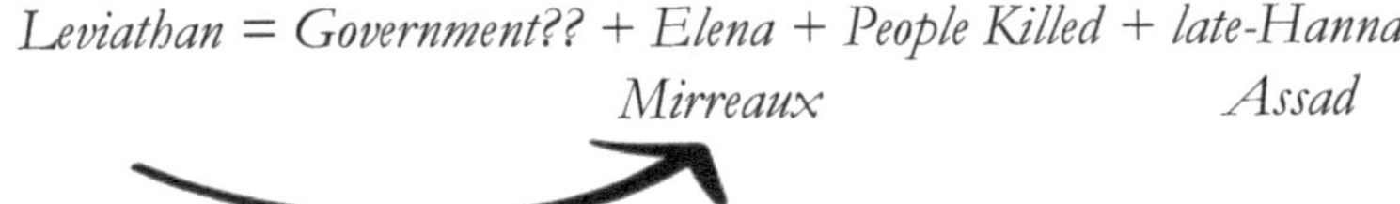

As he looked at the note, he remembered the note she made a few days ago—a revised note. Looking up from the notebook, he asked, "Do you think the government is involved?"

"I'm not sure. But based on my journalistic instincts, it's pretty strange that the two potential nominees to become the next UNSG happen to pass away in close proximity to François Mirreaux. Furthermore, Elena wasn't clear about who Hanna Assad was. It was almost like she knew a secret about Hanna."

Ian nodded. "Could it have been Hanna's vision for whatever is going to happen?"

"Yeah, that might be the case. But we don't know much about Hanna Assad other than she and Elena met at Oxford and both become part of the Leviathan Rowing Club. Then Hanna is murdered, and the case is supposedly still unsolved."

Vanessa paused and looked at Ian. "Are you ever going to tell me what made you leave your company for this conference?"

Ian looked down briefly, then looked up at Vanessa. "It's not a moment in my life that I am proud of. It relates to one of my exes from college. Her name was Sophie. We mutually parted ways. But we kept in contact after college. She went to work for an NGO that focused on women's rights in Syria, while I went into investment banking before starting my company. Sophie called me for a few days straight, and I didn't pick up because I was too busy with a couple of clients. When I finally checked my messages from her, she was screaming that she feared for her life and was being abused by the Syrian government and army that allowed her NGO to work there. I had trouble getting in touch with her and the NGO for a couple of days. When the NGO finally called me back, they said Sophie was unfortunately killed in the line of duty. I immediately called her parents, whom I met several times while we dated. Her parents were distraught. Her father told me that Sophie was abused emotionally and physically during her time in Syria. He told me he told her to get out of Syria and come back home. Sophie had a stubbornness that, when it kicked in, she couldn't be stopped. She told her dad that she could deal with the abuses if it meant saving other women who had no other hope. A little while later, she was raped and killed." Ian looked down again and then up at Vanessa. "I had a chance to save her, and I didn't do anything."

"You can't blame yourself, Ian. You weren't in a relationship with her and had your own work. How could you have known?" Vanessa said as she put her arms around Ian.

"I know I couldn't have known, but I had some contacts in the area that could have gotten her out of there." He paused. "I told myself that if there ever came a time when the world would truly make better laws for women's rights and safety, I would drop whatever I was doing and help the world accomplish that goal."

Vanessa looked at Ian with a tear in her eye. "It is very romantic of you to want to continue her dream."

"I think the romance fizzled, but I believed in what she was working towards." Ian and Vanessa then looked out of the window in silence for a few minutes.

Then Ian turned toward Vanessa. "What about trying to contact Vivi Hadid and asking her what she remembers about Hanna and the murder?"

"Sure, I can do that."

"While you do that, I will go on a walk and call Elliot Brooks to learn more about his investment in Leviathan."

"Good idea," she said, looking through her contacts to find Vivi's number.

CHAPTER 52

Gibraltar
Monday

"Vanessa, I'm so happy you called," Vivi said as she answered the phone. "I've actually been thinking a great deal about the things we discussed in person."

"Good. That's actually why I am calling," Vanessa said. "Is there anything you can tell me more about Hanna Assad and/or about the murder at Oxford?"

"That's what I have been thinking about. I blocked the event of the murder out of my mind. I guess because I had seen so many people murdered, I didn't want to keep a memory of that when I thought about my university days."

"I can't imagine what you had been through before your time in Oxford," Vanessa said.

"It was truly terrible, and I wish war would vanish from this world," Vivi said philosophically. She paused, then said, "Sorry, I am getting ahead of myself. You asked a question in regard to the murder."

"I believe it was Hanna Assad who was murdered."

"Yes, you are right. But the strange part is I swore I saw her around campus."

"Sorry, I don't understand what you are saying," Vanessa questioned.

"Elena and Hanna resembled each other in more ways than one. It almost seemed that they were related. But I couldn't tell since I really didn't see Elena and Hanna walking together. When they were at the boathouse, they were never next to each other." Vivi paused and cleared her throat. "There was a time after the murder when I was walking into Christ Church College to go to their library, and from across the path, I thought I saw Elena. I called out to her, but she looked at me and didn't acknowledge me. She seemed different. Plus, I saw her much later in the day again, and this last time, she was more of her normal self and said she didn't go to Christ Church."

"So, Hanna could have been Elena's twin?"

"From close up, I don't think so. But from a certain distance, one could come to that conclusion."

"But wasn't Hanna murdered?" Vanessa asked as she took notes on her notepad.

"I believe so. That's what the university said. However, I noticed Elena would continue to pick up her mail. Again, around this time, Elena and I stopped speaking. So, I wasn't in a position to ask her about Hanna."

"Was there a memorial service for Hanna? And do you know what cemetery she would be buried in?"

"Blimey. I really can't remember. Something tells me that there might have been a memorial at the university but the actual funeral was private."

"Do you recall what the memorial was like?"

"When I look back on it, I remember there was a candlelight vigil and there were a good number of students in attendance. I don't remember if there were any faculty members."

"Do you recall where the funeral was located?"

"I truly can't remember. But something in the back of my mind tells me that no location was given."

"Thank you, Vivi. Your recollection has been quite helpful. I don't want to take up any more of your time."

"It's no trouble. As I said before, you and Ian's conversation and questions were on my mind recently." She paused, then said, "If you need anything else, please feel free to call me."

"Of course. Thank you again, Vivi."

"My pleasure. Have a good day."

"Have a good day as well." Vanessa then ended the phone call and immediately pulled her computer out of her bag. Once she connected it to the hotel's Wi-Fi, she opened Google and immediately started searching variations of "*Hanna Assad Oxford Cemetery*."

CHAPTER 53

Gibraltar
Monday

Ian exited the hotel and walked toward the harbor. Once he saw the harbor, he noticed that all of the ships were congregated on the sides, and there were no ships in the center. He thought to himself that this was a bit strange in comparison to other harbors around the world.

He was about to cross the street when the green crosswalk sign flashed. He looked to the left and saw a white van, which many Gibraltar tour guides use. He walked over to the driver's side of the van and tapped on the window.

An older man with a scruffy beard who wore a flat cap and had a tour guide ID pinned to his shirt rolled down the window and said, "G'day mate. Can I offer you a tour?"

"No sir, but I have a quick question. Why are all the ships hugging the side of the harbor?" Ian asked, hoping for a quick answer before the streetlight turned green.

"Good question, mate. The Rock of Gibraltar is 426 meters. The middle of the harbor is about double in depth."

"Thanks. Very interesting," Ian said as the light turned green.

"Pip pip." the taxi driver said as he drove off.

Ian then waited until the crosswalk sign turned green again. After a couple of minutes, it did, and he crossed the street, walking closer to the harbor.

As he walked, he pulled out his phone and found Elliot Brooks in his contacts and hit call. The phone rang a couple of times, then Elliot answered, "Hello, this is Elliot—the best investor ever in the world. How can I help you?"

Ian rolled his eyes and then said, "Good morning, Elliot. Do you always answer your phone like that?"

"No, I just want to give you shit for not taking my advice. And look—I pick the best winners out there."

"As if. I'll give you some credit for some of your winners," Ian coughed. "Speaking of your supposed winners, I want to ask you about Leviathan."

"I think I used the word revolutionary when I last saw you and that beautiful woman you were with at my concert. Revolutionary is a tremendous word. You know, when I invest, I know a thing or two about investing, and I look for the best and most fabulous opportunities. This will be the biggest deal ever for Stephanie and me. And I'm bringing Stephanie's personal investment in, too on this so it's definitely going to be the biggest winner yet."

Ian pulled the phone away from his ear to roll his eyes and cough, then he put the phone back to his ear. "Cut the shit, Elliot. Tell me straight up what I want to know."

Elliot laughed on the other end of the phone. "Are you looking for some insider trading information?"

"Nothing like that. I'm looking more for information in regards to Leviathan in general. How were you approached? Who's on their board? What type of ROI were you promised?"

Elliot laughed. "Well, I guess since the company is going public next week, I can talk to you about it." He paused to clear his throat, and then he continued. "About a year ago, I received an email from Jack Samuelson from the White House. He asked for a meeting in Washington. I had been desperately wanting a meeting with the president. For several months, I had been leaving messages with various high-level people at the White House. I almost gave up when Jack emailed me. When I emailed him back stating I could be there the following day, he told me to call a certain number. So, I thought this was some screening meeting before I'd meet the president.

"I arrived in Washington the following morning and then called the number. When I arrived, I called that number. Jack immediately picked up and said, 'Le Diplomate 9 p.m.,' and then he hung up the phone. I did think this was somewhat strange. But to be honest, I loved the secrecy and I was intrigued."

"There was no indication what the meeting was about?" Ian asked, trying to get to Elliot's point without hearing every step in this courtship.

"No. Again, I thought we were going to talk about economic policy and I was going to pitch myself as the best economic advisor the president could hire. So, I get to Le Diplomate at 9 p.m., and I'm escorted to the table. Jack is already seated at a table for two, but I notice that there is only a place setting for me. When I sat, Jack told me he couldn't stay but he ordered me the steak au poivre and a bottle of Caymus. He then gave me a manila envelope and told me to read it while I ate. And that the meal was courtesy of the U.S. government. He told me to call the same number if I was interested in the proposal. But if the contents of the envelope didn't interest me, I was to burn the files immediately. And if I were to expose any of the materials publicly, I would be arrested and charged with leaking state secrets.

"I have to tell you, Ian, I'm not gay, but as Jack walked away, I got so hard from his words that I was ready to say yes to anything he wanted. He didn't even need to pay for my dinner at that point. I was ready to fuck. " Elliot cleared his throat then continued. "When I opened the envelope the first words I saw were 'Top Secret: Eyes Only—Project Leviathan.' This made me even harder. The following pages talked about an artificial intelligence technology that would supersede the United Nations. But they needed an international group of investors. They were seeking $30 billion. The offer included an ROI promise of 40%. I didn't even have to call Stephanie. I knew she would say yes. I just had to figure out how much personally I wanted to put up versus my fund. After I finished the best steak au poivre I've ever had, I called Jack and said, I'm in and that I'd make the investment official the following day. He responded by saying, 'Welcome to the new world order.' And then he hung up the phone. The following day, when I got back to the office, I told all my fund managers to take a million dollars from each of their portfolios and put the funds into the Leviathan account. I also had a talk with Stephanie, and we decided to put $100 million of our own money into this investment."

As Elliot spoke, Ian found a paper and pen and wrote some notes from the conversation. "What about doing some due diligence on this supposed artificial intelligence technology?"

"I don't know if anyone really understands A.I., though it can do some really cool shit."

"Was there anything about economic growth? And scalability?"

"Of course. I'm not an idiot, Ian. It was all in the document. And everything looked great."

"Do you know anything about the founders of Leviathan?"

"All I can say is it's an international group. The lead investors, like me, are from nine countries, and then it's a lot of investment funds."

"Have you seen a prototype of what this Leviathan does?"

"I'm sorry, Ian—I can't say anything about that. I am sure you will see it when it goes public in a couple of days. Actually, I and the other investors will be meeting in Geneva later this week. I probably said too much. You're not going to turn me in to the SEC, are you?"

"No, Elliot. But let's just say I hope you won't be getting that 40% return."

Elliot laughed, "Good man, Ian. I like you even though you never take my advice. How about lunch when I get to Geneva?"

"Sure," Ian replied. "I'm actually not in Geneva right now, but I will definitely be there later in the week."

"Great. Call me on Wednesday."

"Sounds good." Elliot hung up first, then Ian put the phone back into his pocket and quickly walked back to the hotel.

CHAPTER 54

Gibraltar
Monday

When Ian arrived back at the hotel, he saw Vanessa finished eating chips that were taken from the minibar in front of her computer.

"Ian, I need to tell you what I found."

"Let's go grab something to eat and discuss. I have a couple of things to share with you too," Ian said as she closed her computer and followed him out of the hotel.

"How about some fish and chips?" he asked as she followed.

She groaned, then said, "I guess when in the United Kingdom, that is customary. The English cuisine really can't compete with the French cuisine." She laughed.

They walked for about three minutes and found a restaurant called The Angry Friar, which appeared to serve traditional English pub-style food. There weren't too many people around and not many restaurants to choose from. The Angry Friar had a sign out in front of the entrance that stated "Best Fish & Chips in Gibraltar," and it just so happened to be located very close to The Covenant, which was the building that housed the governor of Gibraltar.

As they walked up to the restaurant, they noticed a few tables with patrons eating at tables under the awning. They decided to pick a table on the far end, away from the other patrons. They both looked at each other in silence and smiled. They both wanted to make sure they ordered before they started telling each other what they discovered.

A couple of minutes later, an older waitress came to the table and put down menus. "Here you go. Now, what can I get started for drinks for you both?"

Ian spoke up first. "Actually, we are all ready to go."

"Great. So, what can I get you?"

"We'll have two orders of fish and chips with tartar sauce and two Guinness draughts."

"Perfect. I'll be back shortly and I'll bring some extra sauce for you both."

When the lady walked away, Vanessa looked at Ian and rolled her eyes and made a slight groan. "I think I've had enough of British food for a while. I can't wait to get back to Switzerland and France."

Ian smiled. "It's ironic how much of the world Britain controlled but their cuisine didn't change much."

"Probably so. But also, we French take cooking pretty seriously. Julia Child once said, 'In France, cooking is a serious art form and a national sport.'"

Ian laughed. "Yes, that is probably true."

The waitress arrived back with the two beers. "Here you both are. I'll be back with your fish and chips in a jiffy."

Ian and Vanessa thanked the waitress. When the waitress was out of earshot, Ian looked at Vanessa. "So, I called Elliot Brooks. He told me that it was Jack Samuelson from the White House who got him involved in Leviathan. Elliot doesn't even know what Leviathan will do. Jack Samuelson supposedly gave him some information, but Jack told Elliot if he leaked any of the information from that document, Elliot would be arrested for treason."

"Jack Samuelson is the deputy chief of staff, correct?"

"Yes. Elliot has a power complex and he wanted desperately to be an economic advisor to the president. Looks like Jack gave Elliot a better offer of sorts," Ian said. He took another sip of his beer, then he continued summarizing the rest of the conversation. "At the end of our conversation, he told me that on Wednesday, the investors are meeting in Geneva. He wants to have lunch with me, and said he would bring the file that he mentioned to me on the phone."

"We need to get to Geneva for that lunch. Hope it's not too late before the conference starts."

The waitress came back to the table with both orders of fish and chips. "Here are some extra tartar and brown sauces. Do either of you need anything else?"

"No, thank you," Vanessa said. She then cut some of her

fried fish and dipped it into the tartar sauce before eating it. "This does taste better with the sauce, but nothing like if we French made this."

Ian laughed and ate a couple of bites of his fish and chips.

Vanessa then continued. "While you were away, I did a little more research into Hanna Assad. Most of the articles I found didn't mention how the murder took place, but I found one article that mentioned what happened. The murder occurred in a lab, and the deceased had severe burns to much of her body. The body was wearing a lab coat and in it was Hanna's ID card."

"So, you are telling me that you don't think the person in the lab was Hanna?"

"I'm not sure. It just would be super convenient." She paused. "In that specific article, it mentioned that the murderer could have been another woman. There was an eyewitness who exited the lab prior to the murder and he said he saw Hanna and another woman in the lab."

"What about any DNA testing on the body?"

"I don't know, but Syrians are quick to bury their dead, and the university wanted to put this behind them." She took a couple more bites of her food, and then said, "Plus, I found out that the university changed much of its procedures in the labs around campus."

He looked at her. "So you think Hanna is still alive?"

"I don't know if she is still alive. But she wasn't murdered in the lab that night. It would make a plausible explanation for two things. First, Viyan's interaction in that courtyard that day and secondly, why Elena still had Hanna's mail."

Ian nodded. "That could be plausible. But why?"

"I still am not sure of the why. But I think Elena and Hanna are related in some way."

As they cleaned their plates and finished their beers, the waitress came up to them. "May I get you anything else?"

Ian said, "No, just the check, please. Those were some great fish and chips."

The waitress smiled as she picked up the plates. "Glad you liked it. Will you be paying with cash or a card?"

"Card," he said.

The waitress nodded, "Great. I will come back with the machine shortly."

As they waited for the waitress to return, Vanessa and Ian looked out towards The Covenant. Vanessa gasped as she and Ian saw Elena get out of a black Mercedes and walk into The Covenant.

Vanessa kept her eyes on the entrance of The Covenant and the Mercedes as the waitress came back with the credit card machine and Ian paid the bill. After the waitress walked off, Vanessa looked at Ian. "Let's follow Elena to see what her next move might be."

As Ian and Vanessa walked out of The Angry Friar, Elena got back in the Mercedes. Ian and Vanessa were able to find a taxi quickly.

CHAPTER 55

Gibraltar
Monday

"Thank you, good sir. Your timing was impeccable," Ian said as he and Vanessa got in the back of the taxi.

"Welcome. So, where can I take you both?" the taxi driver said as he looked into his rearview mirror at Ian and Vanessa.

"See that black Mercedes?" Ian said and pointed toward the car. "I want you to follow it."

"Bloody hell. I can't do that," the taxi driver answered.

"We'll make it worth it," Vanessa added. "Whatever is the rate at the end of this ride, we'll triple it." She looked at Ian and he nodded.

"Bloody hell, are you cops?" the taxi driver asked, starting to follow the Mercedes.

"No. I'm a journalist and he works for the United States consulate," Vanessa said.

"So, is this some type of diplomatic chase?" the taxi driver asked.

"No, it's more of a reconnaissance mission," Vanessa replied.

Ian then asked, "What's your name?"

"I'm Richard. I've lived all my life in Gibraltar. I know it inside and out."

"Nice to meet you, Richard. I'm Ian and this is Vanessa."

"It's a pleasure. So, the car we are following, is it some national security story?"

"Not sure," Vanessa said as she looked at Richard and then at Ian.

"You know that Gibraltar is still an active military base used by the Royal Air Force," Richard said. "Actually, when Russia invaded Ukraine, the military antenna that you see near the official base was upgraded in the event Russia made an even broader attack."

"I didn't see any military aircraft at the airport," Ian said.

"Rarely there are aircraft. They will come just for a short time, either for training exercises or NATO forces will use Gibraltar as a stopover." Richard paused before continuing. "You know the Rock has over 200 caves. Few are open to the public. Many are used by the Royal Air Force and closed to the public."

Richard kept his cab about three car lengths behind the Mercedes. Both cars started to meander up the road that ascended the Rock. This was not an unusual path; many cabs and buses used this road if visitors wanted to be driven up to the top rather than using the 6-minute cable car. Much of the road up the Rock had trees on either side, as it was a nature reserve.

Vanessa and Ian noticed a group of white cabs stopped by a lookout. The Mercedes passed the lookout point and continued further up the Rock.

"Richard, why were all those cabs at that lookout point? Was that a special point?" Vanessa asked.

"Actually, it's a good point to see the Pillars of Hercules," Richard responded.

"Pillars of Hercules, like from mythology?" Vanessa asked.

"Yes. According to legend, Hercules passed through this area to take the Cattle of Geryon from the far west and bring them to Eurystheus. It was his tenth of twelve labors. During his journey, he encountered a mountain that was once Atlas. Hercules decided not to climb the mountain. Instead he used his superhuman strength to break it, then he could just go through rather than over the mountain. It was this action that led to the Atlantic Ocean and the Mediterranean Sea becoming connected, and he formed the Strait of Gibraltar."

Richard continued and raised his right hand to point to the right-side window. "Today is not the clearest of days, but right across from Gibraltar is Morocco. On a super clear day, you can usually see the other pillar. It is called Jebel Musa. It is about twice the size of the Rock of Gibraltar."

"Fascinating," Ian and Vanessa said. After a brief pause, Ian asked, "Any idea where that Mercedes could be going?"

"If I had to guess, I would say we are headed to St. Michael's Cave," Richard responded.

"Why do you say that?" Ian asked.

"See the car's license plate? It reads 'G 7867 E.' The 'G' indicates Gibraltar. While some plates start with RN or RA, which means Royal Navy or Royal Air Force, cars with those plates can get to more secure parts of the Rock."

Vanessa then asked, "What's St. Michael's Cave?"

"It is one of the most visited caves on the Rock. The cave is made up of limestone. It is in the upper rock region, which is about 300 meters above sea level. According to the first historian of Gibraltar, Alonso Hernández del Portillo, the name came from a similar grotto in Apulia, Italy where the Archangel Michael is said to have appeared." Richard paused and said, "If you go into the cave, there is a formation of limestone that looks like an angel's wings. It is pretty special if I might add."

The car started to slow down. "Looks like I was right. We are coming up on the entrance to St. Michael's Cave," Richard said as the car slowed to a stop. He still kept the car a little distant from the Mercedes.

They all watched as the Mercedes stopped and Elena got out of the car and started to walk toward the cave entrance.

"Will you be getting out here?" Richard asked.

Ian and Vanessa looked at each other and nodded. "Yes, we will be getting out. Is there a way you can stay?" Ian asked.

"Of course. Taxis usually wait in this area," Richard answered and reached for some wristbands. "You both will need these." He handed them to Vanessa and Ian. "These bands will allow you to enter the cave."

"Thank you," Vanessa said, and then she and Ian exited the car.

Ian and Vanessa walked past the Mercedes and into a gift shop. Some tourists looked at different souvenirs. On the other end of the gift shop, Elena walked through the security gate to enter the cave. Vanessa and Ian made their way toward the cave entrance.

Once they entered the cave, a damp coolness gave Vanessa and Ian both chills. Elena kept walking and Vanessa and Ian kept a safe distance away. The cave had several large chambers, some with ceilings around 40 feet high. The minerals in the cave had formed many different shapes, many of which hung from the ceiling. At one point, they walked by the minerals that formed the angel wings, which were about 16 feet in height.

"That's really beautiful," Vanessa said as she looked at the wings.

"It is—and it is natural too. But I think now is not a time to discuss philosophy and religion," Ian said and started to walk further into the cave.

Vanessa smiled and followed Ian. "Definitely."

They walked into a cavern that looked like an auditorium. On the far end, there were multilevel seats. It looked like there could be concerts, plays, and other events held in the room. They saw Elena go to the middle row and sit in the middle.

Vanessa turned to Ian. "Let's split and sit behind Elena a few rows up." Ian nodded as he walked to the left, and Vanessa then walked to the right. They found a couple of seats apart, two rows behind Elena. Some tourists were taking their seats nearby. The lights then went off for a few moments, and then a light show came on with soft music and highlighted much of the mineral formations in that area of the cave.

In the middle of the light show, a lady came and sat next to Elena. The lady wore jeans, a white shirt, and a black baseball hat. Ian and Vanessa noticed the lady was about the same age as Elena. Because of their proximity and the fact that not many tourists were around making too much noise, Ian and Vanessa were able to hear part of the conversation.

"Is everything set in place?" Elena asked.

"Yes, except that the conference is still taking place. I thought you said it would be easy to derail," the lady said sternly.

"Yes, I thought it would be easy to at least postpone. I guess Seung Kim is more formidable than I originally thought."

"Do you think anything can stop him now?"

"We could isolate him too, like the others," Elena said as she looked at the other lady.

"That is definitely a thought. But that might draw too much attention. We've isolated two, but three would start to bring attention to the matter."

"On top of everything, that journalist and her so-called assistant visited me on the yacht—but only after Trevor left."

"I thought you had her fired?"

"I did. But somehow that bitch didn't get the message that her career is over."

Elena and the lady sat in silence for a few moments.

"What about the contingency plan we talked about?" Elena asked.

"I think we need to activate that contingency plan but with some extra insurance that it works."

"Extra insurance? What do you mean, Hanna?" Elena looked at the lady.

Hanna reached for Elena's hand and grabbed it. "You don't have anything to worry about, Elena. Just know that I love you and this is for the greater good. Remember in Hobbes we trust."

"Yes, in Hobbes we trust. But what can I do?"

"Take the yacht to Lisbon and then fly to Geneva. I'll make the necessary arrangements." Hanna stood up and looked at Elena. "You've done your part. Thank you." Hanna leaned and kissed Elena on the lips, then silently walked away.

Elena stayed in her seat as she watched the light show for a few minutes and then stood up and walked out of the cave.

After Elena walked out, Ian walked to Vanessa and sat next to her. "Was that Hanna Assad?"

Vanessa looked at Ian. "Quite possibly. It would make sense in some weird way."

"We need to get back to Geneva and warn Seung Kim," Ian said, and Vanessa nodded.

They both got up and walked back to Richard's taxi. By the time they got back to the taxi, the Mercedes was gone.

Richard saw Ian and Vanessa and waved. "I assume we aren't following that Mercedes anymore."

"No. Back to the hotel," Vanessa said. "Unfortunately, we

will be leaving soon."

Richard nodded and started to drive them back to the hotel.

CHAPTER 56

Gibraltar
Monday Evening

The Phantom, who wore a blue jumpsuit, a white helmet, and a backpack, walked on the deck of the *Emma Maersk*, inspecting some of the containers. A few other workers on the ship were also inspecting the containers. The *Emma Maersk* held about 15,500 twenty-two-foot containers, and each one needed to be accounted for before the ship left Gibraltar for its next stop.

The Phantom couldn't care less where the ship was going—he would not be on board for too long. During the ship's stop in Gibraltar, some of the crew rotated on and off. The ship had about thirteen members on board at any one time, and there was room for thirty. When rotations occurred, not all the crew knew each other. For the Phantom, it was fairly easy to hack into the ship's computer and add an alias for himself to the crew.

Before getting on board the ship, he took the rental boat with his buoys and placed them a few hundred yards in front of the ship. No one would give these buoys a second look, and the Phantom knew this. He then took the boat back to the rental spot and found the pick-up spot for the Emma Maersk workers. No one gave him a second look.

As he was inspecting the containers, his phone vibrated. He looked at his phone and there was a text message from an unknown number. The message said, "*GO*." He knew what the message meant and who it was from. He then made his way toward the bridge. When he arrived, he noticed the first officer was patrolling the bridge to make sure everything was running smoothly. He closed the door behind him and walked toward the first officer.

The first officer looked up towards the Phantom. "Excuse me, there's no need for you to be here." The first officer said in a Swedish accent.

The Phantom said nothing, heading to the consoles before quietly starting to work on they ship's systems.

"I order you to stop," the first officer said as he rushed over to pull the Phantom away from the ship's computers.

When the first officer put his arm on the Phantom's shoulder, the Phantom instinctively grabbed the first officer's wrist and twisted it until it broke, then used his shoulder to ram it into the first officer's head, knocking him out. After the first officer fell to the ground, the Phantom then had a little time to work in silence.

Many of the ships today can truly be put on autopilot, even those the size of the *Emma Maersk*. He input the command for the ship to raise anchor and gave the coordinates to which he wanted it to proceed. Those coordinates were those of the buoys. A ship of that size did not move very quickly, and he knew he could get off before it reached that location.

Once the ship started to move, he exited the bridge and quickly walked down to the level where he originally entered. The door was still open, and he grabbed a small device from his backpack and put it up to his mouth. This device would help him breathe underwater. He then jumped out of the ship and started to swim away from the ship towards land. He ended up finding a speedboat nearby where he could rest.

When he was on the speedboat, he watched as the ship started to move. He also saw *The Leviathan* yacht move toward the same coordinates. Everything was going according to plan, he thought. He then jumped back in the water and started to swim towards the shore. Fortunately, he was in shape and had good strength for swimming long distances.

About five minutes later, as he was swimming underwater, there was a deep, resonating boom. Seconds later, he felt a massive shockwave that rattled his bones and pushed him violently forward. He kept his body calm as the sensation passed. After the explosion, the current and waves became more violent, but he continued to swim to shore.

Once on shore, he heard lots of sirens and people screaming for help. He looked back towards the water and saw the *Emma Maersk* and *The Leviathan* engulfed in flames. Several fireboats were rushing to the scene.

The Phantom walked casually back to his rental truck. Once he reached the truck, he drove to the Gibraltar airport, where a black G650, supplied by Damien, was waiting with its engines on, ready to whisk him away.

CHAPTER 57

Gibraltar Airport
Monday Evening

As Ian and Vanessa arrived at the airport, they heard a lot of sirens. They walked up to the front desk.

"Excuse me," Ian said. "Did something just happen?"

The lady behind the desk replied, "Yes, there's been an explosion in the harbor. A ship and a yacht collided."

"Oh my God," Vanessa shrieked. "Do you know which vessels?"

"No, madam," the lady said. "Which flight are you here for?"

"I'm Ian Steele. There should be a private jet under my name," Ian said.

The lady looked at her computer and then up at Ian and Vanessa. "Oh yes, Mr. Steele. Your aircraft recently landed. You can walk to the plane. It's the grey aircraft, tail number N65GV."

"Thank you," Ian said. Then Ian and Vanessa walked out of the building and towards the aircraft.

As they walked, Vanessa pulled out her phone and called Richard. "Hi, Richard. I just heard there was an accident in the harbor. Do you know what yacht was involved?"

"Vanessa, I was just about to call you," Richard said. "After I dropped you and Ian off at the hotel, I did some more detective work. The car you had me follow went to the yacht that just has been in an accident. The yacht was *The Leviathan.* I'm not sure about any survivors, but it looks really bad."

"Shit, I was afraid of that," Vanessa said as she tapped Ian's shoulder. "Thank you, Richard. You have been very informative."

"You're welcome. 'Til next time." Richard said as he hung up the phone.

Vanessa put her phone down and looked at Ian. "The yacht

was *The Leviathan.*"

Ian looked at her in shock. "Shit. Any survivors?"

"Richard didn't say. Maybe we can find some more news once we get on board the plane."

Ian nodded. As they started to walk to their plane, they saw a man walking to a black G650 next to theirs. Ian looked at Vanessa. "The man walking towards that other plane—doesn't he look familiar?"

She looked in the direction of the other plane, then back at Ian. "Yes, I think it's that guy who we saw at the Geneva airport with the Leviathan Cross watch."

"What are the odds of that?" he asked as they stepped towards their plane, and turned his attention to the flight attendant and pilot. "I'm Ian Steele, and this is my guest, Vanessa."

The pilot and flight attendant welcomed them both and took their bags. "Anything we can do for you before we leave?" The flight attendant asked.

"By chance, can you tell me where that black jet next to us is going?" Ian asked as he and Vanessa sat in plush executive-style reclining chairs.

Since the cockpit door was open, the pilot overheard and came out. "From the control tower information, it looks like that plane is headed to Geneva too." The pilot paused. "Too bad you didn't coordinate with that passenger. You all could have saved on the money and gas." The pilot laughed.

Vanessa and Ian nodded cautiously and Ian said, "We are ready to be wheels up anytime."

The pilot looked at them and nodded. "Yes, sir. We will be wheels up shortly after I finish some paperwork." He said and walked back to the cockpit.

The flight attendant then looked at Vanessa and Ian. "May I offer you both something to eat or drink?"

"Single malt Scotch if you have it," Vanessa said as she rubbed her head.

"Make that two," Ian said. The flight attendant nodded and walked to the back of the plane.

Ian turned towards Vanessa and turned on the TV. When he

turned on the TV, BBC was on with breaking news. "*Yacht accident in Gibraltar - Elena Mirreaux unaccounted for.*"

They both looked at each other as the plane started to move. "This was no accident. And that guy on the plane…what the fuck is going on?" Vanessa said.

CHAPTER 58

Airborne - Gibraltar to Geneva
Monday Night

Vanessa and Ian spent the first part of the flight on their computers, watching the news for updates as they sipped on their drinks, which the flight attendant had given them. Since the accident had just happened, there was not too much to report other than the initial shock of the accident.

"Good evening. This is Oscar Roberts with GBC News. I'm at the port of Gibraltar bringing you some breaking news. In just the last hour, the Emma Maersk, a cargo ship, and a private yacht collided. Both vessels are engulfed in flames with fireboats currently trying to extinguish the fires. GBC News cannot confirm how many people are aboard either vessel and if there are any casualties." The TV camera panned to the ongoing fires on both vessels. Some of the *Emma Maersk's* containers had fallen into the water.

"GBC News is reporting that the private vessel was *The Leviathan*, but we are trying to get a secondary confirmation," Oscar reported through the TV. "We are also trying to figure out if any of the contents in the containers are hazardous."

Vanessa put the TV on mute and looked at Ian. "The BBC is reporting that it was Elena Mirreaux's yacht. But they don't say anything about whether she was on board or not."

Ian looked up from his computer. "This was definitely not an accident. We need something more on Hanna Assad."

"I know this is crazy to consider. That kiss, could Elena and Hanna have been in love?" She said as she leaned down to put her chin on top of her arms.

"That could be possible. But how to prove it?" He said as he leaned back in his chair. "But that kiss could have just been something friendly between them. Maybe it was something culturally for them?"

"Really, Ian? A kiss like that is a friendly gesture?" She smirked at him and said sarcastically.

"I don't know. I'm just trying not to jump to any conclusions too quickly." He paused. "Either way, how can we prove it?"

"You mean besides seeing them hold hands and kiss?" she asked.

"Yes. It would be our word against theirs if they deny it." He paused, then continued, "Plus, let's say they were lovers. Why would their contingency plan be to kill Elena? That is—if she is indeed deceased."

"Obviously, another way of trying to stop the conference, since Elena had worked hard to make this conference happen. Yet, Elena didn't seem like she knew her impending death was about to happen."

They both stared at each other for a couple of moments in deep thought. "No confirmation has been reported about Elena. So, I think we have to assume both could still be alive, and/or Hanna is going to try something in Geneva," he said. "Remember the Leviathan Rowing Club photo in Oxford? Elena and Hanna did look similar."

Vanessa nodded. "The way we can do this is if Viyan can identify her," she said.

"But Viyan thinks Hanna died decades ago. How will she know for sure?"

"True, but at least Viyan will know for sure if she is the real Elena or not."

"So, you want to send Viyan in as bait somehow?"

"Sadly, yes. I don't see another way."

"We must keep a close eye on her if we involve her. I don't want to see her as collateral damage."

"If we can find a way to get into that Leviathan investors meeting, I'm sure Viyan could try to identify her without getting noticed," she said, then paused. "Did Elliot say when that investors' meeting was to be held?"

"Good point about that meeting. I will contact Elliot, and maybe you can contact Viyan."

They both nodded to each other, and then returned to work on their computers.

CHAPTER 59

Multiple Undisclosed Locations
Tuesday Morning
Via videoconference

"Swan wants me to inform everyone on this call to report to Geneva," the scrambled voice said.

"I thought the point of this group coming together was to make sure our respective delegations do not go to Geneva," Zaaeem Farouq said.

There was grumbling by others on the call.

"This will be business as usual. The unfortunate accident in Gibraltar and the launch of Leviathan will cause everything else to be derailed," the scrambled voice said.

"This is turning into a shit show," Ibrahim Kane said.

"I humbly disagree," the scrambled voice responded. "Yes, there have been some setbacks, but you all will still be paid, and Leviathan will still have a successful launch."

"Can we have any assurances from Swan about this?" Kabir Varma asked.

Before the scrambled voice could answer, Kane spoke up. "I know we have all tested Leviathan, but how do we know for sure that this can be rolled out on a global scale immediately?"

"The programmer who built it has high confidence that it will do what it needs to," Jack Samuelson said. "He has put extra assurances in place to set off right before the launch to make sure."

All the individuals on the screen began to smile. Then the scrambled voice said, "Swan will be in Geneva to celebrate with each of you."

"Should we go to the investors' meeting?" Nakia Ahmed asked.

"No, your anonymity is still key in this venture." The scrambled voice answered. "The meeting place with Swan will be sent to each of you."

"When will the news of Elena's departure be circulated?" Kabir said.

"It is starting, but some groups prefer to find a body first," the scrambled voice responded.

"Isn't that your job to make sure they do?" Kabir sternly asked.

"Yes, but it has been dark in the harbor. Once the sun is in full sunlight, the extent of the damage will be done."

Each individual nodded. There was a brief pause, then every member said, "In Hobbes We Trust."

CHAPTER 60

Geneva Airport
Tuesday Late Morning

Once the plane landed in Geneva, Vanessa and Ian noticed that the black G650 was parked and closed. Its passenger had already left.

"I'm going to go find out where our mysterious passenger went," Vanessa said as she looked at Ian.

Ian looked at his phone and then up at Vanessa. "I have a few missed calls from Paul Greene. I need to see what's going on with the conference."

"Go see Paul, and we can meet up later."

"Be careful." He looked at her. "If you are in trouble, call me."

"I will." She leaned towards him, pecked his lips, and smiled as she walked toward the black plane.

He smiled, pulled out his phone, found Paul's contact, and hit the number to call.

The phone rang a couple of times before Paul answered. "Hi Ian, I've been wondering where you are. An accident in Gibraltar might be creating an economic panic."

"I have some information about the accident." Ian paused. "Are you in your office? I have something I need to talk to you about in person."

"Yes, come over."

"Be there within the hour." Ian then hung up the phone before Paul could respond. Ian then walked to the main terminal to find an Uber.

Vanessa walked to the black G650 and saw the pilot and flight attendant about to get into a parked car near the plane.

"Excuse me," Vanessa called out in French. "I think there's been some mix-up. I'm looking for the passenger who was on your flight."

The pilot and flight attendant looked at her. "Sorry, he left in a hurry," the pilot said.

"Do you know where he was heading?" Vanessa asked as she stepped closer.

"No, sorry, madam, I don't know," the pilot said. "You should call him if you were supposed to pick him up."

Vanessa looked at the pilot and then at the flight attendant. "This is just not my day. I know you aren't going to believe me," Vanessa said. "My phone battery died, and I'm really in a bind."

"Sorry, I don't know," the pilot said and got into the car.

The flight attendant came up to Vanessa. "The man stayed very silent for the flight. He just kept writing in a journal and reading over it," the flight attendant said. "When I brought him a drink during the flight, I saw what he wrote on one of his pages. He wrote 'InterContinental Hotel.'" The flight attendant paused. "I'm not sure if this helps, but that is the most information I can give you."

Vanessa smiled. "Thank you so, so much. I really appreciate it." She paused. "Now that you mention it, I do recall that's one of the places he is going. I'm such a klutz today."

The flight attendant smiled. "You're welcome." She then got into the car and closed the door.

Vanessa watched as the car drove away. She then turned to walk toward the terminal to get an Uber. As she walked, she thought about who could be the next target. She knew that the InterContinental Hotel was one of the most secure hotels in Geneva and where most diplomats stay during high-level conferences.

CHAPTER 61

Geneva
Tuesday Late Morning
U.S. Mission to the United Nations

Paul was sitting at his desk when Ian walked in. "Well, Ian, this has become a clusterfuck."

Ian took a seat in the chair opposite Paul. "What do you mean?"

Paul cleared his throat and said, "I'm not sure this conference will happen. Have you heard about the shipping disaster in Gibraltar?"

"Yes, I did," Ian said. "I was there and left just before the accident."

Paul continued talking as if not hearing all of what Ian had said. "The ship's contents are all over the harbor and floating in the straits. This is going to mess up international trade for a while. Plus, the yacht at some point carried Elena Mirreaux, but no one knows if she was on board." Paul paused, and Ian's words finally caught up with him. "Wait a second, you were in Gibraltar?"

"Yes, I thought I mentioned that on the phone earlier," Ian said.

"You probably did. But I've been pulled in many directions since the accident there." Paul paused. "What brought you to Gibraltar anyway?"

"I have been following up on a story with the Financial Times journalist Vanessa Dupont. It relates to the upcoming conference, the new company Leviathan, and Elena Mirreaux."

Paul looked straight at Ian. "First, Ms. Dupont is no longer associated with the Financial Times. Secondly, are you pitching me some conspiracy?"

"I believe it is, and they are all connected. Even Vanessa's dismissal from the *Financial Times*." Ian briefly explained his recent travels and events.

"My God," Paul said. "I've been wondering where you have been the last few days. Have you been chasing some crazy conspiracy?"

"I'm not sure if I would call it crazy. I think there is a very real threat to the conference."

Paul looked at Ian from across his desk. "What proof do you have?"

"I gave you the facts, but I need your help."

"What type of help? Look, I want to believe you, but I am having difficulty recognizing that Elena Mirreaux and this Leviathan company are connected. Let alone the fact that they are trying to bring down this conference. Furthermore, a directive was sent out to everyone associated with the United Nations that Vanessa Dupont is persona non grata."

Ian frowned. "Excuse my language, but who the fuck do you think ordered that?"

"I don't give a fuck, Ian. But as a government employee, I don't want to rock the boat, especially when a conference is on the line to create something great for the world."

"I, too, don't want to rock the boat. I think this group has been trying to rock the boat, though. I must credit Seung Kim for not caving in so far. But I think he could be in danger."

Paul looked at him briefly before he responded. "Look, I don't know you that well, but trust me, all of our security intelligence says there is no threat to this conference and Geneva."

"I think the threat hasn't surfaced yet but is here in Geneva." Ian paused. "I just need a favor."

"What's that?" Paul asked apprehensively.

"I need you to do a background check on Hanna Assad."

"You mean the Oxford student who died years ago from the events you mentioned?"

"Yes. Vanessa and I believe we saw her in Gibraltar, and she is connected to everything I just mentioned."

"I can't just order background checks for no reason of suspicion."

Ian grew frustrated with Paul. He tried not to show his frustration. While people in government have the power to do some remarkable things, they get bogged down in the red-tape nature of the system. Ian took a deep breath and then responded. "As I explained, I think there is a connection, and it is quite possibly a matter of international security." Ian looked at Paul. "Look, I came here to help this conference take place. I'm trying to save it."

Paul looked down at his desk and then back up at Ian. "Okay, I'll run this up the flagpole with CIA and Interpol and let you know."

Ian made a small smile. "Thank you, Paul. Please express the urgency."

"I'll do my best and let you know—hopefully in a couple of hours."

"Great. Let me know as soon as you hear anything," Ian said as he stood up.

"I hope you're right, otherwise, this is an abuse of power." Paul said, seated at his desk.

Ian nodded, then walked out of the office and checked his phone. There was a text from Vanessa that said, "*InterContinental Hotel*." He looked at his watch, and decided to stretch his legs and walk about twenty minutes to the hotel. He thought it would be easier than taking the bus or Uber, as security for the conference was beginning to close off some streets.

CHAPTER 62

Geneva
Tuesday Afternoon
Intercontinental Geneva

Ian walked into the hotel lobby. The lobby was very busy with people checking in for the conference. The lobby exuded a blend of contemporary luxury and understated elegance. As Ian walked into the lobby, he was greeted by high ceilings and an expansive space bathed in natural light due to the large floor-to-ceiling windows.

Plush seating areas on the left side of the lobby were arranged to invite conversation or relaxation. Large sofas and armchairs were arranged around low coffee tables with fresh floral arrangements. Artwork adorned the walls, providing touches of European culture and style, enhancing the lobby's atmosphere without overwhelming it.

A chandelier at the lobby's center was a focal point; its soft illumination enhanced the luxurious feel. The reception desk in the middle of the lobby was polished and minimalistic and staffed by courteous and professional staff. On the left side of the lobby, where the bar would normally be located, were two tables draped with light blue United Nations logos. One table had a sign indicating "Media Check-In," and the other had a sign indicating "Speaker Check-In." The diplomats going to make the official negotiations and sign any official resolution would not have to check in at the hotel; rather, they would go to the United Nations meeting rooms. The hotel was hosting additional women's rights informational sessions that rode the coattails of the conference.

Ian looked around the lobby to see if he could find Vanessa. He spent a few minutes looking around. Most people scurrying around had their bags, as they seemed to have just arrived from the airport. He finally found Vanessa and walked up to her.

"That guy from the plane is somewhere here," she said, looking at him without trying to appear concerned.

"Did you see him come here?" he asked.

"No, but the flight attendant from his plane told me that she saw something written in his journal about his hotel."

"If he's here, he must be after someone or something. Let's try to blend in and see if we can find him."

She nodded at him and then walked to the check-in desk. He followed.

"Are you both checking in?" the lady at the table smiled at Vanessa and Ian.

"Yes and no," Vanessa said. "Our bosses said there's some mistake with our registration, but it should be rectified soon. By chance, do you have any guest passes we could have in the meantime?"

The lady smiled. "But of course. Sorry that has happened to you both." The lady pulled two guest badges with lanyards and gave them to Vanessa and Ian. "You can wear these for public networking events, but they will not allow access to secured events."

"Thank you. You've been a major help," Ian said.

"It's my pleasure. I hope your registration gets sorted out soon." The lady smiled and turned to another attendee.

As Vanessa and Ian walked away from the table, Ian said to Vanessa, "Smart thinking about the badges."

"Oh, I wonder what you would do without me." She smiled, "Now we can blend in-well enough." He nodded as they circled the room, quietly studying the attendees.

Some governmental diplomats wore lapel pins with their country's flag. They both could tell there were no high-level diplomats around, as the security wasn't over the top.

As they walked to another section of the lobby, Ian noticed a few people with the Leviathan Cross lapel pin. He tapped Vanessa's shoulder and casually pointed in the direction of the couple of individuals who were wearing those pins. "I wonder if any of them are part of the investors Elliot is a part of?" he asked.

"We could ask if they know Elliot, maybe?" Vanessa asked.

"That's a way to get them talking." He said.

Before he turned away from her, he heard someone calling his name behind him. "Ian Steele!" The voice sounded familiar as Ian turned and saw Elliot approaching him and Vanessa.

"Elliot, I didn't think I'd see you till tomorrow. I told Vanessa I needed to text you about our lunch tomorrow," Ian said as he shook Elliot's hand.

Elliot then took Vanessa's hand and kissed the top of it. "It's so nice to see you again, Ms. Dupont."

Vanessa smiled. "You have a good memory."

Elliot smiled at Vanessa. "It comes easy when remembering someone as attractive as you."

There was a brief silence, and Elliot said, "I'm glad I found you. Due to some misunderstandings, the Leviathan investors' meeting is this evening, not tomorrow. We can forgo the lunch. Why don't you both come to the meeting tonight?"

Ian responded, "Sure, if it won't be an imposition."

"You're the one who will be put in awkward imposition for not investing in this wonderful company," Elliot responded.

"I'm not sure about that, but I'd like to learn more," Ian said.

"Well, meet me in the lobby of this hotel at 7."

"Perfect. Is the meeting in the hotel or elsewhere?" Ian asked.

"In a secured room of this hotel." Elliot paused. "Make sure you both wear something nice; it will be like a cocktail party."

Vanessa and Ian looked at Elliot. "Sounds great," Vanessa said. "Since I'm French, I promise not to disappoint."

Elliot smirked, "See you tonight." Then he walked away to greet a couple of other people.

Ian looked at Vanessa. "Well, I guess we have a reception to attend, too. Do you want to meet here at about 6:30?"

"Sure. I might bring something to record what happens."

"Good idea, but be careful."

"A French woman who happens to be a journalist can be quite resourceful," she said, smirking at him.

CHAPTER 63

Geneva
Tuesday Evening
InterContinental Geneva

Wearing a navy suit with a white shirt and navy tie, Ian waited in the lobby for Vanessa's arrival. As he waited, the lobby bustled with an evening crowd of unassuming tourists, diplomats, and the press. Most of the people were having drinks at the bar or getting ready to go to dinner. He looked around to see if he could tell if anyone was there for the investors' meeting. No one caught his eye.

After a few minutes, Vanessa entered the lobby and grabbed Ian's attention. She wore a black V-neckline dress that stopped just below her knees and black high heels. She also wore a silver necklace with a rectangular pendant that dropped in the center of her neckline.

"Wow! You look beautiful," he said as he hugged her.

She smiled. "Thanks. You don't look too bad yourself." As she hugged him, she leaned to his ear. "My necklace has a listening device in it."

He smiled as he looked at her. "I didn't know you were like James Bond."

She smiled. "I think I have better journalistic skills than Monsieur Bond."

"That you do, Ms. Dupont." He laughed. "Good to be home?"

She looked at him. "Yes, but when I left Geneva, I was an employed journalist, and the traffic wasn't as bad as it is now."

"True about the traffic. I didn't know Geneva's traffic could get this congested." He paused. "As far as your job, if we foil this plot, I think a journalism award is on your horizon."

She blushed. "It's ironic. I just wanted to be a biographer to someone I thought I admired."

"Well, I still think there are ways to admire people even if they aren't perfect."

"But we are talking about a murderer and a global conspiracy."

"We still don't know how she and Hanna are connected."

She looked at him, and before she could respond, they both heard Elliot loudly calling their names.

"Vanessa and Ian! You all are becoming some of my favorite people right now. I can't wait to prove you wrong. You know I love a good deal when I see it. I make deals and investments better than anyone. If anyone tells you anything else, it's a hoax." Elliot said as he gave Vanessa and Ian a hug.

"I still don't understand how you are friends with him," Vanessa said as she looked from Elliot to Ian.

Elliot laughed, and Ian said, "We've known each other a long time. But he's acting more strange than normal."

Elliot laughed again and put his arm around Ian's shoulder. "It's all in good fun. I'm just so jacked from this investment."

She looked at Elliot wearily. "D'accord." She paused and asked, "Is your lovely wife Stephanie joining us?"

Elliot smiled. "Yes, of course. She should be at the reception." Elliot said as he started to guide Ian and Vanessa towards an elevator whose doors were guarded by a man with a serious look on his face and an earpiece in his right ear.

"Excuse me," the man said. "This elevator is off limits."

Elliot smiled at the man, pulled a metal card from his wallet, and showed it to him. The man didn't say another word and immediately used a key to call for the elevator, and the elevator door opened. Elliot walked in first, followed by Vanessa and Ian.

When the doors closed, Ian asked, "Is that some sort of membership card?"

Elliot smirked and held out the card for Ian and Vanessa to see. The card was metal, with only the Leviathan Cross engraved on it. "Isn't this some cool shit?" Elliot said as he dangled the card in front of them for a moment before putting it back into his wallet.

Ian smiled. "I guess. But I find it cooler when I had a check for $500 million in my hand when my first company was bought."

Elliot quickly retorted, "I think the returns on this will be even more."

Vanessa and Ian silently looked at each other as the elevator reached the correct floor.

When the elevator doors opened, they were greeted by large banners with the Leviathan Cross on them along a long hallway with cocktail tables wrapped with white covers every five feet. There were about seventy-five people, mostly men and some women. The men were dressed in suits, and the women were dressed in cocktail dresses. There were about ten servers who walked around giving drinks and small appetizers.

One of the servers approached Vanessa, Ian, and Elliot with a tray of champagne. "Some champagne?"

"Yes, please," Elliot roared as he took a glass of champagne. Vanessa and Ian then took a glass for themselves. The waiter then walked off toward the other guests.

As they took the first sips of their champagne, Vanessa asked Elliot, "The people here—are they just investors in Leviathan, or are they also employees?"

Elliot sipped his champagne and said, "These are just the investors."

Vanessa nodded, "D'accord. Have you seen how Leviathan works?"

"Not yet. Though I know that the board has tested it and has approved that it works," Ian said and smiled.

"So your investment is still a roll of the dice?" Ian asked.

"You know, Ian, that any investment is a leap of faith," Elliot responded.

"Yes, but before I invest, I like to touch and feel a prototype at least," Ian said.

"You need to be an investor like me, Ian. Take a leap of faith and you will have wealth like you can't imagine."

"How did the due diligence work for Leviathan?"

Elliot gulped the rest of his champagne and said, "Leviathan was different. It wasn't just about looking at spreadsheets; we delved deep into market dynamics. We analyzed consumer behavior, talked to industry experts, and explored emerging technologies.

"Besides gathering data, we trusted our instincts. It's about understanding the bigger picture and taking calculated risks. Sometimes you have to see the vision and go for it. That's what separates successful investors from the rest."

"You mentioned industry experts. What type of experts?" Vanessa asked, looking at Elliot.

"Government, news, and tech experts."

Before Vanessa or Ian could ask another question, Stephanie came up to Elliot and gave him a hug and a kiss on the cheek. She wore a black dress that had a V-neckline with spaghetti straps and a slit just above the left knee.

"So good to see you, Ian and Vanessa," Stephanie said to Ian and Vanessa as she looped her arm around Elliot's arm.

"Same. That was a beautiful concert you sponsored at your home," Vanessa said to Stephanie.

"Glad you enjoyed it. We love giving to charity and will do much more soon," Stephanie said and kissed Elliot's cheek.

Vanessa rolled her eyes and said, "Not all charitable giving is the same if you have blood on your hands."

Stephanie and Elliot looked at Vanessa quizzically. "It's always brought us joy and the others around us," Elliot said.

There was a silence, then Stephanie said to Elliot, "Hanna is here."

"Oh wow! I was wondering if she was going to be here. So, Leviathan must be ready for launch," Elliot responded, looking at Stephanie.

"Who's Hanna?" Ian asked.

"She's the brains of this operation. She is the person who sold me on Leviathan," Elliot said.

"I would love to meet her. Do you think you can provide an introduction?" Ian looked at Elliot and Stephanie with a smile.

"Abso-fucking-lutely," Elliot said with a giant grin. "Let's go find her." He took Stephanie's hand and they started to walk down the hallway. Vanessa and Ian followed.

Elliot said hello to a few people as they walked but did not introduce them to Stephanie, Vanessa, or Ian. They walked toward a crowd that hovered around Hanna. Hanna had black hair and wore a sleek, short-sleeved, streamlined black dress with a split crew neckline.

After a couple of minutes, Hanna started to walk off. Elliot got her attention and walked over to Ian, Vanessa, and Stephanie. "I'm so glad you are here. I have a potential investor for you to meet," Elliot said. "Hanna, this is Ian and Vanessa."

Hanna extended her hand to Ian and Vanessa. "Nice to meet you both. Have we met before?"

Ian and Vanessa shook Hanna's hand. "No, I don't believe so," Ian said.

"You both just look so familiar." Hanna paused. "Vanessa, aren't you a former journalist?"

Vanessa smiled, "Yes, I am a journalist."

"Well, no journalists are allowed at this event," Hanna said sternly.

"Well, I'm not here in any official capacity. My boyfriend Ian is interested in investing."

Ian smiled and put his arm around Vanessa's shoulder. "Yes, I need a new money-making opportunity."

Hanna looked at Vanessa and then at Ian. "We aren't taking any new investors until after the launch, which will be momentarily. But if you did invest, the equity options won't be as good as the ones Mr. Brooks will receive."

"Of course. I want to learn more about Leviathan and see a prototype before considering an investment, even at a smaller equity position."

Hanna smiled. "Well, I don't have a prototype to show you. Leviathan will go live later this evening, and you can judge your investment options then."

Ian looked at her. "I didn't realize that Leviathan was ready for launch."

"The board decided it would be better to launch earlier than anticipated for a better market valuation." Hanna paused. "Very nice meeting you both. I'm sorry, tonight is very busy. I have to make a quick call before the presentation. I hope you will consider an investment."

Vanessa, Ian, Stephanie, and Elliot told Hanna goodbye as she walked off.

"She's fantastic. I think you will really be impressed," Elliot said. "Let's go find seats for the presentation." Elliot led the way to the conference room.

Hanna found a secluded corner at the far end of the room and pulled out her phone. She dialed a number; the phone rang once, and she heard breathing on the other end. "They are here. I don't want them to see how my presentation ends." She then hung up the phone and composed herself before returning to the crowd of investors.

CHAPTER 64

Geneva
Tuesday Evening
InterContinental Geneva

When the phone cut off, the Phantom knew what his next action would be. He went to the closet and pulled out a hotel waiter's uniform. He procured the uniform earlier in the day even though he didn't know if he would need it. Before he left the room, he picked up a plastic vial filled with a clear liquid from his bag and placed it in his pocket. The liquid in the vial was the same potent poison that he used on François Mirreaux. However, the vial only held half of the dose that killed François Mirreaux. The Phantom thought only half a dose of the poison would be needed.

He left the room and headed to the staff entrance from his floor. No one gave him a second look as he walked confidently. Since he had studied the schematics of the hotel, he knew how to get to the Leviathan reception area as he used the staff corridor. He walked into the kitchen area and approached the place where trays of champagne were prepped to be picked up and brought out. He pulled the vial out of his pocket and put it into one of the champagne flutes. He then put the empty vial back in his pocket, picked up the tray, and brought it into the presentation area.

When he brought the champagne tray into the reception area, the attendees went to the presentation room. The Phantom quickly glanced around the room to find Ian and Vanessa. Once he spotted them in the center back of the room, he approached them.

A few investors took some of the glasses as he walked by with the tray. He made sure no one picked the flute with the poison. He also made sure there were two glasses left as he approached the table where Ian and Vanessa were seated.

Ian's glass was empty, while Vanessa's was still half full. The

Phantom reached Ian's left, picked up his glass, and replaced it with a full glass.

Ian said, "Merci." The Phantom nodded and started to walk back to the kitchen.

Ian turned his head toward the stage, but he felt perplexed in his gut and took a sip of his champagne.

The crowd started to clap as the master of ceremonies introduced the board chair. The applause lasted for a few moments, and then, from the curtains, Hanna began to emerge and walk to the podium. A few people stood up as the applause continued.

Hanna motioned for everyone to be seated. "Thank you all for coming. But most of all, thank you for your belief in Leviathan. If it weren't for your support, we would not have been able to achieve greatness."

The applause finally quieted, and Hanna continued, "Before I discuss more about Leviathan and what your generous support has helped build, I have some unfortunate news." She paused and looked around the room. "It has come to my attention that it is with great sadness that I announce the passing of Elena Mirreaux. It has been a hard time for the Mirreaux family, but Elena has helped us get to where we are now in many ways. Please raise your glasses as we honor Elena." Hanna raised her glass with everyone.

Ian and Vanessa raised their glasses to avoid drawing attention to themselves. As they both took another sip of their champagne, Ian started to cough uncontrollably. Vanessa looked over to see if Ian was okay. He drank some water, but he kept coughing and motioning to his throat so that he couldn't breathe. She then started to hit his back. She thought he might have choked on something.

He leaned towards her between coughs, "I need to go. I'm dizzy too."

She immediately helped him up from the table, put his arm over her shoulders, and slowly walked to the back of the room. A few people looked at them as they walked, but Hanna kept talking to draw everyone's attention to her and not them. A few workers rushed to them.

"Madame, do you need help?" One of the servers said as two others had taken Ian's arms from Vanessa.

"Oui, s'il vous plaît. Il a dit qu'il était très étourdi," (*Yes, please. He said he is very dizzy,*) she said with a worried look.

"Let's go to an outside room," the server said as they all moved quickly to the outside room.

Ian was guided to a bench and sat down, still coughing. The waiter asked Vanessa, "What happened?"

Vanessa looked at the server and said, "One of your colleagues gave him some champagne, and then after a few sips, he started coughing uncontrollably." The server nodded, looked at one of the other servers, and said, "Prends la trousse de secours." (*Get the first aid kit.*) One of the other servers dashed to a side hallway and returned to them in less than two minutes with the first aid kit.

The server beside Ian looked through the first aid kit and found what he wanted. He took out some black pills and gave them to Ian with some water to swallow.

"What's that?" Vanessa asked as Ian took the pills and downed them with the bottled water.

"It's activated charcoal. It's used in the event someone might be poisoned," the waiter said.

"Poisoned?" Vanessa gasped as she looked at Ian and then at the waiter.

The waiter nodded. "Since the hotel caters to some very important guests, we must be prepared for any situation."

Ian's cough started to subside, and he drank more water. After a couple of minutes, he turned to Vanessa. "I think it was something in the champagne." He coughed a couple more times. "The server who gave me the champagne—I recognized him from somewhere."

The server replied, "Monsieur, you think one of our staff members poisoned you?"

Ian coughed a few more times and wiped the sweat from his forehead. "Well, someone dressed like a staff member." He coughed a few more times and turned to Vanessa. "It could have been that man from the plane."

Vanessa nodded, then turned to the waiter. "There's a man here that we think is an assassin. We know he's somewhere in this hotel, but we have not been able to find him."

"Mon Dieu," the waiter shrieked. "Shouldn't we inform the others?"

Ian shook his head, and Vanessa replied, "No, I think that was meant for us."

The waiter looked confused. "Do you want to go to the hospital?"

Ian shook his head. "We need to get back inside."

Vanessa looked at him. "I can go back in if you want to go to the hospital."

He shook his head. "No time to separate." He stood up and started walking back towards the investors' room. Vanessa quickly followed.

They opened the door and closed it quietly. Hanna was still talking from the podium. "And that is how Leviathan and the board will make you all wealthy and powerful." Everyone then stood up and gave a big round of applause. Everyone then started to socialize with each other. Hanna meandered through the crowd to find Ian and Vanessa.

"Mr. Steele, I am sorry you and Ms. Dupont missed the crux of the presentation," Hanna scornfully said. "I didn't think you'd have the energy to return. I would have thought you'd have more pressing matters."

Ian coughed several times, then replied, "Rowing has taught me how to compartmentalize pain when the finish line is in sight."

Hanna smirked, then said, "You have some amazing strength. But remember, Leviathan is only the beginning." Then she walked off to talk with the other investors.

CHAPTER 65

Multiple Undisclosed Locations - Geneva
Tuesday Night
Via videoconference

"Let us have a moment of silence for Elena. This endeavor would not be possible without her," Ibrahim Kane said.

After a few minutes of silence, Hanna spoke up. "I think the investors were thrilled and are eager to see more than just a demonstration."

Everyone on the call nodded, and then Zaaeem Farouq said, "Agree. But what about the two impostors? How did they get in?"

Hanna quickly replied, "One of our current investors invited them. He thought Mr. Steele would be interested in investing."

"Should we be concerned with this investor who invited them?" asked Kabir Varma.

"No, the investor is very committed to our cause. But he seems clueless regarding what Mr. Steele and Ms. Dupont are investigating," Hanna said as she tried to calm the group's concerns.

"Should we take extra insurance so that they are neutralized? It's already gotten too close for comfort. We were never supposed to be in Geneva at this time," said Jack Samuelson.

Hanna responded, "I have taken some extra precautions and keep the faith that everything will come together."

"But like Jack said, we were never supposed to be in Geneva right now," Farouq said. "I thought the Gibraltar incident would have stopped everything."

Others on the call nodded their heads. "Yeah, everywhere I look, the discussion now is about the economic and supply chain issues that these are causing and will cause," Samuelson said.

"Yes, as you all know and signed up for, this was a worst-case scenario," Hanna responded. "You all can see that the attention is turning. So, when Leviathan launches, no one will think otherwise. It will be seen as a savior."

"So, how do you foresee the final stage?" Varma asked.

Hanna calmly replied, "As I said a few minutes ago, I see everything still going according to plan. The goals are still the same. I will just have to take a few extra steps to make sure. It is nothing for you all to worry about."

She paused and surveyed everyone's faces. "I just need someone from this group at the first session of the conference to bring up a resolution to postpone the conference due to pressing worldly economic needs." She paused again, then added, "Be sure that the conference will never occur. It will give us the perfect way to launch Leviathan."

A few people looked at each other on the screen, and then Ibrahim Kane spoke up. "I will make sure the delegation from Mali makes this resolution."

Quickly, Nakia Ahmed added, "And I will make sure Egypt is a co-sponsor."

Everyone started to nod, and then Hanna replied, "Faith will keep this together."

As if on cue, everyone said, "In Hobbes, We Trust." Then the screen went black, with only the Leviathan Cross logo.

Hanna then stood up from her computer, pulled out her phone, and dialed a number. After one ring, Damien answered, "How can I be of service?"

"Speed up the final act," she said curtly.

"Yes, Swan. It will be done," Damien said, then hung up the phone.

CHAPTER 66

Tuesday Night
Geneva

Ian and Vanessa quickly left the hotel and found a taxi to take them to Vanessa's office in the back of Cornavin. As they were walking into her office, Ian's phone rang. Ian looked at the phone; it was Viyan Hadid.

Ian picked up the phone and said, "Hello, Viyan."

Viyan responded, "Sorry it's so late, but I did come across some interesting details regarding Hanna Assad. Can you come to the Fairmont Hotel now?"

"Of course. Vanessa and I are on our way." He hung up the phone and looked at Vanessa. "We need to get to the Fairmont now."

Vanessa and Ian left the office and found a taxi to take them to the Fairmont. Once in the cab, it took them about five minutes to get to the hotel; there wasn't much traffic so late at night.

The Fairmont Hotel was a big hotel on Lake Geneva. Ian and Vanessa walked into the spacious lobby. The lobby was adorned with cream marble flooring, and the furnishings provided a warm and inviting atmosphere. Even though it was 10:45 p.m., the lobby was still bustling with people. At this time of night, there were primarily conferencegoers and young professionals. One of the more sophisticated bars in Geneva, the Floor Two Bar, was located on the second floor of the hotel. Tonight, a DJ was playing in the bar. The music could be heard from the first floor. Ian and Vanessa could tell that some people in the lobby were headed to the bar.

Ian pulled out his phone and called Viyan. The phone rang once, and then Viyan picked up. "Yes? Are you at the hotel?"

"Yes, where would you like to meet?" he replied.

"I think you should come to my room. I'll meet you in the lobby and take you up since you can't use the elevator unless you are a guest. Give me a few minutes."

"Of course. See you soon." He hung up the phone and turned to Vanessa. "Viyan is coming down and will take us to her room."

Vanessa nodded as she looked around the lobby.

"The news about Elena's passing. Did that hit the newswire yet?" he asked Vanessa.

"I didn't hear anything official before what Hanna said earlier." She then took out her phone and did a couple of searches. "It looks like it's just hitting the news now."

Before Ian could respond, Viyan came out of the elevator. "Sorry for calling so late and asking for a meeting. Please come with me."

Ian and Vanessa followed Viyan into the elevator. Viyan used her room card to activate the elevator to the sixth floor. They rode the elevator in silence. Then Ian and Vanessa followed Viyan down the hall to her room.

Viyan opened the door and let Ian and Vanessa enter the room. They then came into the room and locked the door. The room was a standard room with a queen-sized bed facing full-length windows that overlooked the Jet d'Eau. Viyan had the drapes pulled over the windows. Between the bed and the windows, there was a TV.

"Please have a seat," Viyan said, motioning to the couch on the other side of the bed.

Ian and Vanessa walked over and sat down.

Viyan looked frazzled, picked up her laptop, and brought it over to Ian and Vanessa. "This evening, I received an alarming message."

"Who sent the message?" Vanessa asked.

"That's the first interesting part. It's from Elena." Viyan said as she opened her computer and turned it around to show Ian and Vanessa. "This evening, I received an email from Elena's personal account. Look at what it said."

Ian and Vanessa then leaned toward the screen and read the message.

Dear Vivi,

Please watch the video, and everything will be explained.

I'm sorry it has had to come to this.

I wish I were meeting you in person instead of you watching the video.

By the will of Allah, we shall all meet again.

Love,

Elena

Ian and Vanessa nodded in silence toward Viyan. She then clicked on the video link. The link pulled up the video on a secured cloud service similar to a Google Drive account. Viyan hit play and then moved to let Ian and Vanessa have an unobstructed view.

Elena's face immediately appeared. In the background were bookshelves like those in her office in New York. She smiled before she started to speak.

Hi Vivi. If you are seeing this, then it means I have died. Everything that has occurred to François and me recently has not been random. Rather, it was well orchestrated and planned for some time. I have deep regret for the role I played in this. I have tried to stop what is about to happen. And it is for this reason that I have been killed.

Let me start from the beginning. At university, I fell in love twice. Once to Hanna Assad and another to François Mirreaux. At Oxford, I felt finally free to be myself and had an epiphany that I could change the world. The experience of being a refugee and the plight of that experience never left me. While in secondary school, I was teased a lot. At Oxford, I started to be myself and was accepted for being me.

During my first year at university, I met this beautiful young woman. Her name was Hanna Assad. She was so bright and talented. She also happened to be a refugee. I had never felt this way about any woman until I met her. I wanted to spend all my time with her. She was in the sciences while I was in international relations. During class was the only time I wasn't with her.

She was an exceptional athlete, too. She was a rower and convinced me to join a rowing club. The club was called the Leviathan Rowing Club. Vivi, I think you were part of the club for a time. I had never rowed before, but Hanna helped me. She was a caring person. But it was in this club that I became one for philosophical debates. As you know, this club mainly comprised international students who were not from first-world countries. During the rows, we would have philosophical discussions in the middle of the water and would not have anyone around to listen and criticize us. It was like our personal safe space. Much later, discussions became about alternative histories and explored ideas from major scholars like Thomas Hobbes.

I think it was at that point you left the rowing club. Granted, the discussions did get far-fetched at times. But Hanna seemed always to take note and be interested in the possibility that some of this could become a reality.

Around that same time, I fell in love a second time. I attended a guest lecture by a United Nations assistant secretary-general on Middle Eastern Affairs. His name was François Mirreaux. The way he talked about his work and the issues he faced daily made me want to ask him so many questions. On top of that, he was handsome. From the first time I saw him speak, I could tell he would go far in the U.N. system and make a difference. I thought I could help him achieve those possibilities.

Soon after that lecture, I made a move on him, and since that point, we have started to have a relationship. It became serious early on. We were madly in love with each other. It was hard for us to be apart.

Hanna became very jealous and manipulative. When she saw how close I was becoming to François, she started playing games to get in between us. She agreed that François was going to change the world. She started talking to François behind my back about some of these philosophical discussions from the Leviathan Rowing Club.

There was a point when I thought Hanna was cheating on me with François. I became more upset with her than with him. But as I said, I was in love with both Hanna and François. I couldn't see how they both could fit in my life. On top of that, I was getting more frustrated with Hanna because of how manipulative she had become.

So, I tried to end it with Hanna. I told Hanna one night, and then she left in silence. I thought she understood what I wanted, then the next day, there was a suspected murder in the lab where Hanna worked. There were messages from every department at the university stating that students should stay away from that lab. There had been a horrific event; I think those were the words the university used in its messaging. The university made an announcement later that day that Hanna had died in a terrible event and said there would be an investigation. The next several days, a memorial was set up to honor Hanna.

I was very sad during that time. I couldn't believe that right after I broke things off, she died in a horrific accident. I did love her but began to love François more for his idealism. This idealism propelled him and me to do great things at the United Nations. Even in a dark, realistic world, idealism can succeed if some people believe and act.

Fast-forward many years, and when François became Secretary-General, I was elated and making progress with helping refugees and other women's rights initiatives. François was genuinely becoming a transformational leader, unlike the United Nations had ever seen. I was ecstatic to be by his side. Even though he had the title, we were partners.

I was in Dubai for a conference where François would join me a few days after I arrived. On one of the days when François was not with me, I received a letter at the hotel that stated an old lover wanted to say hello. This confused me as the only other lover I ever had was Hanna. And I knew she died. I disregarded the message and went to have a drink at my hotel. While I was having some wine, a lady approached me and sat down. She said her name was Hanna Assad. I didn't believe her. Then she told me great details that only the real Hanna would know. I was in utter shock. She then told me that she felt very threatened at Oxford and that people were after her. That is why she had to fake her death. She then spent the next few years hiding out and building a network to destroy the establishment and create a new world order. She said those philosophical discussions with the Leviathan Rowing Club were coming true.

I couldn't believe my eyes and ears, but she was so persuasive. I felt the same feeling in my chest as when I first saw her and the first part of our relationship.

She told me that the missing piece to making her dreams come to reality was that François had to disappear. Now, thinking about it, I have realized that she is the devil, not the savior she professed.

I willingly went along with her plan. At first, I didn't realize that she was going to kill François until it was too late. I thought at first she would create a mechanism to kick him out of the U.N. Once I realized what would happen to François, I tried to stop Hanna but couldn't. The wheels were already set in motion. The killings that took place after François' passing are all connected to Hanna's organization.

I know this message has been long, but I want to give you the background. I don't deserve François' love for how I betrayed him. That regret will never leave me, no matter what comes next.

Hanna has created a machine that will destroy the world. It will bring her and a few others a fortune at the expense of the world. No one will know what will happen if someone doesn't stop them. It is an artificial intelligence system called Leviathan. If it launches, it will be irreversible as it will disable other systems worldwide.

I don't know what you can do, but I needed to tell you this as I don't think I will be able to meet with you in Geneva as planned. If possible, I will do my best to get to Geneva to stop Hanna. And if I can stop Hanna and Leviathan, I promise to confess to the world what happened. I don't want to be seen as a savior after my actions, but I want to make things right.

The video screen then went black. Ian and Vanessa sat in silence as they absorbed the video. Viyan looked at both of them, waiting for their reaction.

Vanessa broke the silence. "Fuck. I've never seen a confession like that."

Ian nodded and looked at his watch. "We don't have a lot of time. Leviathan goes public today when the New York Stock Exchange opens."

Viyan said, "I don't understand how a company can go public without having a product already in the market."

Ian looked at Viyan and said, "That is unusual. I have been asking that question since I first heard about Leviathan. They must have something big planned."

Vanessa nodded. "We can't let that happen. We need to find Hanna."

Ian nodded. "Yes. I'm going to call Paul Greene at the U.S. Consulate. He needs to see that video."

Viyan nodded. "Do you think he can be trusted?"

"Yes," he said. "I will get Paul to come here."

Viyan nodded, and then Vanessa looked at Ian. "We need to go quickly. Where do you think we can find Hanna at this hour of the night?"

"The event was at the InterContinental, but I doubt Hanna would be staying there," Ian replied.

They looked at each other, and then Vanessa replied, "I heard some people from the investors' party mention something about The Woodward."

Ian replied, "That is one of the nicest hotels in the city, and it has all suites, so maybe we should try it there."

Vanessa nodded. "Viyan, stay here til Paul gets here."

Viyan nodded, and then Vanessa and Ian left the room.

CHAPTER 67

Tuesday Night
Geneva

Vanessa went towards Viyan to talk with her and reassure her about the next steps. Ian pulled out his phone from his pocket and called Paul.

The phone rang twice, and then Paul groggily said, "Ian, what the hell? What time is it?"

"It's 11:30. It's urgent."

"I know the conference is coming up, but at least get some sleep. Just for a few hours. And no, I haven't heard back about your Hanna Assad question," Paul said as his voice became more alert.

"I have the evidence or confession you need. Get to the Fairmont Hotel as fast as you can. I'll text you the number of Viyan Hadid. She is a guest at the hotel and was friends with Elena Mirreaux. She has a video you need to see."

"Okay. Text me the number, and I'll arrive in 20 minutes," Paul said as he started to find some clothes to change into.

"Thanks. Call me once you see the video. I have to find Hanna," Ian said, then hung up the phone.

After changing, Paul found his keys and left the house to go to his car. He got into the car and started to drive to the Fairmont. No vehicles or people were on the street, as it was 11:40 at night. He stopped at the stoplight, and didn't dare run the light even though he was in a rush. Since moving to Switzerland, he learned that the Swiss people stay at red lights and crosswalks until the lights turn green, even if no one is around.

As he waited for the light to turn green, the Phantom, wearing a hooded sweatshirt, approached the car and knocked on the window. Paul looked, and rolled down, the window and said, "May I help you?" The Phantom quickly pulled out his silencer and shot

Paul twice in the chest.

With Paul slumped over the steering wheel, the Phantom put the car in neutral and pushed it to the side of the road. Then he stepped away, managed to lock the car from the inside, and closed the door. He scanned the vehicle one more time before he walked away. The Phantom guessed it would be another three or four hours before anyone would investigate the car and find Paul.

As he walked away, he pulled out his phone and looked at his email. He had a message from an unknown sender. He clicked on the message. The message said, *Someone is looking into Hanna Assad. Take care of it.* He hit the reply button and typed the answer with one hand: *Done.* The Phantom then returned to his car, which was parked a few blocks away.

CHAPTER 68

Tuesday Night/Wednesday Morning
Geneva

Ian and Vanessa exited the Fairmont and turned left toward The Woodward. The Woodward was about a five-minute walk from the Fairmont along the lake. As they walked at a hurried pace, they looked at each other.

"So, what's the plan? We can't just ask to go to Hanna's room, especially this late at night," Ian asked.

"Maybe you can go to the front desk and say you are the male she ordered for the evening?" Vanessa smirked.

"As if I could pull that off," he replied. "But seriously, what can we do?"

"Hey, I just needed to laugh a little." She paused, then said, "We could still use a similar play. We could go to the front desk and say that she expects us for some briefing. Or we can see if anyone else from the meeting is in the lobby."

"I think our chances might be better finding someone in the lobby with a nightcap."

She nodded as they approached the entrance to The Woodward. When they walked into the lobby through a wrought-iron door, they were greeted by sparkling Baccarat crystal chandeliers and furniture with red fabrics and rich ebony wood. The lobby also had floral arrangements to help create a welcoming atmosphere.

They walked into the lobby without drawing attention and immediately went to Bar 37, which was located on one of the hotel's verandas. A few patrons were there, finishing their nightcaps as they listened to someone playing the piano. The bar closed at midnight.

A man in a suit with a Leviathan Cross lapel pin quickly approached Ian and Vanessa. "Excuse me, but the bar is closed due to a private event."

Vanessa quickly replied, "Oh, sorry. We must have misplaced our invitation. We were at the event earlier this evening at the Inter-Continental. We are with Leviathan."

The man kept a stern face and walked closer to Vanessa and Ian. "We are at capacity. No one is getting in."

"You will be in big trouble. Do you know who I am?" Vanessa declaratively said.

The man kept his stern look. "My apologies, madame. I know all of our guests for this event, and they are already in the bar. So, madame, please take up your issue of being left out with your organization."

Vanessa huffed in protest and turned away from the man. Ian followed.

They saw the Phantom walk into the lobby and approach the elevator as they walked away. They quickly approached him and waited next to him at the elevator.

The Phantom entered as the elevator door opened, and Vanessa and Ian followed. The Phantom hit a floor number, and Vanessa turned to Ian in her Texas accent, "Well, look at that, honey. This nice gentleman is on our same floor." Vanessa smirked at Ian and then at the Phantom.

The Phantom looked at Ian and Vanessa as the elevator moved, but he said nothing. Ian and Vanessa noticed the Phantom wore the same watch as the Leviathan Cross from the Geneva airport.

When the elevator doors opened, the Phantom allowed Vanessa and Ian to exit first. Once in the hallway, Vanessa said to Ian, "Honey, do you have our key? I think I misplaced it."

"Let me check," Ian said as he pulled out his wallet.

The Phantom left the elevator and went down the hall to his room. Ian and Vanessa watched which way he went and followed him. They almost ran to be sure they could catch up to him.

As the Phantom opened his door, Vanessa tapped him on the shoulder. As he turned, she sprayed him in the face with pepper spray that she had in her purse. Then Ian and Vanessa pushed him inside the room and closed the door behind him.

"What the fuck?" the Phantom said as he stumbled into the

room and onto the floor. He tried to rub his eyes.

She sprayed some more into his face. "Ian, get him into a chair."

Ian dragged the Phantom into the room and closed the door with the latch behind him. The room was a junior suite, and upon entering, a small hallway led into a living area with a couch and coffee table. The bathroom was to the right of the couch, and on the left was the king-sized bed. He dragged the Phantom to the edge of the bed as Vanessa quickly grabbed two lamps.

"Can we use these to tie him up?" she asked, holding the lamps with the electrical cords.

"I've never done something like this. But we could try," Ian responded.

She gave him one of the lamps and each of them tied his wrists with the electrical cords around the bedposts. The Phantom still squirmed, and she resprayed his face with pepper spray.

Ian looked into the Phantom's jacket and saw a gun. "Who is this guy?"

Vanessa grabbed the back of the Phantom's neck. "Who are you? And what do you know about Leviathan?"

The Phantom squirmed and moaned. "What the fuck?" He tried to pull his arms but they were stuck to the bedposts where the whole bed frame jolted.

"Is Geneva not a safe city? Why the gun?" Vanessa authoritatively asked.

Ian began to look around the room to see if he could find any clues about who this man was. Looking around, he said, "It would seem like this guy is a ghost."

The Phantom started to cough and regain a bit of consciousness.

"Who are you?" Vanessa asked as she lifted the Phantom's head.

The Phantom looked at Vanessa, smiled, and then spat into her face. "You're an amateur. I'll get out, and you both are dead."

She looked at him without having the spit affect her. "Maybe so. But right now you're the one tied up." She paused, then asked, "Who are you? What do you have to do with Leviathan?"

The Phantom stared in silence at her.

At the same time, Ian kept looking around the room for anything he could use to start a conversation. He found the safe, which was locked.

He walked back to Vanessa. "The safe is locked. Something must be in it."

Vanessa then took one of the electrical cords and made it tighter. "What's the code?"

The Phantom's arm jerked as she pulled the cord, and he just looked at her.

"Looks like he is playing hardball," Vanessa said.

"Let me try," Ian said as he approached the Phantom. Ian pulled up a chair next to the Phantom's face. "Do you have a name?"

The Phantom smirked at Ian. "Does it really matter? You both will be dead soon." He said as he tried to move his arms.

Ian stayed calm. "I never thought of being assassinated. But I think if I did, I'd want to know the name of my assassin."

The Phantom laughed. "Fucking amateurs. No names make it a lot easier in my line of work."

"We might be amateurs, but just appease us. Would you?" Ian asked. He looked at Vanessa as she handed him a phone. The phone was a small black flip phone.

"This fell out of his pocket when we dragged him into the room," Vanessa said.

Ian held the phone in his hand and flipped it open. "I haven't seen a phone like this in a long time." Ian paused, then said, "For a guy with such a nice watch, I thought you'd have a smartphone. It is the industry standard."

The Phantom looked at Ian. "I've never been into phones. I don't use them for long."

Ian kept looking at the phone and saw it was blank except for one number in the contacts. "This number—who does that call?"

The Phantom looked stoically. "You won't find any answers from that number."

"Then why is that number in your phone?" Ian asked as he looked more at the phone.

"I don't ask you why the fuck there are certain numbers are

in your phone," the Phantom retorted.

"That's true. But I'm not the one under interrogation." Ian said.

The phone started to ring, and Vanessa walked back into the room. Ian looked at the Phantom. "I need to answer that," the Phantom said.

"We may be amateurs, but then you don't know what we are capable of. Don't say anything about us." Ian responded, then waited to hand the phone to the Phantom. The Phantom then nodded.

Ian hit the answer button and turned up the volume so that he and Vanessa could hear the conversation. She held a fire extinguisher.

The Phantom breathed into the phone, and the man on the other line spoke, "It's been a busy night. One more job. We found the target at the Fairmont."

Ian and Vanessa looked at each other, knowing who the probable target was.

The man on the phone continued, "Like earlier this evening, this is extra, and you will be compensated accordingly. The information on the target will be in the usual place."

"It will be done," the Phantom responded. Then the line went dead.

Vanessa stepped closer to the Phantom with the fire extinguisher. "Who's your target? What happened earlier tonight?"

The Phantom smirked. "As if I would tell you, amateurs."

Vanessa's frustration started to show. She lifted the fire extinguisher and slammed it on the Phantom's shoulder.

"Fuck!" the Phantom screamed.

"What happened earlier?" Vanessa screamed.

The Phantom stared at her. She then picked up the fire extinguisher and slammed it again on his shoulder.

"Bitch! I think you broke my shoulder!" he screamed.

Vanessa then repositioned herself to try for the other shoulder. "Care to answer our questions? Or your other shoulder will be broken."

Ian looked at the Phantom. "I would answer the questions. There is a better chance you will come out of this alive."

The Phantom thought for a moment, and then his mouth started to move. "Earlier tonight, I was asked to take care of a U.S. diplomat. Regarding the next target, I need to log into a secure site to find the target."

"Where's your computer?" Ian asked.

"In the safe," the Phantom said.

"What's the code?" Ian asked.

"I still won't tell you," the Phantom responded.

Vanessa then raised the fire extinguisher, "You really want me to break your other shoulder?"

The Phantom looked at her and knew she was serious. He then shook his head, and she lowered the fire extinguisher. "The code is 1651."

Vanessa watched the Phantom as Ian walked to the safe. A few moments later, Ian returned to the room with a laptop and a journal.

While Ian opened the laptop, Vanessa quickly said, "Show us where to go for the information."

The Phantom looked at both of them and knew he had been outsmarted. "I need to use my fingerprint to open the computer, and then I can show you where to go."

Ian brought the computer to the Phantom's right hand and placed his right index finger on the computer pad so that it would open. The laptop then displayed the Leviathan Cross at the center of the screen for a couple of minutes as it loaded. Ian could tell from the time it took to load that the computer was encrypted.

The Leviathan Cross disappeared, and the home screen appeared. This screen displayed something similar to that of a Mac OS device.

"Hit the Internet icon and type in ProtonMail," the Phantom instructed.

Ian clicked on the Internet icon and typed in ProtonMail into the search engine. He was familiar with ProtonMail, as it was one of the better end-to-end encrypted email services currently in use.

When the sign-in screen appeared, the Phantom said, "It can only be accessed by my fingerprint." Ian gave him the computer, and the Phantom placed his finger on the pad. Within seconds, Proton-

Mail opened, and there was one unread message. The subject line of the message said, "ASAP."

Ian took the computer, and as he opened the message, Vanessa looked over his shoulder. The message read, "Fairmont Hotel, Viyan Hadid. Extra compensation." Ian and Vanessa then looked up at the Phantom. "Why are you going to kill Viyan?" Ian asked the Phantom.

The Phantom looked at Ian and Vanessa and said, "I have no idea who that is. Usually, I have time to plan. But in cases like this, I don't know."

Vanessa then struck one of the Phantom's shoulders. "Why her?"

He screamed in pain and then said, "I have no clue. It's just an assignment."

Vanessa looked at Ian. "I think I believe him. He's just a hired hand."

Ian nodded and then looked at the Phantom. "Who hired you?"

"Leviathan," the Phantom said as he winced in pain.

"Where is Hanna Assad?" Vanessa asked as she stared into the Phantom's eyes.

"Who?" the Phantom said.

"Hanna Assad. The head of Leviathan." Vanessa answered as Ian watched the Phantom and looked at the computer screen.

"I have no idea who you are talking about. I don't know who is Leviathan. All I know is it is a company," the Phantom responded.

Vanessa put her hand on his shoulder and pressed down. He started to wince in pain and asked, "What do you want?"

"How do I get to Hanna Assad?" Vanessa asked.

Before the Phantom answered, Ian said to her with the laptop in his hand. "Come over here. I think I may be able to see where this email was coming from." He walked with her to the table in the living room area of the hotel suite and put down the computer.

He sat in front of the computer and started typing and opening different screens, confusing her as she tried to follow. "What are you trying to do?"

He was glued to the screen as he answered, "I'm trying to

find who sent the email. I was able to find the sender's IP address. From what I can tell, the sender is not in Switzerland, which doesn't make sense if Hanna is here in Geneva."

Vanessa looked at the Phantom and then back at Ian: "Our friend in the next room mentioned that Leviathan hired him. Could his director, who may be a third party, send this message to him?"

He nodded. "That is very plausible. It would create ways of plausible deniability if anyone were ever caught."

Vanessa then walked back into the bedroom. "Who's your boss?"

The Phantom's head was slumped over. There was white foam dripping from his mouth.

"Fuck!" Vanessa screamed, and Ian ran into the room and immediately saw the Phantom.

"Damn. Let's get back to Viyan. Let's make sure she's okay." Ian said.

Vanessa nodded, and before they left the hotel room, they picked up the Phantom's computer and journal.

CHAPTER 69

Wednesday Morning
Fairmont Hotel
Geneva

Ian and Vanessa quickly returned to the Fairmont and knocked on Viyan's hotel room door.

"Hi. I thought your colleague from the consulate was going to contact me?" Viyan asked as she opened the door.

"That's not going to happen. He's been permanently detained," Ian said.

"I don't understand," Viyan responded.

"We just left his killer's hotel room. He murdered Ian's colleague, and you were going to be his next target," Vanessa said.

"Oh my God! Should I go into hiding?" Viyan said worriedly.

"No, we think you should be fine with us," Vanessa answered as Ian sat at the desk with the Phantom's computer and started to work.

"Did you both kill him?" Viyan asked nervously.

"No, he died from a cyanide pill or something he had in his mouth," Vanessa said.

Vanessa looked at Ian. "How did you get into the computer? I thought it was only his fingerprint."

"I disabled the feature." He paused, then looked up at Vanessa and Viyan. "I have an idea; it might be crazy. But we are trying to find Hanna. What happens if I write back to whoever sent the message asking for a meeting with Hanna?"

Vanessa looked at Ian strangely. "That doesn't seem like it was how that guy operated in his work. Wouldn't whoever is on the other end know it's not him?"

"True. Maybe it's a risk worth taking. We could even say

something that she said she was Leviathan."

Viyan looked strangely at both of them. "Who's she?"

Ian and Vanessa looked at Viyan. "You," Ian said.

Viyan's face turned white. "I'm not a spy. I don't know what I would be doing."

Vanessa looked at her. "We aren't either." She paused, then turned to Ian. "It would be one thing if these emails were being sent from Hanna. But the assassin said he was a hired hand There would be no incentive for the person on the other end to point us toward Hanna."

Ian nodded. "That's true."

Vanessa said, "I know we got kicked out of the function. But what about calling your obnoxious friend?"

"You mean Elliot?"

"Yeah."

"Who's Elliot?" Viyan inserted herself into the conversation.

"He's sort of a business friend of mine who is an investor in Leviathan. He's in it just for the money. He doesn't care about the product, just that it brings him and his wife a lot of money." Ian paused. "I'm not sure he would know where Hanna would be. The event was probably his first time meeting her."

"Leviathan is supposed to go public today on the New York Stock Exchange when it opens. Wouldn't there be a sort of party for the investors?" Vanessa asked and looked at Ian.

"Not really. Though sometimes the head of the company going public and some of the big investors will ring the New York Stock Exchange bell."

"Do you think Hanna would go to New York for that?"

"If the U.N. conference were delayed, she would definitely be in New York. But I think she's still in Geneva with tomorrow's conference."

Ian and Vanessa continued discussing different options when Viyan's phone suddenly began to ring. She looked at her phone but didn't recognize the number, so she answered it. "Hello?" she said nervously.

"Hi, Vivi. It's Hanna." Hanna paused, and Viyan quickly raised her hand to Ian and Vanessa to get their attention and be quiet. She put the call on speakerphone.

"Hanna, wow. I didn't know you were alive. I thought you were dead," Viyan said into the phone.

"Cut the bullshit, Vivi. I know you missed my colleague last night with some help. Since it has been some time since we last saw each other, why don't we meet for breakfast today and catch up?" Hanna said.

Ian and Vanessa looked at Viyan and nodded. Then Viyan responded, "Sure. It would be great to catch up for old time's sake."

"Let's meet at the Foundation Martin Bodmer at 10 a.m. I'll bring the coffee," Hanna said.

"Sure. I'm looking forward to it," Viyan responded.

"Also, Vivi," Hanna paused. "Come bring your friends too."

"Okay," Viyan responded, but the phone went dead.

CHAPTER 70

Wednesday Morning
Henderson, Nevada

The man wore all black, with a San Francisco Giants hat and a fake Google badge on his shirt, which he had made with a 3D printer to give him access to the data center. The few people he saw didn't question his casual dress, as it was late at night or early morning, depending on their perspective.

The data center, about 750,000 square feet and open 24 hours a day, every day of the year, supported several Google services, including YouTube, Google Calendar, Gmail, and Google Cloud. The facility employed various people, from full-time and contractor positions, like computer technicians and engineers, to maintenance and security staff.

The man walked down the row of server racks with a backpack, a clipboard, and a computer—standard items for a contractor doing a system upgrade. Each rack held thousands of servers with blinking lights. The servers were housed in cabinet-like structures with locks on all the doors.

He stopped in the middle of the row and turned toward the servers. He reached into his backpack and retrieved a key-stolen earlier that day from an actual Google contractor he'd met at a Las Vegas conference. He then pulled out a computer stand located near the servers. He placed his laptop on the stand.

He then unlocked the door and pulled out one of the servers. When he pulled out the server, many wires connected to it. He surveyed the cables, disconnected one, and plugged his laptop into the server with a cable near it.

Once the laptop was booted up, he looked around to see if anyone was nearby. If anyone walked by, they would think he was doing a system upgrade. When he saw no one was around, he opened the server's file on the computer. Then he found the Leviathan file on the laptop's hard drive and told it to migrate to the Google server. He was prompted several times with messages asking if this was what he requested. Each time the window popped up, he hit ok. The Leviathan file proceeded to merge onto the server.

It took a few minutes for the file to be merged. Once it had merged, he unhooked the wire and plugged it back into the main server. He put his laptop in his bag and walked out of the facility. With the Leviathan file on the Google server, it would take a couple of hours to go into effect fully. By then, he would be away from the facility and could disappear without anyone finding him. Google employees would spend more time trying to undo the file than finding out who put it on the server.

Once outside, he found a trash can and threw the identification badge into it. Then he got into his car and drove back to Las Vegas.

CHAPTER 71

Wednesday Morning
Foundation Martin Bodmer
Cologny

Ian, Vanessa, and Viyan drove to the Foundation Martin Bodmer in an Uber. The foundation was known as one of the most significant private libraries in the world, dedicated to preserving and showcasing humanity's intellectual and cultural heritage. They wanted to ensure they were not late for their meeting with Hanna. During the drive, they discussed potential scenarios. In the end, they decided to be cautious and listen to Hanna.

The Foundation was elegant and understated—the outside blended modern design with the serene surroundings of the area. The main building was low-slung and partially built into the hillside. It featured clean, geometric lines of stone, concrete, and glass. It was set in a lush, green garden overlooking Lake Geneva and the distant Alps. The vibe embodied elegance, functionality, and harmony with its picturesque surroundings.

They walked through the gardens toward the foundation's entrance when they exited their Uber. The actual entrance was a level below them, and one would take the stairs to get there. However, Hanna waited at the top overlooking Lake Geneva with four coffee cups.

As they approached Hanna, she turned and said, "Good morning. I'm so happy you all were able to join me here. Isn't this beautiful?"

Viyan looked at Hanna in shock. "Hanna, is that you? What happened?"

"I had to get away from society's shackles to know what society needs," Hanna said.

"You could have withdrawn from university and led a solitary and meaningful life. You didn't have to manipulate Elena."

"She was my ticket to get to where I am today. I did it for love. Elena was too idealistic. But we together complemented the idealism with the realism."

"What are you planning?" Viyan asked as she stepped closer to Hanna.

Ian and Vanessa stayed close.

"To quote Thomas Hobbes, 'where there is no common Power, there is no Law; where no Law; no Injustice.'"

"What are you saying, Hanna? The United Nations might not be perfect, but it can still be a force for good," Viyan paused. "Look at the women's conference tomorrow. It will be life-changing for so many women around the world."

"The United Nations has led many people astray, and it's time to set it right. The technology today is unmatched and will revolutionize the world."

"While making you and a select few uber-wealthy," Ian inserted.

"I would lie to you if the money weren't appealing," Hanna responded.

"Isn't what you are describing an oligarchy?" Vanessa asked.

"I wouldn't call it an oligarchy. The artificial intelligence program will make the decisions; we will have a small group that will financially benefit from its decisions," Hanna responded. "Remember, Viyan, during our rows, the quotes we would recite from Hobbes. 'The original of all great and lasting societies consisted not in the mutual goodwill men had toward each other, but in the mutual fear they had of each other." She paused, then said, "We will put the fear back and let everyone listen to just one voice."

"What the hell happened to you? You might be more of a realist than others, but this has gone too far," Viyan responded.

"The three of us saw Elena's confession. We know what you did and are planning," Vanessa added.

Hanna pulled out her phone and typed on the screen before she responded. "Leviathan is live. There's no stopping it. Leviathan will now make everyone's decisions."

Ian looked at Hanna. "So, you want humanity to become

unanimous drones?"

Hanna smirked. "I wouldn't say a drone, but we'd want them to believe what we want. It will make the United Nations more united."

"Yes, the United Nations isn't perfect, but the differences and opinions help improve the world," Viyan said.

"Why bother with these opinions? That's what's made the UN stall and not react to crises. We have made it better now," Hanna retorted.

"There are other ways to reform the organization, Hanna," Viyan said.

"No, that's where you are wrong. The world needs one leader. Thomas Hobbes gave us the road map. And now we have a Leviathan that will do just that."

Viyan shook her head. "No, you're wrong. You've gone too far. This is more than just a rowing club conversation."

Hanna turned to take in the view. She smiled and then turned to respond to Viyan.

Whizz! Whizz! Pop! Pop! Whizz! Whizz! Pop! Pop!

Ian, Vanessa, and Viyan immediately ducked and moved toward the concrete barrier. After getting to the concrete barrier, they looked back, and Viyan screamed. "Oh, my God!" They saw Hanna on the ground, lying in a puddle of blood.

CHAPTER 72

Wednesday Morning
Foundation Martin Bodmer
Cologny

"I thought the assassin died at the hotel," Vanessa said.

"Could there be someone else?" Ian asked as he looked around to see if he could see where the bullets came from.

"If Hanna pulled Leviathan together, why kill her?" Viyan asked.

They then heard a car peel out of the parking lot. Ian looked at the black Mercedes and saw only the license plate, CD GE 0201. They then cautiously stood up and looked at Hanna's body.

"Maybe someone had a grudge against her, or it has something to do with greed," Vanessa responded.

Ian looked at Viyan and Vanessa. "I saw the license plate. It's a diplomatic car."

Viyan looked quizzically at him. "How do you know?"

He looked at her. "The license plate started with CD in white lettering with a blue background. CD means Corps Diplomatique."

Viyan nodded, and Vanessa asked, "Did you see the rest of the plate?"

He nodded. "Yes. The full plate was CD GE 0201." He paused, then said, "I know GE means Geneva. And I know the first two numbers indicate the vehicle number. The last two numbers indicate which country or organization."

"It's a WTO vehicle," Vanessa interjected. "01 stands for WTO."

"So, we are looking for someone at the WTO who can use the carpool?" Viyan asked.

Ian and Vanessa nodded. Then Ian said, "We need to find out who signed out the car. Let's go."

"What about Hanna?" Viyan asked.

Ian looked at Viyan. "I think we need to leave her behind, or someone is bound to spin this on us."

They then walked toward the bus stop. They waited silently as the bus took them back toward the city.

On the bus, Ian looked at Vanessa and Viyan. "Do you think the car is back at the WTO?"

"I think not to draw attention, the car is probably back at the WTO. Was it a WTO employee who took it?" Vanessa responded.

"No idea. It could be anyone. WTO is one of the sponsors of the conference. So, anyone could be using those vehicles," Ian responded.

Viyan looked away from the bus window and faced Ian and Vanessa. "Everything is such a blur. I think there is a lunch for the speakers at the WTO today."

"Perfect cover for Vanessa and me to investigate," Ian responded. "Viyan, you must go to that lunch and act as normal as possible." He paused again, then said, "What I don't understand is—why take out the CEO of Leviathan on the day it goes public? If and when the news comes out, the opening will be a mess for the investors."

Viyan nodded and then stared out the bus window.

CHAPTER 73

Wednesday Morning
Geneva

Emily drove away in the black Mercedes from the Foundation Martin Bodmer as her hands shook. She tried to keep her hands calmly on the steering wheel. She had never killed anyone before. She had shot a gun on several occasions in the past, but only at shooting ranges.

She drove in silence as she drove down Rampe de Cologny toward the lake. When the car stopped at a stoplight before turning left on Quai Gustave-Ador, she reached for the bottle of Evian in the drink holder. After taking a sip of Evian, she breathed a sigh of relief.

The stoplight took longer than expected as there was much morning traffic congestion on Quai Gustave-Ador. Since she had sat through a few lights without moving, she pulled out her phone and opened her Notes app. Before the app opened, it prompted her for a passcode. She looked at the phone screen using her facial recognition, and the app opened to her notes. The first note was a list of names. The top of the list was Hanna. With her finger, she put a check next to Hanna's name.

Right before the light turned green, she put the gun in her purse and pulled out her conference badge. Then the light turned green, and she continued to drive to the WTO. It took her about forty minutes to navigate the traffic and pull into the WTO car lot.

In the car lot, she pulled up to the security gate. The security at this entrance wasn't as strict as at the main entrance. She then lowered her window, and flashed her badge.

"Bonjour. I was told to bring this car to this parking lot," she said with a smile.

The security guard scanned her badge. "Bonjour. Yes, I need

to look around the car before you enter." He then walked around the car with an under-vehicle inspection mirror.

When the security guard returned to the driver's side window, he said, "You are all clear. You may proceed." He then hit a button, and the security gate lifted.

"Merci," she said as she raised the window and drove into the parking lot.

She drove carefully through the parking lot and found the empty parking spot where she had picked up the car.

Before leaving the car, she grabbed her badge, which was attached to a lanyard, and put it over her head and around her neck. She then grabbed her purse and exited the car.

She pulled out her phone and opened an U.N. parking app as she walked toward the elevator. She then hit a button in the app that indicated that the car had been returned.

She entered the elevator and opened her notes app. The following person on her list was Nakia Ahmed. She then locked the phone, put it in her purse, and hit the elevator button to take her to the luncheon.

CHAPTER 74

Wednesday Afternoon
Geneva

The bus stopped at the Jardin Botanique, where Ian, Vanessa, and Viyan exited. The WTO entrance was about a three-minute walk. Ian turned to Viyan.

"Viyan, go to the luncheon and act normal. If you see anything strange, let us know. Vanessa and I will try to figure out who took that car."

Viyan nodded. "Will do. But I think it's best if you walk in with me."

Vanessa nodded, pulled out two conference badges, and gave one to Ian. "I took a few when I was at the hotel. They are just participant badges. Viyan has a speaker badge."

They all put their badges with lanyards around their heads and around their necks.

There was a long security line as they walked up to the WTO. The line moved efficiently but slowly on a long driveway lined with flags of WTO member countries. At the end of the driveway was the WTO building, which was surrounded by lush greenery and manicured gardens.

The security checkpoint was in a unique lobby with high ceilings and large windows that let natural light through. This created a professional yet welcoming atmosphere.

Once through the security checkpoint, they followed the signs towards the luncheon. As they approached the luncheon area, Viyan proceeded to a speaker entrance while Vanessa and Ian started to veer off.

Ian and Vanessa started to ask around for any WTO employees. Once they found a man who said he worked for the WTO, Ian said, "A car belonging to the WTO hit my car and drove off. Can you see who might have used the car if I have the license plate number?"

The man looked at Ian and nodded. "My apologies for what happened. If you have the plate number, I can look up who was using it."

Ian then smiled. "That will be a big help. The plate number was CD GE 0201."

The man opened an app and typed in the plate number. A couple of moments later, he looked up. "It looks like that was one of the communal cars at the WTO. The last person who just returned it was Emily Shannon." He paused. "It looks like she is a WTO visitor."

Ian and Vanessa looked at each other and then at the WTO employee. "Thank you. What a small world. We know Emily. We know her boss so we can look for her."

The man looked at them quizzically, then nodded. "Bien sûr. If you need anything else, please let me know."

Ian and Vanessa nodded and walked away. Vanessa pulled out her phone and typed in Emily Shannon into Google. A moment later, she looked up at Ian in astonishment. "Fuck!"

"What is it?" Ian asked.

"Emily Shannon is Elena Mirreaux's assistant."

"You mean the Emily we met in New York?"

Vanessa nodded. "Yep." She then showed Ian her phone, which showed Emily's LinkedIn page.

"Text Viyan a photo of Emily; maybe she'll be at the luncheon," Ian said. Vanessa nodded and texted Viyan.

CHAPTER 75

Wednesday Afternoon
WTO
Geneva

"What's Emily's involvement in this?" Vanessa asked as she and Ian walked quickly toward the luncheon.

"I'm not sure," Ian responded. "It doesn't make sense to take out the CEO of a company right before it goes public. Hypothetically, it could happen if someone was trying to short the stock."

"But do you think Emily knows about Leviathan's goals?" She asked.

"I really don't know. We need to find her," he responded as they walked into the luncheon room and started to look around.

The luncheon room was ample, with about two hundred people seated at large round tables, with about ten people per table. Towards the back of the room was a long table for the food buffet, and there were two areas for drinks. Since it was lunch, the drinks were water, tea, and coffee. A large staff scurried around the room to clean up and serve food to those who couldn't carry their food from the buffet.

From what Ian could recall of the conference schedule, there would be a more formal dinner for the speakers and diplomats once the agreement had been signed.

They looked around the room attentively but in a way that wouldn't draw attention to themselves. Around the tables were large banners that said "Free Women = More Trade." Another banner imitated the famous WWII Rosie the Riveter poster. Instead of an American woman flexing her arm, there were two Arab women, one wearing a hijab and another wearing a burka, flexing their arms with the statement "More Trade" underneath.

From a distance, they saw Viyan at the speakers' table, talking to other attendees. As they scanned the room, they saw Emily enter at the far end. They quickly walked towards her.

Emily did not see Ian and Vanessa approaching. Instead, her sight was on Nakia Ahmed, who was about to sit at a table with other Middle Eastern individuals. Emily walked up and tapped Nakia on the shoulder.

"Yes?" Nakia said as he turned toward Emily. He wore a dark suit with a Leviathan Cross lapel pin.

"Excuse me," Emily said. "You have a call from the ambassador."

"Call?" Nakia asked. "He usually calls my mobile if he needs me."

Emily quickly thought on her feet. "I'm not sure, sir. I am just a messenger. He said it is quite urgent."

Nakia nodded and then stood up. "Please show me," he said, following Emily as she led him outside. She turned to see if Nakia was behind her as she approached the door. She saw Ian and Vanessa closing in. "Sir, right this way," Emily said, leading him outside.

Ian and Vanessa quickly navigated the crowd to get to the door where Emily exited. Once outside, they didn't see where Emily and the other man were.

In the distance, they heard Nakia scream, "What the—" Then silence.

Once Nakia lay on the ground, Emily returned the chloroform napkin to her purse. She then pulled out a plastic bag to put over his head. As she placed the bag over his head, Ian found Emily.

"Emily, drop the bag and let him live," Ian said, keeping eye contact with Emily.

"What are you going to do? Are you part of Leviathan, too?" Emily said as she continued to place the bag on Ahmed.

A few seconds later, Vanessa jumped on Emily from behind, and they wrestled to the ground. Emily then let go of Ahmed as she tried to fight off Vanessa.

Nakia stumbled, and Ian went to catch him, taking the bag from his head. Ian discovered that Nakia was unconscious.

Vanessa finally pinned Emily to the ground.

"Who the hell are you?" Vanessa asked as she held Emily on the ground.

"Fuck Leviathan," Emily retorted. "This is for Mrs. Mirreaux."

"What do you know about Leviathan?" Vanessa asked.

"That they caused Mrs. Mirreaux to die, and that bastard is one of them." She pointed to Nakia, who was unconscious and being held by Ian.

Ian walked up. "We need to get out of here. Let's interrogate them both somewhere else."

"I'm not going anywhere with you two," Emily retorted. "How do I know if you both aren't working for Leviathan?"

"You would have shot at us and not just Hanna," Ian replied.

"I was trying to cut off the snake's head," Emily said as Vanessa tightly held her wrists.

Ian looked around and saw a sign that said "Parc William Rappard." "Let's take them to the park to find some answers."

Vanessa nodded, and they followed the path and signs to Parc William Rappard.

CHAPTER 76

Wednesday Afternoon
Parc William Rappard
Geneva

The park featured well-maintained gardens and lush greenery. The mature trees gave the lawn a serene escape from the bustling city. Several sculptures, art installations, monuments, and plaques were scattered throughout the park.

Due to the conference, the public entrance to the park was closed, and benches were placed so that the diplomats and conference attendees could sit and converse easily. The park served as a reminder of the city's role in fostering global dialogue.

Ian and Vanessa brought Emily and Nakia to sit on two benches that faced James Vibert's *The Human Effort* sculpture. The sculpture portrayed a group of figures engaged in a unified, strenuous effort. This was to symbolize the collective human struggle and the pursuit of progress.

Nakia was still passed out as he sat next to Ian, and Vanessa continued to hold Emily's wrists as they sat on the other bench.

"What do you know about Leviathan?" Vanessa sternly asked.

"I don't know. But they killed Mrs. Mirreaux," Emily retorted.

"I know you were her assistant. But what do you know about her connection to Leviathan?" Ian asked.

"Why the fuck should I tell you both anything?" Emily asked.

"We know that the launch of Leviathan will take down the United Nations," Vanessa said.

"We are trying to save the conference and the U.N.," Ian said. "We need more information." He paused. "If you thought Vanessa and I were threats, why didn't you shoot at us earlier today?"

"You both weren't on my list. What information? Let me finish what I started," Emily said.

Vanessa and Ian looked at Emily. "What list?" Vanessa asked.

"I'm going after all the people who hurt Mrs. Mirreaux like the bastard sitting next to you." Emily pointed to Nakia, who slowly gained consciousness.

"How do you know these people?" Ian asked.

"I overheard Mrs. Mirreaux talking to them one night when she thought I had left. And later, I saw her making a confession video." Emily said.

"We just saw the video," Vanessa responded. "She is still a hero."

"Who else do you know is part of Leviathan?" Ian asked.

Emily looked at Vanessa and then at Ian. "I have seven names. But I think there are more."

"Were you planning to kill each of them?" Ian asked.

Emily nodded. "Yes, I thought it was my duty."

"Why not go to the authorities?" Ian asked.

"No one would believe me." Emily paused. "You both aren't the police."

"She has a valid point," Vanessa said, and Ian nodded. "But we aren't actively trying to kill anyone."

"What was going to be your plan after you killed the people on your list?" Ian asked.

Emily looked down. "I don't know. Maybe disappear, but I would know that I successfully avenged Mrs. Mirreaux's death and helped secure her legacy for women's rights."

"If I can access Leviathan, maybe I can see how it works and maybe stop it," Ian responded.

"Wake the bastard up and let him tell you," Emily retorted.

Nakia started to squirm and cough. Ian's eyes caught Nakia's eyes. "Welcome."

"Who the hell are you? What do you want?" Nakia said.

"Why the fuck did you kill Mrs. Mirreaux?" Emily screamed.

Vanessa then held Emily back and looked at Emily. "Take it easy."

Nakia smirked. "She was just a pawn."

"What do you mean?" Ian asked.

"What does it matter?" Nakia arrogantly answered. "Leviathan has launched."

"What do you mean it's launched?" Emily said.

"Take out your damn phone and look. Nothing can stop it now." He paused. "And in a few hours, when the company goes public, I and a few others will be worth a fortune."

Emily and Vanessa pulled out their phones as Ian watched Nakia. A couple of moments later, Emily and Vanessa's eyes widened in astonishment. "What the fuck?" Vanessa said.

Ian looked over to Vanessa. "What's going on?"

"When I open my browser, I get a website called Leviathan with a search engine." Vanessa showed Ian. On the screen, a search field with the Leviathan Cross took up a large part of the page. "And when I type in Google, it says the site is invalid and directs me back to Leviathan."

Emily stood up, walked to Nakia, and punched him. "What the fuck is this? You and Leviathan are murderers."

Vanessa quickly stood up and grabbed Emily to pull her back, while Ian grabbed Nakia. "Emily, calm down," Vanessa said.

Nakia smirked. "There's no stopping it." He then looked out at the lake and the mountains in the distance.

"We have a confession video from Elena Mirreaux, and she explains her role in Leviathan," Ian told Nakia.

"What would the confessional prove? Even if you put a so-called video out there, Leviathan will ensure no one ever sees it." He paused. "We can dictate what people see and will change how they think." As he pontificated, he felt his pant pocket.

Ian took notice. "What are you hiding?"

Nakia smugly looked at Ian. "It's nothing." He put his hand in his pocket.

Ian then grabbed his hand and pulled it out. "Show it to me."

Nakia looked at Ian as he opened his hand and showed Ian a small thumb drive. "Leviathan."

"What do you mean, Leviathan?" Ian asked as Vanessa and Emily focused their attention on Nakia.

"Leviathan." Nakia smugly said and crossed his arms.

Ian quickly looked at Vanessa and Emily. "Vanessa, let's take our friend to your office with the drive. Emily, track down everyone you know who was on that call. But don't hurt any of them, understand? Find Viyan Hadid. She knows what is going on."

Emily nodded. "Okay."

Ian helped Nakia as they both stood up. "We will discuss somewhere a little more private with your drive."

Emily and Vanessa stood up. "You will bring justice for Mrs. Mirreaux?" Emily asked.

"We are going to try," Ian said. "Keep the faith."

CHAPTER 77

Wednesday Afternoon
WTO
Geneva

As the crowd sat for several informational sessions, a few attendees started to grumble and mumble to each other while they looked at their phones and a few were on their computers.

"What's going on?" a male attendee asked.

"Is something wrong with the Wi-Fi?" A female attendee asked.

"It's everywhere; how do I make this go away?" someone else said.

"This is a bunch of lies!" another person loudly said.

Viyan looked around to try to figure out what was going on. She saw that the people who were being disruptive were either on their phones or computers. She then took out her phone and gasped—she almost threw her phone to the ground. She immediately saw the Leviathan Cross. She opened her phone's browser, and it took her to the Leviathan search engine. She looked up Google, only to see a message saying the site no longer existed, which led her right back to Leviathan. She then tapped the screen of her phone to look up something, and immediately several articles came up, but they were all fake news.

She looked around to see if she could find Ian or Vanessa. With no luck, she tried to text them. The text went through without a problem, but it went unanswered.

She tried to stay calm and act normal while hoping Ian and Vanessa were on the trail to taking down Leviathan.

CHAPTER 78

Wednesday Afternoon
Vanessa's Office
Geneva

Ian, Vanessa, and Nakia took an Uber to Vanessa's office. No one said a word during the short ride. Nakia looked out the window and then back at Ian and Vanessa. "You know there's nothing you can do."

Ian and Vanessa did not respond. Once the Uber pulled up to the office, Vanessa led the way, and Ian guided Nakia.

Once in the office, Vanessa ordered Nakia to sit in a chair on the far side of the room, and she pulled out some zip-ties.

"Where did you get those?" Ian said.

She smirked as she tied Nakia's wrists together and his ankles to the chair. "Don't ask."

Ian looked at Nakia. "Can I have that drive?"

Nakia jerked his arms. "You know this is illegal."

She looked at Nakia. "What you are doing is more illegal."

"Hobbes set out to stop political violence. Leviathan will set things right," Nakia said.

Ian reached for each of Nakia's pockets and found the thumb drive.

"In Hobbes, we trust," Nakia said as Ian walked to the computer on the other side of the room with the thumb drive.

Vanessa walked behind Ian to the computer. As Ian sat in the chair in front of it, Vanessa reached across and opened the laptop with her thumbprint.

Ian put the thumb drive in the computer. He opened the file and was prompted with a password field to fill in before the file opened.

Ian turned toward Nakia. "What's the password?"

Nakia laughed. "Why the fuck should I tell you?"

"I don't think you have much choice," Vanessa said. "You are zip-tied to a chair and in my office."

Nakia looked at Vanessa and Ian. "Do what you will. I won't break."

Ian turned to the computer screen. "Let's not bother with him then. I'm going to try something."

Ian looked at the thumb drive and noticed an SH-2 hash written on it. He then focused on Vanessa's glowing MacBook Pro. He thought this was standard security, but it was far from unbreakable.

He opened Safari, pulled up Google, and found his way to download a rainbow table. Cracking a password using the old-fashioned brute force would take too long. On the other hand, a rainbow table was different—a precomputed database of hashes and their corresponding plaintext passwords. It was a shortcut to breaking weak security.

He loaded the table, an immense file, and stored it on an external drive connected to the computer. He didn't think Vanessa would mind.

He then ran his script: *./rainbow_crack-i hash.txt -t sha2_table.rt.*

The drive whirred as it processed the hash and compared it against billions of precomputed values. The progress bar on the computer screen inched forward. Ian looked back at Nakia and Vanessa. Nakia was still stoic while Vanessa tapped her fingers impatiently on the desk. For Vanessa, the seconds felt like minutes.

All of a sudden, the screen flashed. A match was found. Ian and Vanessa inched closer to the screen. The password then appeared: *Pharaoh1651!*

Ian smirked. For someone from Egypt, why use something as easy as Pharaoh? And 1651, was that in reference to the publication of *The Leviathan*? Maybe Nakia was a sentimental fool? Either way, Ian didn't care. He copied the password, pulled up the thumb drive document, and tried logging in.

Access granted.

The document unfolded before him. It revealed the Leviathan coding.

As Ian stared at the computer screen, he said, "Oh my God."

"What is it?" Vanessa said as she leaned over Ian to examine the computer screen and scroll the pages. "This is a bit too complicated for me."

Ian pointed at the screen. "If I'm reading this correctly, it will destroy the U.N. and the member countries." Ian paused as he read more of the code. "It also looks like once countries opt in, this software will gain access to each member country's federal reserves and military institutions and their arsenals."

"What the fuck?" Vanessa said, and then she turned to Nakia. "Is what Ian said the real reason for Leviathan?"

Nakia laughed and looked at Vanessa and Ian. "Possibly."

Vanessa put her hand on the back of Nakia's neck. "Don't play coy with me, you son of a bitch."

Ian walked up to Nakia and looked at him. "Why not launch Leviathan without killing the Secretary-General and his wife?"

Nakia smirked. "They were just pawns. No other use. They needed to get out of the way."

Vanessa kept her hand on the back of Nakia's neck. "That's not what Elena's confession video said."

Nakia turned his head and looked at Vanessa. "What confession video?"

"The one where Elena confesses her part in this fiasco," she responded.

"You're lying," Nakia said and shook his head. "Hanna said there would be no trace."

Ian looked at her. "I think I believe him. He has no idea about the confession."

"Where is this video?" Nakia asked.

"That would be too easy, wouldn't it?" she said. "I guess you'll just have to trust us. But I can assure you it exists and will be broadcast to the world soon."

Nakia shook his head. "You won't be able to do that once Leviathan is live and goes public. The system pushes fake news and such. Leviathan will dictate what people see, read, think, and do." He then laughed. "So you might as well let me go."

Ian looked at Nakia. "I see that the Leviathan code is in a

read-only file. Where is the workable version?"

Nakia laughed. "You don't think we were given the real copy to edit, do you?" He laughed some more.

She then grabbed his neck more tightly. "Where is the other version?"

Nakia winced and responded, "I have no clue. The hacker probably made it, but he's ready to become a millionaire when Leviathan goes public."

She grabbed his neck again. "What hacker?"

Nakia winced again. "I have no idea. It was the American in the group, who found the hacker. I think he's in California." He looked around the room and saw a pair of scissors on top of a desktop within arm's reach.

Ian tried to think quickly on his feet. He guessed that the hacker helped take down Google and such. He didn't think Nakia or any other conspirators were smart enough to know how Leviathan worked. They were just in it for the power and the payday.

"Would Hanna have a workable copy?" Ian asked as he looked at Nakia.

"I have no clue. But you're too late. Leviathan has launched, and it is just a matter of time till the world sees its full potential." Nakia laughed again.

Vanessa forcefully let go of Nakia's neck and then walked toward Ian. "Is there anything in the code you could use to break into?"

Ian turned his focus back to the computer screen and studied the code. "Not really. I see some weak points, but I will need the real code to test it."

Vanessa put her hand on Ian's shoulder as she looked at the code. "I can't say I know anything about code, but isn't there some type of virus you can give it?"

"Well, the only way for Google and other sites to go down is a virus." He paused. "You could have the virus self-destruct if the correct commands were given to it."

While Ian and Vanessa had their backs to Nakia, he raised his tied hands above his head and forcefully brought them down towards his stomach. This action broke the zip-ties, and he quietly reached for the scissors. He then was able to cut the zip ties around his ankles and quietly stood up.

He clutched the scissors and quietly snuck up behind Vanessa. He put the scissors next to her throat. "Don't scream. Now the tables have turned."

Vanessa shrieked as she and Ian turned to Nakia. "Don't do anything stupid now."

"It's two against one," Ian said.

Nakia pressed the point of the scissors a little into Vanessa's neck. "That may be. But if you attack me, I will slit her throat."

Vanessa winced and looked at Ian. "If I have to die for Leviathan to be taken down, do it."

Ian shook his head. "No, I'm not going to let you die." He then turned his attention to Nakia. "What do you want?"

"I want you to zip-tie each other first," Nikia demanded.

Ian then grabbed the other zip ties on the far end of the desk. He tied Vanessa's wrists, and Nakia watched as Vanessa then zip-tied Ian's wrists.

"Good," Nakia said and looked around the room. "Now lie down and remember I still have scissors."

Ian and Vanessa obeyed, and Nakia came behind them and zip-tied their ankles together.

Nakia then stood up and took out his phone while looking at Vanessa's desk.

"We have a problem. I need you to pick me up with some packages. I'll send out my location." He took the phone away from his ear and then texted his location.

"What are you going to do with us?" Ian asked.

"I shouldn't have let go of your neck," Vanessa said.

Nakia saw two pillows in the corner. He walked over to the corner, took the pillowcases off the pillows from the daybed, and took them toward Ian and Vanessa. "Would you both shut up?" He placed the pillowcases over each of their heads.

Finally, he sat in the desk chair and waited.

CHAPTER 79

Wednesday Afternoon
WTO
Geneva

The noise in the room was a cacophony of sounds as people talked to each other, and some called on their phones. They were still trying to figure out what Leviathan was and why it had taken over their phones and Internet searches.

At times, different individuals screamed, "This is all fake news. It's a virus of misinformation!"

Viyan looked around the room and tried to figure out how to keep everyone calm. She needed to develop an idea quickly but not tell everyone what Leviathan was. She wasn't sure if anyone from the cabal was in the room.

She rechecked her phone to see if Ian or Vanessa had texted or called her. She found no notifications and wondered if she should try calling them.

"Excuse me, are you Dr. Hadid?" a young woman asked, tapping Viyan on the shoulder.

Viyan turned to face the young woman. "Yes, I am. And you are?" She nodded and stuck out her hand.

"My name is Emily. I was Mrs. Mirreaux's assistant." Emily shook Viyan's hand. "Can we go somewhere more private to talk?"

Viyan nodded. "Nice to meet you. Yes, follow me." She then led Emily to an empty hallway and turned to face her.

"You are Elena's assistant? But she's dead. Why are you here?" Viyan asked.

"Long story, but Ian and Vanessa told me I should find you," Emily answered.

"I haven't heard from them in a couple of hours. I don't know where they are, but Leviathan has launched."

"I know who the Leviathan members are, and some are in the room."

Viyan looked at Emily. "You do? Let's follow them. Everything else is at a standstill and in a panic."

Emily nodded. "Yes, I would try to kill them, but I was advised against it."

"What do you mean?"

"I know how Mrs. Mirreaux was set up. I saw her make the confession video in New York. She never saw me. And I have a list of those who were on those Leviathan calls."

Viyan nodded. "Wow! Show me who they are."

Emily nodded. "I will. None of the members were well-known public names, but they all worked in high places for their respective governments."

"Not sure if you know that Hanna Assad is dead."

"I killed her," Emily said, cutting Viyan off.

Viyan stopped and looked at Emily in shock. "You what?! You were the one shooting at us this morning?"

Emily nodded. "Yes, but Hanna was my target."

` "Are you a spy?"

Emily shook her head. "No, I'm just doing this to avenge Mrs. Mirreaux's death. Her mission and achievements should not be forgotten along with her husband's impact."

Viyan grabbed Emily's hand. "If any authorities find out, maybe I can help you get diplomatic immunity."

"Maybe. But let's take down Leviathan first, and I will face consequences for my actions."

"Okay. Let's go back and see what we can do."

Emily and Viyan walked back into the room and casually conversed. Emily spotted a couple of Leviathan members and carefully guided Viyan toward them without making their approach obvious.

Two men were standing next to each other, talking. They each wore a Leviathan cross.

Emily leaned toward Viyan to whisper, "The two men with the Leviathan cross pins were on the conference calls with Mrs. Mirreaux. The man on the left is Jack Samuelson, and the man on the right is Zaaeem Farouq."

Viyan casually looked at them and then turned to look at Emily. "I know of them. They are both high up in their respective governments."

A cell phone rang from Jack's pocket. He looked at the caller ID and ended his conversation with Zaaeem. Emily and Viyan listened but looked in the other direction.

"Yes?" Jack looked at Zaaeem as he listened to the person on the other end of the call. His face went from a smile to a frown. "Fuck. He said what? Fuck. I'm on my way." He then ended the call and looked at Zaaeem.

"That was Nakia. There's been a complication. I think we should both go." Jack said, and Zaaeem nodded.

They then turned to walk out of the room. Emily and Viyan followed.

CHAPTER 80

Wednesday Early Evening
Villa Diodati
Geneva

Ian and Vanessa stayed silent as Nakia and two other men seized them and pushed them into a car. After a fifteen-minute drive, the men pulled them out again.

One of the men took the pillowcases off Ian and Vanessa's heads. The lights on their faces blinded them. The man then walked out of the room. Ian and Vanessa had a hard time determining where they were.

Once Ian's eyes could refocus, he noticed he and Vanessa were sitting in two chairs back to back to each other, and their hands were zip-tied to the chairs. Ian looked around the room. They were in what looked like the main salon of a villa. The sunlight entered the room via tall windows overlooking the lake and the Alps. A large fireplace was on the other side of the room, opposite the windows. There were large bookcases on either side of the fireplace.

He also noticed that this villa had no air conditioning, although it had electricity.

"Vanessa, are you okay?" he asked as he tried to pull on his wrists.

"Yeah, but my wrists hurt. Are you okay?" she answered as she tried to move her chair.

"Yes, any idea where we are? Seems like some literary villa."

Before Vanessa could answer, Nakia entered the room and slowly approached Ian and Vanessa. "I'm glad you both could join us," he said sarcastically.

"Where are we?" Vanessa asked.

"Wouldn't you like to know?" Nakia said. "I think my questions are more important at this point."

"What questions?" Ian asked.

"Let's wait until my colleagues get here," Nakia said as he looked out the large windows. As the sun set, gray clouds started to roll over the mountains, and thunder could be heard in the distance.

"What questions?" Vanessa asked.

Nakia turned back toward Ian and Vanessa. "Please be patience. You both will find out in due time." He then walked past them and out of the room.

Ian and Vanessa tried to wiggle more in their chairs.

CHAPTER 81

Wednesday Early Evening
Villa Diodati
Geneva

Emily drove Viyan in one of the WTO cars as they followed Jack and Zaaeem, who were in a black chauffeured Mercedes. Emily drove aggressively but stayed a few car lengths back so they did not get noticed. The public buses made it a challenge a couple of times, but Viyan helped to identify where the black Mercedes was.

They drove along Quai Gustave-Ador, which gave them a nice view of the Jet d'Eau. The traffic dissipated, and the road started to incline slightly as they entered Cologny. The road was two-way, and next to the opposite lane was a sidewalk for people to walk on.

The black Mercedes turned left and entered a private estate nestled among trees. Emily passed the entrance and pulled onto the sidewalk to park the car, ensuring it did not block traffic.

Emily and Viyan exited the car and started walking back to the estate.

"What's the plan?" Viyan asked as they walked.

"Follow me. I know a way in," Emily said as she started to take the lead.

"How do you know this place?" Viyan asked as she followed Emily up the driveway.

"I was here for a tour."

"What is this place?"

"It's Villa Diodati," Emily said as she crouched and walked further.

Viyan crouched like Emily. "Villa Diodati—isn't that where *Frankenstein* was written?"

"Yes."

"How could you get a tour of the villa? I thought it was private?"

Emily looked at Viyan as they approached a side door. "Yes. Actually, I think it still is private. It must have been during an event that Mrs. Mirreaux was attending."

Viyan nodded and continued to follow Emily up the driveway. Emily then turned to the garden and walked further toward the window.

"Let's see if we can see anyone, then we can figure out how to get in," Emily said as she looked at Viyan.

Viyan nodded. "Sounds good." While they hid behind the shutters, Emily leaned over to look through the window. She then turned back to Viyan. "I see Ian and Vanessa. They are tied up."

"What should we do?" Viyan asked.

"I don't see anyone around. There's a door on the other side of the window; maybe we can get in undetected. Let me go first to see." Emily didn't wait for Viyan's approval and immediately headed to the door. Viyan stayed and watched Emily.

The sky started to get darker, and the thunder became louder.

Between a couple of thunderous sounds, Viyan heard Emily scream in the distance, "NOOO! Vivi!"

Viyan's adrenaline kicked in, and she ran toward the door. Right before she turned toward the door, she was hit on the head with a fist, and she lost consciousness.

CHAPTER 82

Wednesday Evening
Villa Diodati
Geneva

The rain and thunder intensified as sunset approached. When Viyan started to gain consciousness, she noticed she was zip-tied to a chair, and as she moved her head, she saw two other people.

"Ian?" Viyan said wearily.

"Viyan! You're up. How did you get here?" Ian said.

"What's going on?" Viyan said.

"We've all been kidnapped," Vanessa said.

"Where's Emily?" Viyan asked as she looked at Ian and Vanessa.

"What about Emily? Emily was never here," Ian said.

"Yes, she was," Viyan said. "She seemed to know where to go, and I followed her when I heard her scream."

"We haven't seen Emily. We thought that was you when we heard the scream," Vanessa said.

"If Emily is here, do you think Nakia is torturing or even killing her?" Ian said.

"Why would he do that?" Vanessa said.

"I don't know. Does she know something about Leviathan?" Ian responded.

Viyan shook her head. "I don't think so. All she told me was she was avenging Mrs. Mirreaux's death."

"That's what she told us, too," Vanessa said.

There was a loud sound of thunder, then the door opened. Nakia and two other men walked in holding a chair with Emily zip-tied.

Nakia and the men put Emily down close and left the room.

"I'm so happy to see you all," Emily said. Her lip was bleeding, and her left eye was swollen.

"What happened?" Viyan said over Ian and Vanessa.

"They interrogated me and asked why I was here," Emily responded. "They then asked me about the confession video."

"What did you tell them?" Vanessa asked.

"I told them that I know Mrs. Mirreaux created one. But I said I don't know where she put it and who's seen it."

Ian looked at Viyan and Vanessa. "Is this what they are after?"

Before Vanessa or Viyan could respond, Emily said, "They mentioned something about being upset that one of you mentioned there are faults with the Leviathan code. They said it's impossible for there to be an error."

"Vanessa and I saw a read-only file of the Leviathan code. It's an interesting code, but it's crackable. One does have to be very skilled to hack it, though. I think I can access the workable file," Ian said.

"Have any of you been interrogated?" Emily asked.

"No, we've just been tied up in this room. We haven't seen anyone," Vanessa said. The sound of rain intensified.

"Who interrogated you? Was it just Nakia?" Ian asked.

"Nakia hit me a couple of times. But the other two were asking me questions," Emily answered.

"Do you know the other two?" Vanessa asked.

"They are part of Leviathan. I remember them from the video conferences," Emily responded.

"Do you remember their names?" Ian asked.

"Jack Samuelson and Zaaeem Farouq," Emily said. "Jack is from the United States, and Zaaeem Farouq is from Saudi Arabia."

"Jack is the deputy chief of staff at the White House," Ian said.

Emily nodded. "Yes. In between their forceful interrogation, they said others from Leviathan would be here to interrogate us."

Viyan said, "Is it just us who know about the confession video?"

"I think so." Ian nodded.

"You told me to show it to your colleague Paul, but he never showed up," Viyan said.

"So, if it's just us, how do we get the video?" Emily asked.

"It's on a cloud, and we will distribute it once Leviathan shuts down," Ian responded.

"What about giving them the video and finding a way to make everything right?" Emily asked.

"How do you know they will let us live?" Vanessa asked.

Ian shrugged. "Not sure, but maybe I can offer a deal to keep you all safe in exchange for showing the problems with the code."

"That might work," Viyan responded.

Vanessa looked around. "Never mind that. How do we get out of these zip ties?"

The sounds of thunder shook the room.

"What's that?" Viyan asked. "Some smoke is coming through the door."

"I don't smell anything burning," Vanessa said.

The smoke quickly filled the room. Before anyone could respond, everyone passed out.

CHAPTER 83

Wednesday Night
Villa Diodati
Geneva

Ian was stirred awake by another sound of thunder. Opening his eyes, he noticed he was still in the same room, but a computer had been set up on a desk. At first, he did not see Emily, Vanessa, and Viyan. He turned his head and then he saw Vanessa and Viyan with bags over their heads, still in their chairs but on the opposite side of the room. But he didn't see Emily. He hoped she wasn't interrogated more.

"Vanessa, Viyan, are you both okay?" Ian called out.

"I'm okay. I can't see a bloody thing." Vanessa called out.

"I'm okay, too. Where's Emily?" Viyan responded.

"I'm not sure. She's not in the room," Ian said.

Then, the door to the room opened, and Nakia, Jack, and Zaaeem entered.

"Where is Emily?" Ian said as he looked toward Nakia.

"She's in a safe place," Nakia said.

"I hope you didn't hurt her," Vanessa shouted.

"You'll see her soon," Nakia said.

Jack then cleared his throat. "Let's quit the fucking small talk. Ian, I can help you if you help me."

Ian looked at him. "I can't help you because I'm tied to a chair."

"I think we can get enough out of you while you are in the chair," Zaaeem said. "I've seen it work in other situations."

"What's the incentive for me?" Ian asked.

"I don't understand. What do you want?" Ian asked.

"I want to know what the fuck is wrong with Leviathan?" Jack said.

"I need to see it. I just saw it briefly," Ian said. "I don't have a photographic memory."

"Why should we believe you?" Zaaeem said.

"Well, if I'm seeing something wrong, I'm sure any coder from their bedroom can find it too. You can't take the chance of me being right now," Ian responded.

Nakia and Jack approached Ian, picked him up, chair and all, and brought him to the desk with the computer.

"So fucking tell us," Jack said impatiently as Zaaeem held the computer mouse.

"Not so fast. I need to do my own scrolling, or do you know how to code?" Ian responded and looked at Zaaeem.

Zaaeem looked back at Jack and Nakia and they nodded. "Before you can freely scroll, we are going to show you our security," Nakia said as he walked to the door.

"What do you mean, security?" Ian asked.

"You'll see," Jack said.

A few minutes later, Nakia came back to the room with Emily. Emily had cleaned up her appearance. "Emily has something to say."

"Emily, are you okay?" Ian said.

"Emily!" Vanessa and Viyan said from under their head covers.

Emily walked over to Vanessa as Nakia walked to Viyan and picked her up to set her down next to Vanessa.

"I'm more than okay," Emily said as she pulled out a knife from her pocket and put the knife up to Vanessa's neck.

"What the hell is going on?" Vanessa said as she felt the metal sharpness next to her throat.

"What is that?" Viyan shrieked. Nakia pulled out a knife and placed it along Viyan's neck.

"So, Ian, please proceed. We might let you all go if you show us what's wrong." Jack said.

Zaaeem started undoing Ian's zip ties. Ian didn't make any sudden movements. "Emily, what happened?"

Emily looked back at Ian and smirked. "Money and love. It's a capitalistic world. You should know that, Ian."

"What do you mean? What about the Mirreauxs' reputation? I thought you wanted to ensure that history is correct in how they see her and her husband." Ian responded.

Jack, Nakia, and Zaaeem started to laugh. "She's been our inside woman with Elena," Jack said.

"What? Emily is what?" Vanessa and Viyan called out.

"Emily is with Leviathan," Ian said.

"That can't be," Vanessa said.

Emily pressed the knife a little more into Vanessa's neck, still not breaking the skin. "I will admit, I took the job with Mrs. Mirreaux when I had idealistic ambitions. Then, while working for her, I fell in love and was shown the future."

"Who did you fall in love with?" Viyan said.

"I met Nakia, and we fell madly in love. He then showed me what he and others were working on. He asked me to be his eyes and ears next to Mrs. Mirreaux and ensure she did what they wanted."

"Did this include watching François?" Ian asked.

Nakia shook his head. "No, we took care of François. We wanted to be sure Elena stayed in line."

"I still don't understand," Ian said. "What was the point of killing Hanna? And if you wanted Elena gone, why not get rid of her earlier?"

Zaaeem then said, "Hanna's time with us needed to end. Her plan did not work, and her ideas were being second-guessed."

Before anyone could respond, Nakia added, "Emily told us about hearing a confession video. But she had no idea who had seen it or where it had gone."

"When you both came to see Mrs. Mirreaux in New York, I got suspicious that she might have told you both something about the confession," Emily said.

"Take these head covers off of us. And I want to see your betrayal face," Vanessa demanded.

Emily and Nakia looked at each other, nodded, and removed the head covers. "You bitch," Vanessa said as she spit on Emily's face.

Emily kept her composure. "I should slit your throat."

"I wouldn't do that," Ian roared. "If you hurt either of them,

I'm not helping you with Leviathan."

Emily and Nakia kept their knives on Vanessa and Viyan's throats.

"Now, show us," Jack said forcefully, shoving Ian towards the computer.

Ian rubbed his shoulder and looked at the computer. He saw the Leviathan code. It was similar to what he had seen earlier, but he could tell it was now in an editable format.

"Go ahead. If it's so simple, show us," Zaaeem said.

Ian began to scroll the code freely, typed some things and the screen changed.

Jack and Zaaeem looked at Ian. "What the fuck is happening?"

Ian looked at them calmly. "Nothing right now. All you are seeing right now are SQL injection queries. I'm testing the vulnerabilities." Ian kept working on the computer as Jack and Zaaeem looked at each other.

"What's going on?" Nakia said.

"I'm just testing the vulnerabilities and doing a security test. I have to say, this program is very sophisticated from the outside, but when I dig a little deeper, it's not that good."

"If you are screwing with us, I will have no problem slitting both of your throats," Nakia said.

"Why would I screw with you?" Ian said calmly. "You have our lives in your hands."

Ian then proceeded to open a few other tabs and log into a few different networks.

"I don't like what I'm seeing," Jack said.

Ian turned from the computer. "If you know what I'm doing, please tell me where the mistakes are."

Jack stomped his feet in frustration. "No, I don't. I pay people to tell me what's wrong."

"Hey! It's your lucky day. I'm trying to fix your problems and won't even ask for payment." Ian laughed and then turned his attention to the computer screen.

After a couple more minutes, Ian looked up. "I have a question."

Zaaeem looked over. "What is it?"

"In my security diagnostic, I see a list of names. Who are they?" Ian said and let Zaaeem look at the screen.

Zaaeem's eyes grew larger as he looked at the computer screen. "What the fresh hell is this?"

"What's going on?" Nakia said.

"Our fucking names are listed," Zaaeem responded.

Nakia, Emily, and Jack rushed to see Zaaeem's screen. Ian quickly looked over at Vanessa and Viyan. With his eyes, he tried to tell them to try something to get out of their zip ties.

"How the fuck is this here?" Nakia and Jack screamed and slapped Ian. "This is your fault."

Ian took the blow of the hit but tried not to show his pain. "I just found it in the source code. It was buried, sure, but it could be found if you looked hard enough."

Nakia then turned to Jack. "I fucking trusted you and your coder to get this done."

Jack looked at Nakia. "You can trust me. I will take care of the programmer when I get stateside. I did bring in a lot of investors."

Zaaeem tried to keep things from getting out of hand. "Ian, fix it, or we will kill you and your two friends."

Ian nodded. "Sure." He thought for a moment, then added, "I'll also show you the confession video."

"What?! Ian, what are you doing?" Vanessa and Viyan called out.

Ian didn't respond and looked at Nakia, Jack, Emily, and Zaaeem. "Let me work, and I'll show you all. I want my friends and me to be safe."

"Don't be another traitor, Ian," Vanessa yelled.

"Why, Ian?!" Viyan screamed.

As Ian worked, Nakia, Jack, Emily, and Zaaeem paced the room. "I'm just curious. I see that there are two other individuals. Where are they?" Ian asked.

"They are at the InterContinental with their delegations," Nakia begrudgingly answered. "Are you done yet?"

Ian looked back at the computer screen. "Almost. Just a couple more things, and Leviathan should be the most secure thing in the world."

A couple more minutes passed, and Jack took a knife from Emily and placed it on Ian's throat. "Show us now!"

Ian calmly backed away from the computer. "I see that patience isn't one of your virtues." A black video file came up on the screen. "The video is ready for you to see, and I've fixed the Leviathan errors." Ian paused and looked at Nakia. "While you all watch the confession, can I at least see Vanessa and Viyan?"

Nakia didn't look at the others and kept his eyes on Ian. "Sure. But remember, we will kill you if something goes wrong."

Ian nodded. "Of course. Just hit play, and you will see everything you asked for."

Nakia turned to the computer and nodded to Jack to hit the play button. At the same time, Ian slowly walked toward Vanessa and Viyan.

The video started to play with Elena coming on the screen. When Ian reached Vanessa and Viyan, he helped undo their zip ties and whispered to each of them. "When I say run, I want you to run towards the door and outside."

"What?" Vanessa and Viyan asked as they got free from the zip ties.

"Just be ready to run," Ian said, looking at Nakia, Jack, Zaaeem, and Emily, who were focused on the video.

CHAPTER 84

Wednesday Night
Villa Diodati
Geneva

Nakia, Jack, Zaaeem, and Emily watched the video more intently. "Elena is trying to be a martyr. How do we delete this video?" Jack asked and looked toward Ian.

"It can't be easily deleted," Ian responded. "Keep watching."

Ian then looked at Vanessa and Viyan and whispered, "Move slowly toward the door now."

Vanessa and Viyan moved slowly toward the door.

As the video played, it then automatically moved to the right of the screen, and on the left, a source code started to scroll. "What the fuck?" Jack screamed.

"Run! I'll be behind you shortly," Ian said to Vanessa and Viyan.

Vanessa and Viyan briefly paused and looked at Ian.

"Run!" Ian reaffirmed. Vanessa and Viyan then proceeded to run out of the room. After they left, Ian blocked the exit and turned toward Jack and the others.

"I would keep watching," Ian called out. "I made the source code public. And, by the way, when you hit play earlier, the video and the source code went live and out to the world."

"You fucking bastard," Jack screamed and started to run toward Ian.

Ian didn't move immediately. He waited until Jack was almost within arm's reach when Ian moved to the side. Jack slammed himself into the wall and fell to the ground.

Nakia and Emily kept watching the video as Zaaeem started to come after Ian.

"You're going to want to pay attention to the end," Ian said as he stepped over Jack and picked up a chair to throw at Zaaeem.

Zaaeem fell when the chair hit him, and Jack started to get up again. Ian then picked up the other chair and threw it at Jack.

The end of the video started to play. It showed pictures of everyone involved in Leviathan and where they were located. "What did you do?" Nakia screamed. Ian made his way back to the door.

At the same time, the sound of each of their cellphones started to ring. Nakia and Emily looked at their phones. "What do I do?" Emily asked as she looked at Nakia.

"It's the Prime Minister," Nakia said.

Jack slowly started to get up and pulled out his phone. "It's the White House."

Zaaeem ignored his cell phone and looked up at Ian. "I should've killed you when I had the chance."

"Well, then I wouldn't have fixed your problems, and you would never have seen the confession video," Ian said, then ran out of the room.

"Fuck! What do we do?" Jack asked as he looked at Nakia, Emily, and Zaaeem.

"We need to run," Nakia said.

"I have a plane we could use," Zaaeem said.

"We need that plane. Now!" Nakia said. The sounds of police cars could be heard in the distance.

EPILOGUE

A Week Later
Wednesday Morning
Geneva

Ian sat on a bench and sipped his coffee as he looked at the Jet d'Eau. He picked the bench that had a tree covering it. It was a sunny morning, and any shade was a big help. A few minutes later, Vanessa approached Ian with a coffee and kissed Ian on both cheeks. She then sat next to him.

"Have you gotten any sleep lately?" he asked.

"No, I have had a lot of work to do. It's hard writing the full grasp of everything that happened," she responded. "Leviathan's rise and dramatic fall. I've never seen a stock crash that fast. The investors are in shambles. Arrests were made at the airport, and the authorities invaded hotel rooms. The U.N. escaped its downfall and ended up changing the world for women's rights."

He nodded. "Very true. It sounds like something you'd read in a book or Hollywood. Definitely not what I thought I was walking into when I took this job.."

She nodded. "Yes. You came at a complicated time. I don't think Geneva has experienced this much public action. This is something that can't be hidden from the press."

"It's a massive story with so many layers. I have a feeling you're going to rack up awards for your reporting."

She blushed. "It's the story that matters and needs to be told. I'm not in it for the prizes."

"Also, thank you for keeping me anonymous. I'm just glad this conspiracy has been put to rest."

"Of course. Only a select few knew who was involved. I wouldn't be surprised if Seung Kim asked for your guidance again."

"Do you know what Seung Kim asked Viyan?"

"He asked her to be the permanent head of the U.N.'s new

women's rights division. I think it will be called UNWR."

When her phone began to ring, she looked at it. "I really need to take this. These calls don't stop," she said.

As she stood up, he asked, "What are you doing about your book?"

"I think I'm going to change course a little. I'm going to focus on François and Elena Mirreaux. I want to show that they were the ultimate power couple and heroes for saving and strengthening the U.N."

"That sounds great." He paused and kissed her on both cheeks.

"Are you going to stay in Geneva for long now?"

"I'm not sure. I think I need to get back to my company for a bit." He paused. "I'll let you know."

"Geneva will miss you if you go." She smiled, paused, and looked at her phone. "I really have to go."

"Go. I'll call you before I leave," he said, a smile forming as he watched her walk off, already answering phone.

When she was out of his eyesight, he sat back on the bench and looked out again at the Jet d'Eau. "Making the world better never comes easy, no matter what industry you're in," he said to himself as he finished his coffee and took in the beautiful scenery.

ACKNOWLEDGEMENTS

Most writers say that writing is a lonely journey. There are those moments when the journey is lonely, whether with headphones on in coffee shops or at my desk, as I get lost in the world where my characters reside. Yet, at the same time, it has been an amazing experience to create this world and story. Most, though not all, of the places and events mentioned in the book I have visited and experienced. The idea for this book began to germinate in my mind as I completed my master's at the Geneva School of Diplomacy and International Relations. There were many times I would walk by the Jet d'Eau, sit on a bench to admire the view, and think, like Ian does a few times in the book.

I kept a journal that outlined this story. I came to a point where I did not know how it would end. I happened to watch a TED Talk with David Baldacci. During his talk, he mentioned that when writing fiction, one should start to write, and the characters will begin to talk to you. I followed this advice, and I must say, it was effective. While I am happy with where the story ends, I do not think I could have planned every step for the characters before writing.

There were other times during this journey that were more social—either through learning in greater detail about topics brought up in the book or by making sure the story was exciting. Thank you to Florian Bikard, Thomas LaGrange, Viyan Sido, and Benjamin Walker.

Furthermore, I would like to thank Maria Anna Adamiuk, Yazan Alquara, Karim Boros, Soji Iledare, Will and Caitie Klatte, Ghazal Maghareh, Jeremy Meyer, Karim Sbaa, Sebastian Vargas, and Charles Varnishung, who listened to me share countless thoughts about this story, even when they did not want to hear it.

I want to extend a special thank you to Barbie Derebery, who was my first reader and continued to review sections and drafts, providing feedback to help improve the story.

Thank you to the people who inspired certain characters.

Thank you to Rebecca Kastl for introducing me to a wonderful editor, Katie Connolly, whose insights helped strengthen this book. Thank you, Katie. I am also grateful to David Ter-Avanesyan for creating an excellent cover.

Finally, a special thank-you goes to Mom, Dad, and Nina, to whom the book is dedicated. Thank you all for your patience and support during this process. I could not have done it without you.

www.ingramcontent.com/pod-product-compliance
Lightning Source LLC
Chambersburg PA
CBHW060807310726
48980CB00002B/262
9798993058313